THIS KIND of LOVE

ASHLEY DETWEILER

This book is a work of fiction. Any references to historical events, real people, or real places are used fictitiously. Other names, characters, places, and events are products of the author's imagination, and any resemblance to actual events, places, names, or persons, is entirely coincidental.

Text copyright © 2025 by Ashley Detweiler

All rights reserved. For information regarding reproduction in total or in part, contact Rising Action Publishing Co. at http://www.risingactionpublishingco.com

Cover Illustration © Cover Ever After
Distributed by Simon & Schuster

ISBN: 978-1-998076-58-1
Ebook: 978-1-998076-59-8

FIC027020   FICTION / Romance / Contemporary
FIC027240   FICTION / Romance / New Adult
FIC027000   FICTION / Romance / General

#ThisKindofLove

Follow Rising Action on our socials!
Twitter: @RAPubCollective
Instagram: @risingactionpublishingco
Tiktok: @risingactionpublishingco

For Don:
Who made me believe in love at first sight
But will never make me believe mac and cheese is better with shells.
#TeamSpirals

A Note from the Author

Thank you for reading *This Kind of Love*. While I hope you enjoy every bit of it, it is important to note that this book is *not* for everyone. Books can be magical, but they're also full of words, and words, whether they mean to or not, can hurt.

Please read the content warnings with care and only read if, and when, you can.

If you're struggling, please know you're not alone. There is no shame in asking for help.

Call or text ~988. Day or night.

Content Warnings:

This Kind of Love includes alcoholism, mental and emotional health, generational trauma, cancer diagnosis and treatment, death (off-page), grief, and strong language. These topics may be triggering, so please read with discretion.

THIS KIND *of* LOVE

Chapter 1

Now

Everyone makes mistakes. My forty-five-pound husky-mix judges me for mine. For example, last week I forgot to pick up dog treats, and she didn't talk to me for *days*. Yesterday, my skirt was stuck in my underwear (#SundayScaries), and Hyla didn't even give me a warning bark. She just let me walk to the subway, where I was catcalled for blocks by middle-aged, beer-gut hanging-out construction workers. Now, there's a rugged, half-naked stranger sleeping in my bed while I rummage around all five hundred square feet of my New York City studio apartment looking for my other boot and instead of helping, Hyla's giving me a hard side-eye. The *sass*.

Breathe in. Breathe out. Focus. Find the matching boot and get to work. I stretch my arm as if it's an elastic band to get a little further under my bed and sigh. I love my job, my co-workers, and going out to celebrate "team wins," birthday parties, and #SingleSunday nights ... but I'm going to need a large amount of caffeine to get through the day.

"Kate, babe, why don't you come back to bed?" City Boy peeks one eye open and gives me a lazy grin.

Babe. So, he's one of *those* guys. The kind of guy who thinks one night is more than it is. The kind of guy who has a pet name in his back pocket because he thinks I'm looking for a relationship, some sort of commitment, and that a night of sex, no matter how great (and it was *not*), means giving a situationship a label in a matter of days. I've been through this over and over with guys who call me babe. This *particular* guy—Austin? Orlando? Memphis?—seems just like the rest. And even though I imagine my mama's eyes rolling into the back of her head at the sight of this, I'm not a hopeless romantic you can oblige with a white picket fence. Not anymore. Nowadays, you don't just meet the guy next door, fall in love, and live happily ever aft—

"Babe?" he asks again.

"Oh, I can't. I'm running late. Where is that boot?" I glance at City Boy, then continue searching under the bed.

He pulls my long-lost gray, knee-length favorite out from under the covers and (honest to God) caresses it. "This one?"

I pull it from his grasp. "Mhm."

He holds the covers open for me.

What if I leave him here?

Hyla sighs.

Ughhh, she's right. She deserves better.

I reach for City Boy's elbow, encourage him to stand, and—*mistake*. This stranger is standing there in full ... glory ... manhood ... nakedness at attention, and my head is pounding.

This is the moment—*this* right here is when it hits me: twenty-four is too old for one-night stands and all the bullshit that comes with 'em.

Spotting his boxers by the nightstand, I toss them City Boy's way. "Please put these on."

"Yes, ma'am." He salutes.

THIS KIND OF LOVE

I grab my clutch and pace toward the door. When he doesn't follow, I gather his clothes in a small pile and push him and his clothes into the hallway. My fingers linger on the metal knob for a few seconds.

"This was ... *yeah*." I add a smile for good measure but peel it back when he opens his mouth.

City Boy wiggles his eyebrows. "Maybe we can do this again tonight?"

I try not to wince at what may be turning into my second stage-five clinger this month.

Hearing Hyla's less-than-silent judgment, I click my tongue. "This week's not good ... but maybe sometime soon."

I don't wait for him to answer before I push the key in the lock, barrel down the three flights of stairs, and run out into the cool air of New York City in early October. While it hasn't been the best start to the day, I freaking *love* fall in the city. It's not too hot, not too cold, and is the time precisely between summer vacationers and holiday tourists. I pop in my earbuds and mentally run through my to-do list:

-Starbucks
-Monday morning meeting
-Note sharing session
-Copyedits for the New Year's piece
-Case of the Mondays blog
-Pick up Bone Appetit for Hyla
-Call Mama

The fragrance of freshly ground beans and baking croissants radiates through my nostrils as I rush through a set of familiar green doors.

Paradise. My grin fades when there isn't a single name tag I recognize on the staff.

"Oh hey, Nick, your usual?" a barista asks someone in line behind me, blinking her pretty, brown eyes.

"Yes, Betty, thanks ... and whatever this lady would like." His voice is deep but calm. *A voice for radio,* my mama would say. As I turn my shoulder toward him, my mouth falls open. He's close to a foot taller than me, with chocolate brown eyes, a well-kept crew cut, and a black suit that fits in *all the right places.*

"That's sweet, but I can't let you do that," I object. Please let the drool stay *in* my mouth.

Nick smiles, and one dimple forms on the right side of his perfect face. "I insist. Anyone trying to run people over for Starbucks needs it."

There's scuffling further back in line, and my palms moisten.

Betty the Barista taps her finger on the register. "Miss, what'll it be?"

I order all in one breath: "A Grande decaf Americano with room for cream, a Grande blonde roast with room for cream, two Grande pumpkin spice lattes, and one venti vanilla latte with no foam. *Please.*"

There's heat behind me as Nick chuckles.

Glancing over my shoulder, I send an awkward, apologetic smile.

He shrugs. "Hey, a deal's a deal." After handing his credit card over to Betty, he walks to the other side of the store to wait with me. He extends his hand. "Nick Scott."

"Kate Dailey." I close my hand over his. "I..."

He speaks before I can find the words. "Tell me, Kate Dailey, do you always need such a copious amount of caffeine in the morning?"

I hope he's joking, but my palms start to sweat anyway. "I, um, most of them are for a big meeting at work."

The bells on the door ring as a few new patrons enter, and Betty nearly sings, "Nick!"

I hurry to the counter to grab the five that are mine, murmuring a "thank you" while heat rises to my cheeks. "Well, I should be going. Thank you for all of this." I nod to the carrier.

Nick rushes to the door and holds it open for me. "See you around, Kate Dailey."

"I, uh ... We'll see."

"Well, you do owe me half a dozen coffees." He adds a wink that's cuter than it has any right to be.

"Touché." I shuffle across the street to the office, glancing back to find him looking my way, too.

The spark between us was almost as electric as the energy that consumes me when I first step foot inside the *Q Magazine* lobby. The familiar smell of must, sweat, and tears hits me instantaneously. I almost crave it when I'm not here: the hard work and success of writers, editors, publishers, photographers, and assistants who put everything on the line, day in and day out. *My people.* I take a deep breath, and the espresso-filled tray of drinks takes over my senses. The initial whiff is always gone too soon.

I'm late, again. Shit.

As my phone vibrates through my handbag, I shift and stack the coffee to one-handedly dig in my purse for my cell. I slide it to "talk," put the phone on my shoulder, and keep walking. "Hey, Ame, what's up?"

"Where the hell are you?" Amy whisper-screams.

"In the lobby, headed up."

"I'll meet you at the elevators."

I slip the phone back in my bag, re-adjust my hold on the cups, and step foot into the waiting elevator car to go up eleven floors to magazine headquarters.

True to her word, Amy Park, the shoulder-length, raven-haired, amber-eyed, bombshell editor at *Q*—and my boss, confidant, and best friend—is waiting. She's fidgeting with her cadet blue blazer before she reaches out to take the tray from my hand.

We rush down the hall to the Monday morning meeting as I smooth out my skirt.

She leans in and whispers, "What happened? Do you have any idea what time it is?"

"Sorry, the line was out the door today."

"I don't think anyone else noticed, but we need to get in there."

Take a deep breath, I accept the coffee carrier back from Amy. As we pace by the white wall showcasing framed issues from the past year, I can't help smiling at the latest issue of *Q*. It's a special one, not just because it has my first mag-published piece, but because of what it stands for and who helped inspire it. I blink the thought away before it has a chance to linger too long.

Amy pulls at my arm. "Wait a minute. You have a *look*."

I tilt my head. "What look?"

"An 'I just got laid' look."

"I do not have a *look*. I was just thinking Selena's November issue looks great next to Taylor's October cover."

Amy waves her arm. "Yeah, but did you get laid last night?"

My silence confirms it, and she screeches.

"I *knewww it*. Who is he? *How* was he? Was this at Encore after we left? Or did you go to The Saloon again?" She shoots question after question, one after the other, without taking a breath. A few people look up from their cubicles, glaring one by one.

"Amy, we're late. If we don't get to this meeting, I may be fired. Hell, I'm late enough; I may be fired anyway." I freeze in place as her last question hits my brain. "Wait, why do you say The Saloon like it's toxic? It's the best bar on the Lower East Side."

"'Best bar' is debatable. They can't fire you ... they need you. *I* need you." She pauses and checks her watch. "Whew, we need to get in there, but we're not done with this conversation, Kate."

"Second time I've heard *that* today."

Amy raises her eyebrows in a *'we will be talking about this'* kind of way, opens the conference room door for me, closes it as she follows behind me inside, and takes her seat near the front of the room.

"Kate. How nice of you to join us at nine-twenty-seven." Amy's boss, Lucy, is an intimidating woman despite her five foot and size zero frame.

"I'm sorry, Lucy." I keep my head down as I distribute the coffee.

"I suppose you just *forgot* the meeting starts at nine sharp *every* Monday."

"I—"

Lucy cuts me off. "Don't bother. I'll take the tray, and you can sit."

I grab a chair away from the table, which is reserved for editors and full-time contributors. As one of the assistants, I pick up coffee, take notes, and do anything else Amy needs. Lucky for me, Amy is as cool a supervisor as she is a friend, and she tries to make my life at work not only bearable but enjoyable. Not every editor/editorial assistant relationship here is as functional as ours. Part of it, the part everyone sees, is Amy's the youngest editor in the history of the magazine, so she not only busts her ass to show she's earned it (and she has), but she also lifts everyone around her. She doesn't talk down to anyone, from the janitor to her assistant (Hi). While there's no denying how wonderful Amy is at work, it's the other part, the one no one sees; that's my favorite part of who she is. It's the long nights at the office, Jose Cuervo-induced Kelly Clarkson karaoke nights at a local pub, and the girl talk. It's her being the same person, no matter if she's in the office or if we're hanging out at each other's apartments to discuss non-work-related things like relationships (or lack thereof) or having long-standing marathons of the Bachelor/Bachelorette while splitting a bottle of Moscato.

I owe Amy a lot, so as soon as the meeting ends, I hustle into her office. I know we'll be digging into details from last night, why I was late this morning, and meeting notes all in one fell swoop—and I kind of want to.

"So ..." Amy begins.

"Okay. I brought someone home last night; it's not a big deal." I shrug and set down the water bottle I picked up while leaving the meeting.

She gives me a pointed look. "Don't give me the 'it's not a big deal' or 'this happens all the time,' or 'it was just some guy I met at The Saloon' speech."

I raise my finger toward her. "One, while The Saloon slaps, two, it was Encore, and three, it *was* a random guy. It was a one-night stand, truly not a big deal, and I've had better."

"See? This is what I am talking about. You say it's a random hookup, but you come in here all 'cat ate the canary' look on your face, which says it was more than some random guy you want to forget."

I take a long sip of water and stare at Amy. There's no way she's going to let this go. I sigh. "Okay. You're half-right."

"I knew it!" She shouts.

"Shhh!" I rush to close the door. She may have a 'private' office, but it doesn't mean the rest of the open-concept floor plan won't hear everything she says.

"Okay, keep it down," I whisper. "It wasn't the guy from last night."

"What?" She stares wide-eyed.

"It wasn't the guy from last night."

"There's someone else?" Her eyes dart around the room.

"It's not what you think. I met someone at Starbucks this morning. He paid for our entire coffee order and said he'd be 'seeing me around,' full air quotes. Nothing serious, and I doubt I'll ever see the same stranger again in Manhattan, but there's something about him."

Amy slaps my knee. "Unbelievable. In one of the most single cities in the world, I can't find someone—anyone—to spend a nice dinner with, but you're fighting them attractive men off with a stick. It's not fair."

"What happened to Alexis?"

She shrugs. "Eh, it fizzled. The next time we go out, you need to be my wing-woman. I can't be the only person in the city not getting any action."

I slap my palm to my forehead. "I can't believe you said, 'getting any action.'"

"What? It's true."

"It's also very ... old, and you're twenty-six. Do what any other twenty-something is doing and download Tinder."

"Eww. No. I do not have the energy for that."

I slouch in her guest chair as I start thinking of alternatives. "Oh! What about that new guy? I thought I sensed a vibe between you two?"

Amy blushes and avoids my gaze. "Leo? No. Not an option."

I straighten my back. "What do you mean not an option?"

She changes the subject. "Tell me more about Coffee Guy."

"What's to say? I just met him."

"What's his name?"

I shrug. "Nick something."

Amy inches her keyboard closer to her. "Mhm, not much to go off of, but I still think I can find him."

My jaw drops. "Amy Marie, you are not cyber-stalking this man."

"Oh, come on," she objects. "What if he's a serial killer?"

"It's not like this is Sloane. I doubt I'm going to see him again in the city."

She clicks her tongue. "You never know. What's he look like?"

"Dark, slicked-back hair, big, brown eyes, clean shaven, tall, handsome, fills out a suit well."

Her eyes light up. "Sounds delicious."

I sigh. "Yeah."

Amy points a finger at me. "Okay, what is that?"

"What is what?" I point back.

"The disappointment I'm picking up in your voice." Her eagle eye doesn't miss. "What's wrong with him?"

"Nick's ... nice. I'm sure he's perfectly datable if I ever see him again."

"Perfectly datable? Where's the heat? The passion? A hot man bought you and four other people in the office coffee, and not cheap coffee, I might add—good coffee. If it happened to me, I would have jumped him right there, witnesses be damned."

"How are you still single?" I divert my eyes.

Having a best friend who's known me for years means I don't have to say anything—she'll say what I'm thinking for me.

She narrows her eyes. "It's *him*, isn't it? He's not Jase?"

I meet her question with silence, confirming her suspicion. It's not that there wasn't heat with Nick, but it was brief, a fluke, a ...

"Kate, what's it gonna take to get over that asshole? He broke your heart, what, six years ago? You've got to move on."

"I am moving on." And it's not that simple ...

"Cheap one-night stands do not count."

I shoot her a look, but I know she's right. Jase isn't knocking down my door, but I'd be a fool if I ever let someone get that close to me again. I take another sip of water and change the subject. "By the way, did I tell you what the guy from last night said this morning?"

She lifts her coffee and taps the lid. "I wanna have your babies?"

I wince. "Close?" I say with one eye closed. "First, he called me babe, and you know how much that makes me want to hurl."

She nods, ever the supportive friend.

"Then, he asked if he could see me again and, I quote, 'tonight.'" I make air quotes with my fingers.

Amy fumbles with her cup. "He asked what? Whatever happened to one-night stands being cool, casual, this-is-no-big-deal kind of people?"

"Thank you!"

"What'd you say?"

"I think I said, 'We'll see.' I don't know, I kind of pushed him out in his boxers and left."

Amy half-claps. "Atta girl, we don't need guys like that getting ideas ... with Jase still tying up your mind."

I roll my eyes. "I told you I'm working on it."

"Yeah, yeah. All I'm saying is if you see Nick again, you should go for it."

I raise my eyebrows. "Okay. *If* I ever bump into him again, I'll consider letting him buy me a drink."

"And dinner. Okay ... meeting notes."

Our conversation shifts toward headlines, deadlines, and how *extra* Lucy was during the morning meeting.

After the shop talk, Amy jumps up. "I've got to run to another meeting, but I'll be over for *The Bachelorette* tonight."

"Perfect. I have plenty of wine and frozen pizza."

She scrunches her nose and, on our way out of her office, says, "We'll spring for the good stuff."

To Amy, the "good stuff" is Dominos. A city full of pizza options, and she'll order Dominos.

"For the millionth time ..." I lower my voice on my way to my cubicle, "... you can get Dominos anywhere. If we're ordering, let's try a big ol' oozing slice from Nina's. Please?" I all but beg. "One time?"

"We'll see," she sings, then in a serious tone, "Nice buzzword, but no oozing. That's too much—even for me."

"Move." Lucy sprints down the hallway in her black stilettos, glasses never moving off her face, bun standing firm.

"Where do you think she's going ... and how does she make it look graceful in heels?"

Amy shakes her head. "Lucy never has a single run in her stockings, did you notice?"

I laugh. "Now wouldn't that be a great blog topic?"

"Sure would, but you better get me the 'New Year, New You' article first."

My smile falls. "How's tomorrow?" I'm half-joking.

"Five o'clock, today." Amy counters.

I look down at my half-bitten nails. "Yeah, I've got some plans at five ..."

"If you've got time to think about oozing pizza ..." She grimaces. "You've got time for a five-hundred-word article I know for a fact is on your to-do list, Kate Dailey."

Touché. "One New Year's piece headed your way."

Ten minutes to five, I Slack the *New Year, New You: Letter from the Editor* article Amy's way with a note asking for feedback. I glance at my reflection in the hall mirror and release an audible *phew:* my long, auburn hair has managed to stay straight in its pony, my black eye makeup hasn't run too much, and my skirt spent the entire day covering my underwear instead of tucked in it. Miracles do happen. I plug my earbuds in and draft my latest blog post on the way to the subway.

Have you ever had one of those days?

You know the ones, where you need to put on pantyhose, hosiery, stockings ... it doesn't matter what you call them: hell sticks. Ask any woman. They suck. Sure, they may "look nice" ... for, maybe, five whole minutes. Then, they become the bane of a woman's existence. If you've ever watched The Princess Diaries—*particularly, the scene in which Princess Mia is in the back of the limo, rolling around trying to get the damn things on, cursing, screaming, and unable to sit still—well, the image you have in your head is exactly why ... There is no "good" way to put on a pair of stockings.*

I'm home in record time, even after a stop at Bone Appetit for Hyla. The key turns in the door, and I hear her collar jingle. She runs over to greet me as soon as I step into the all-white space.

"Hey, sweet girl," I say, leaning down to scratch her tan ears. She rolls over for belly rubs, and I can't deny her fluffy self all the pets. "I'm sorry about this morning, babes, but I got you the good treats to make up for it."

Hyla sniffs the Bone Appetit bag and stretches. She hops when I grab her leash and let her out.

We're no sooner back inside with Hyla's crunchies poured and my bed sheets changed when Mama calls, right on time for our weekly chat.

"Hey, Mama, how are you?"

"Hey, sweetie, I'm miserable as usual; thanks for asking."

A Pop-ism. It brings a smile to my face thinking of the sweet man my grandfather is and how his 'catchphrase' that never suits his personality has become a *thing* in our family. Even for his daughter-in-law.

"What're you writing for the blog this week?" Mama's question brings me back to reality.

"The trouble with stockings." I put my phone on speaker while I plop the comforter back on the bed.

"Oh, Lordy, that's gonna be a good one." Occasionally, my mama's Southern accent comes out strong. "How's my sweet grand-dog?"

I glance over at Hyla, who's finished her dinner and passed out in her dog bed, a smile on her face. "She's good, off to dreamland."

My mama audibly sighs. "So cute. Send me pictures when we hang up." She is almost as obsessed with my dog as I am.

"Will do. How's everything there?"

"Everything's fine, sweetie. Just grabbing some groceries for dinner, and—oh joy, there's Matilda. I should go before she harasses you, too. Love you, sweetie. Can't wait to read the newest blog."

"I love you, too, Mama."

She hangs up and I quickly take a photo of a sleeping doggo to send to Mama, as requested, and wish her luck escaping the town gossip as quickly and painlessly as she can.

She replies with two emojis: heart eyes and praying hands, just as Amy rushes in the door with Chinese food and a large bottle of white wine. "I'm early, I know, but I'll get some glasses poured while you work on your blog."

I rush to the kitchen to help Amy with the bags she's holding. "I thought we were throwing in a frozen pizza, or, you know 'getting the good stuff.' I also know I told you I had wine."

"Yeah, yeah, I know, but there's a new place down the block, and it smelled amazing, so I just got us another option. You know, in case you decide you don't want to die from plastic pizza ... and the wine was right there, easy peasy."

I audibly sigh. We've had this *discussion* many times. "It's not plastic. It's amazing, and you know it."

"It's no Dominos."

"Now who's talking about plastic pizza?"

Amy gasps and looks around the space as if she's addressing a crowd, "Kate Elizabeth Dailey—you take that back. The Pizza Gods can hear you; don't make them mad."

I lift my hands in defeat. "Okay, okay. I'm about halfway through this post, so go ahead and get started, and I'll join you when I'm done."

"You got it, sister."

Amy knows her way around my tiny apartment. She moves around my cabinets, grabbing a plate, a napkin, and chopsticks, and selects a variety of food in the boxes and cartons she brought over. She brings everything over to the couch and places it on the coffee table before going back to pour some wine for each of us.

Hyla wakes up and walks toward the coffee table, but Amy's quick and slides right into the spot, grabs her plate, and sits with her legs underneath her on my twenty-dollar, thrift store couch. *Hey, if it ain't broke...*

She waves a chopstick at Hyla and says, "Not today, doggo. You know I like you, but there's no way I like you enough to give you my Mushu pork."

As if on cue, Hyla tilts her head to the side, looking impossibly cuter.

Amy just snorts and looks at me. "Are you seeing this shit?"

I nod. "Oh, I see it. She's a master manipulator, especially when there's food involved."

Amy shifts her plate to her left hand and attention to my weekly blog. "Are you going with the stockings post?"

"Sure am."

She takes a bite and tries to speak while she is chewing. "Love it."

My stomach growls, and I close my laptop. My hunger overtakes my willingness to finish the post. I'll get back to it later. I walk the three steps from the sectional to the kitchen counter, helping myself to some General Tso's chicken.

She follows me into the kitchen to top off her wine. "Is the Nick you met Nick Scott by chance?"

I turn to try and grab a water glass. "Oh my God, yes, that's it! How'd you know?"

Amy blinks innocently. "Told you I'd find him."

I exhale. "Okay, let's hear it."

She nearly jumps on the couch from a few steps away. Pulling out her phone, she clears her throat. "Okay, let's see. He's a lawyer, doing well for himself. A lot of connections on LinkedIn. Grew up in Jersey, moved here for work, no recent relationships, so no crazy exes you should worry about."

My mouth falls open. "You found all that on a first name and a vague description?"

Her smile widens, proud of herself. "Yep. I'll do anything for my bestie ... especially when Jase is still haunting you after all these years. You need a good guy to take your mind off him, if you know what I mean."

I roll my eyes. "I told you I'm working on that."

"Yeah, yeah, all I'm saying is if you see Nick again ..."

I take a big chug of my Moscato and raise my eyebrows at her. "Yes, okay," I cave. "I'll give it a try. *If* I ever see him again."

"That's all I ask." She puts her feet up on the coffee table and turns on *The Bachelorette*, "Now, let's see how Hannah does in picking her match this week."

"Hopefully, better than me."

"Hopefully, better than all of us."

Chapter 2

Now

All I'm saying is if you see Nick again ... Amy's words ring in my ear to the point that I'm not sure if I'm hallucinating the familiar stranger standing at the Starbucks counter in front of me ... or if it's really Nick collecting bills back from the barista and a plucking a paperboard cup carrier for his order.

Turning around, he grins and greets me when I walk in. "Hey, there."

I tilt my head and continue appraising the situation. Cups are slung behind the bar, multiple syrups are pumped, and espresso upon espresso is brewed and added to the recipes with urgency.

"I took a chance." Nick bites his lip, and I can't help but smile a little. *Point Nick.*

"And what if I didn't come in?"

He shrugs. "I guess I would have given them to the guy on that last stool by the bathroom."

I spin around to see another regular, dressed in head-to-toe flannel, with his headphones in, typing furiously on his laptop while his leg twitches the entire time like it always does.

"You were going to give the entire order to Dave?"

"You *know* him?" he gapes.

THIS KIND OF LOVE

I shake my head. "Well, I know *of* him. He's always here around this time, dressed like that, way too hopped up on caffeine ... which is why I doubt you would have given him much more than water."

Nick's eyebrows rise slightly into a question. "Well, you don't really know me—I'm pretty generous with coffee."

"You're right. I don't really know you, and that is exactly something a serial killer would say. You're not a closet murderer are you, Nick?" Damn Amy for getting that thought in my brain.

He's quiet.

Damn me for asking. I look down at my watch and shift my feet. "Oh, okay, well, look at the time. I should be going."

I rush out the door. Why did I ask the nicest guy I've met in months if he's a serial killer? Why didn't he say anything? Kate & the Serial Killer—maybe next week's blog. Mama will be proud.

Nick calls after me, "Hey, Kate."

Don't turn around; don't turn arou—

I turn around.

His eyebrows are creased in concern.

"Oh hey. Sorry about that, back there, I shouldn't have said that."

"I'm not a serial killer ... which I know is exactly what a serial killer would say, but I promise: I'm just a guy who likes a girl and wants to impress her with a gesture of goodwill. But looking back now, I can see how this could have been seen as coming on a bit strong."

I fidget.

"Okay, how about this: please hold these." He hands me the coffee and digs his right hand into his suit jacket, coming out with a business card. "Here's my card. You can research me if you want and make up your own mind."

"Sure, but I doubt all the bodies of the women in your basement would come up on a Google search." *Omg, can I not keep my damn mouth shut?*

I hand him his cup and his eyes, honest to God, twinkle. "You'd be surprised."

I stick his card in the middle of the coffee carrier and turn on my heel. "See you around, Nick Scott."

"See you around, Kate Dailey."

I walk a few steps closer to the hustle and bustle of city life, a crowd of people running around to hop in a cab or get on the subway, but today, I don't notice cabs honking or lifelong New Yorkers groaning when tourists cut them off on the sidewalk. I'm too busy trying to hide the smile on my face. I look behind me, hopeful, but Nick's already long gone. "But you," I say to the business card, "you're a nice touch." I add his contact to my phone before I can think better of it and stuff the card in my bag.

I'm still replaying the conversation, flipping his card over in my hand, as I open the door at *Q Magazine*. I walk down the hallway to the conference room and hand Amy the coffee tray for the weekly *Editors Only* meeting, nodding when she utters, "You're an angel."

As I approach my desk, still head up in the clouds, I text Nick before I can talk myself out of it.

> KATE DAILEY: Hi ... It's Kate.

Groundbreaking start.

> NICK SCOTT: Coffee Kate? Long time no talk.

> KATE DAILEY: That's me!

THIS KIND OF LOVE

When did I become so cringe?

> NICK SCOTT: Ha! Hey … any chance you're free tonight? I was thinking of making a stop at my favorite restaurant.

I drum my fingers against my phone. *What would Amy do? She wouldn't even think twice about a hot date with a good meal.*

> KATE DAILEY: That sounds great.

After we get the details nailed down, I try focusing on my work for the New Year's issue, but not even the promise of a Reese Witherspoon feature can keep my attention. At five o'clock on the dot, I fly out of the office to feed and walk Hyla and get ready for the first date that's brought butterflies in the better half of a decade.

The smokiness of sizzling steak fills the air outside of Sully's. Nick's waiting outside when my cab pulls up, the reflection of the city lights shimmering on the glass window behind him. His dark, wavy hair doesn't have a strand out of place, his three-piece suit is a perfect fit, and there's a bouquet of pink roses in his hands.

"Hey there." I stroll over to him in a long, black, silky dress, gray pashmina, and my trusted gray, knee-high boots.

"Hi, beautiful." He smiles.

The same twinkle from yesterday lingers in his eyes, and I can't help but smile, too. "I'm happy you asked to do dinner."

"Ever been here?"

I shake my head. "I have not."

"You're in for a treat." He lifts his eyebrows. "They have any kind of steak you could imagine, and their garlic mashed potatoes are the best I've ever had."

I tilt my head. "Now, now—I'll give you the steak, but my mama's potatoes are pretty damn good."

Nick laughs. "Alright, I know better than to argue with a girl about her mama's cooking."

As the hostess picks up a couple of menus and leads us to our table, I can't help looking back at the man behind me. I can't believe he looks like *that* in a suit.

He catches me staring and tilts his head as though asking, *Checking me out?*

I whip back around, my cheeks heated and flushed.

His hot breath tickles my ear. "I'm glad you said yes."

Nick pulls a chair out for me, and my shoulders relax a bit. It's just a date at a nice restaurant with a guy I'm interested in, who's interested in me, too.

His kind, brown eyes gaze into my giddy blue ones. "Are you hungry? Would you like an appetizer?"

"Sure. What's good here?"

He opens the front of the menu and ponders for a second before offering, "Cheesesteak Eggrolls?"

"Sounds great." I close my menu after deciding on my steak and sides.

"Your tastebuds will thank you later."

"That good?"

"Oh, they're *that* good."

His eyes shine in the light, and I'm captivated by his charm.

The server approaches, and we place our order while I focus on Nick and not my buzzing smartwatch. Whoever it is, they can wait.

"You're a lawyer, huh?"

He snaps his fingers. "Business card gives it away every time."

"What kind of law do you practice?" I unfold the table napkin and place it on my lap.

"I'm a corporate lawyer ... which is a ton of paperwork and threatening to file more paperwork, instead of arguing in court." He chuckles.

"Do you like it?"

His gaze drops. "Eh, could be better, could be worse. I like using the degree I sunk a ton of loans into, and I get to travel, which is cool. But I wish it was more exciting sometimes."

I look down. "I know what you mean."

"Oh? What do you do that you trek around Manhattan collecting coffee every morning?"

I smirk. "I'm an Editorial Assistant at a magazine downtown."

"*Q?*"

"Yes! How did you know?"

The server brings our drinks, and Nick sips his Octoberfest lager, then shifts his hand toward me.

"Lucy Lyons' name has come up around the office," he says.

I wrinkle my nose. "How so?"

"My boss went on a few dates with her. From what I understand, she is a little ... difficult. Anyway, it didn't work out because he can be a bit of a challenge, too."

I extend my glass. "To surviving the day-to-day."

"Here, here." He clinks his drink against mine as our eggrolls arrive.

When my watch buzzes a second time, I tap the side button to send it to voicemail. I take a bite of the appetizer and a moan escapes my throat. "Damn."

Nick nearly chokes on his eggroll.

"This is the best thing I've ever had in my mouth. I think ever."

"Wait until the main course." His eyebrows raise in jest.

My face flames. "Oh. I can't believe I said that."

Nick smiles. "Oh no, I get it. Sully's is the best restaurant in the city, hands down."

I take another bite and sigh in ecstasy.

He lights up when the server brings the main course over. "How long have you lived here?"

I pretend to consider his question like I've forgotten how long it's been, as if I could ever forget. "Oh, I don't know, about six years, I guess. You?"

"Brooklyn born and raised," he replies.

"Yeah? I've always wondered what it was like to grow up in a big city like this."

"Amazing, if you don't mind the constant noise and tourists everywhere." He smirks. "It's engrained in who I am, though. I couldn't live anywhere else."

"I've dreamed of living here my whole life, and now that I'm here, I can't imagine leaving." He cuts into his steak. "Mhm. Where did you grow up, if not a big city?"

"Sloane, Tennessee." I take a bite of the garlic mash and rush to pick up another forkful. "Okay, my mama would be mad at these potatoes."

"I told you they're good." He chuckles. "I've never heard of Sloane, but I go down to Nashville a few times a year for work."

I nod. "Sloane's thirty minutes outside of Nash. I was close enough to bright lights and tourists to crave it but far enough away that Sloane felt like a different world."

"How so?"

"There's all of three stop lights—and by three, I mean three individual lights, not this triage of lights we have here. There's a decorative light on the corner of every house. Everyone knows everyone. You get the gist."

He watches me, his gaze intent. "So, if the movies have it right, there's one high school, football games as 'the thing to do' on Friday nights, and Prom King and Queen who date from the time they were in diapers and live Happily Ever After."

"Exactly." My heart pangs. *But they don't always live Happily Ever After.*

"Ha, beat you!" Nick gestures to his clean plate.

"I don't even know how you did that." I look down at my half-full one. "I guess I'm having steak and eggs tomorrow morning."

He lays his right hand over his chest. "Girl after my own heart."

He winks, and it suits him. I want to smile and believe the sparkle in his eye, but the last time a guy said that to me, he broke my heart a few weeks later. I know better than to swoon or read more into this than it is. He's a random guy in a city full of random guys. It's a first date.

I know better.

Still, I can't help the flutter in my stomach or the hope he's somehow different from the man I left behind. Maybe he can be the one who helps me finally forget Jase.

Maybe.

As Nick helps me hail a cab after dinner, a bit of courage pours over me, and I say, "I had a really great time tonight."

"Me too." He smiles.

The cabbie pulls over, and I step inside the car.

"Hey, Kate Dailey—how about a second date at our Starbucks?"

Our Starbucks.

The sound of having 'our' anything warms my heart. I put my hand up to the window and try winking at him, but I end up blinking an eyelash into my eye. My love life's done a complete three-sixty in the last thirty-seven hours, and I can't contain my grin.

My phone rings, and Amy's image flashes on the screen. "Hey, you were right," I answer. "Went on a date with Coffee Guy, and I'm on my way home now. He's ... remarkable."

"Kate." Amy's clips my name, and I freeze. "Your mom's been trying to get in touch with you."

Everything around me fades except for an oversized lump forming in my throat. "What—what happened?"

"I'm going to be at your apartment in ten minutes. We'll talk in person, okay?"

"Ame, tell me," I plead.

Her voice falls. "It's ... your dad. He's sick, and your mom doesn't know if he's ... going to make it."

My entire body goes limp, causing my phone to crash in the footwell.

I don't remember the rest of what she says, what I reply, when I get back to my apartment, how I remembered to pick my phone off the ground, or how I packed for a trip for an undisclosed amount of time. All I know is a short while later, Amy, Hyla, and I are en route to Sloane.

For the first time in six years, we're heading home.

Chapter 3

Now

Most of the ride home is a blur of highway and oak, maple, and dogwood trees. I fade in and out of a restless sleep, mostly replaying memories I thought I'd buried deep: of 'No. I can't do *this* ... us' and 'No wonder he ended things with you' spinning over and over in my mind.

I blow out a breath and open my eyes.

Amy keeps her gaze on the road. "Oh hey, how're you feeling?"

I grumble.

"It's going to be hard to see your dad after all these years, but Hyla and I are here for you—no matter what happens."

Hyla stretches in the backseat, and I extend my hand to give her head scritches. She leans into me, far too good for this world. "I know. I honestly can't believe you picked me up and split a fourteen-hour drive to *Sloane*, of all places. I don't deserve you."

Amy smacks her lips. "Would you stop already? There's no way I was going to let you do this alone, and Hyla would not have put up with you leaving her for a month *or* boarding her on the back of a plane."

Amy's right. My precious, spoiled girl, who's currently curling up into a husky ball, would *not* have stood for airplane shenanigans.

Amy flicks the turn signal and shifts into the right lane. "Besides, we lucked out with Reese being the next cover. Convincing Lucy to come to Tennessee and wrap up the January article here was the easy part."

"You're amazing."

"Oh please, saving the mag money was all she needed to hear ... and I *may* have bribed her with a few bottles of bourbon we'll need to pick up on our way home."

I pat her right hand. "Thank you."

She grins. "You're welcome."

The clock on the dash reads eleven thirty a.m. right as we pass a sign saying Sloane, TN - 1 mile.

"Speaking of bourbon ..."

Amy finishes my sentence. "Way ahead of you."

My gaze wanders to the backseat. Hyla's awake and ready for a Tennessee pitstop. The one thing I've missed: while New York has plenty of *it* places, few of them will tolerate pets, while the Nashville area is full of dogs—everywhere. It's almost rude if you leave your dog at home.

Amy turns onto Main Street, trying to avoid a few runners in marathon training mode. "When's Sloane's 5K again?"

"In a few weeks, I think."

She clicks her tongue. "I don't think I could ever take up running, you know, because I like food and hate exercise."

"Says my size two friend."

"That shit is all genetics. Skinny doesn't mean healthy."

"Okay, make a left at the light. We'll see what Fran's Diner has on spec—wait, what happened to Fran's Diner? What's Firefly Lounge?"

Amy pulls into a parking spot and shrugs. "Well, *I* have no idea. Are you sure it was here?"

"Positive." With its vintage trolley car design, bright colors, and cheerful owner, Fran's Diner had been a staple of Calhoun County since ... well, forever, and the burgers were the one thing I was looking forward to while in town.

We unbuckle, get out of the car, and walk up the stone path. Amy runs inside for drinks while Hyla and I look for a table.

The new, modern wooden building has a large, shaded patio with white string lights hanging overhead. It's like a weird déjà vu, and I absentmindedly touch my wrist with my thumb.

Amy exits the bar, two Old Fashioneds in hand. She hands me one and lifts the other. "A toast to you facing the past."

I clink my glass to hers. "With help."

She sips her cocktail, sets it on the table, and glances around at the décor. "I know this place has new ownership, but it's exactly like you described ..."

My gaze goes back to the Firefly Lounge sign. There's something about it.

"Kay, is that you?"

Kay. My breath hitches in my throat. There's only one person who used to call me that, but I couldn't be that unlucky to see him within the first five seconds I'm in Sloane, could I?

"Kay?" His deep voice swirls in my ears again. Dammit.

I release my breath, close and re-open my eyes, stand, and turn around. Sure enough, I'm face-to-face with the man I've spent the last six years trying to forget: Jason Cole.

It should be freaking illegal for your ex to look as good as Jase looks now. I'd know his stormy green eyes and buzz cut anywhere. His arms look like they've doubled in muscle mass, and now he has a little scruff on his face. It's not unruly ... just enough to be hot as hell. Screw him. How does he get to shatter my heart and look like ... like ... a damn model?

"I didn't realize you were in town." I catch the drop in his voice. Is he concerned?

"I didn't realize you never left." I snap back at him, wiping my sweaty palms on my jeans.

He doesn't wince, but Amy does.

"Okay." She steps in between us. "Well, this has been fun, but we still have a full day ahead of us and have to get going."

Jase looks down. "Who's this?" He crouches to say give Hyla pets.

She wags her tail and leans into Jase. *Judas.*

"This is Hyla," I grumble.

"Hey, Hyla, you're such a cutie."

She rolls over for a belly rub, and he complies with a smile.

I roll my eyes—hard—and grip the edge of the table. My deeply ingrained Southern manners begin piecing together polite reasons to leave, but my inner New Yorker doesn't have the time or patience for small talk with Jase.

He shifts his gaze up to meet mine, green eyes pleading. "Kay—we should talk."

My traitorous heart skips a beat. "We have to see my mama."

Jase stands and puts his hands in his pocket. If there's one thing he understands, it's that family comes first.

Hyla glares at me, knowing full well I made the petting stop, and she is *not* happy.

I gather our things and walk to the car.

Amy leans in and mutters, "You did great, girlfriend."

"Hey, Kay," Jase calls after me.

I pivot to face him.

"The red suits you."

Out of instinct, I reach for my hair and focus on inhaling and exhaling.

Amy leans in again. "He got to you, huh?"

I don't answer. I don't need to. Amy knows as well as I do that it was more than what he said. It's as much what he didn't say. We have *history*, and sooner or later, we're going to need to talk about it—but that day is not today.

I huff to the car before she catches me.

"I knew it," she exclaims. "You still have feelings for him."

"I do not," I lift my fingers for air quotes, "have feelings for him."

"No?" She puts her seatbelt on and pokes my leg.

"No. Jase is locked in my past, thank you."

Amy gives me a hard stare. "Far be it for me to state the obvious here, but he doesn't appear to be locked anywhere. Nor does he want to be."

I grunt as she puts the car into gear. "It doesn't matter what he wants."

"Okay, fine. Let's not acknowledge the 'do me' eyes you were both giving each other in between giving Hyla love, which I know is your weakness—a hot man who loves your dog."

A deep groan escapes my throat. "He is hot, isn't he? It's not fair. I mean, how does that even happen?"

"I hate to break it to you, love, but I did some Insta-stalking, and Jase has always been fine. But yeah, in person, he is a lot hotter."

"Why are you Insta-stalking him? And how?" I fling my arms outward and grunt. "Aren't there rules in a breakup? Something like the heartbreaker gets old and ugly and the person broken up with gets to ... to *win*. It's not hard."

Amy nods in agreement, but her lips curl into a sly smile. She doesn't believe a word I'm saying.

We ride the last few blocks in silence until we pull into my parents' driveway.

I adjust the seat back and sink into it.

She puts her hand on top of mine. "The sooner we go in, the sooner we have answers and can start working on healing that broken heart of yours."

Taking a deep breath, I open the passenger side door, climb out of the car, and turn to face the life I left behind. Mama comes running from the house, the worn screen door slamming behind her.

"Hey, Mama."

She pulls me into a long, loving hug as if no time has passed.

I lean in and inhale the floral, citrusy punch of her *Sweet Magnolias* perfume. It's one of my favorite scents in the world because it reminds me of her. I gulp and get the courage to ask the question I've been avoiding but know she's been waiting to hear. "How's Dad doing?"

She responds by pulling me into a deeper hug, sobbing.

I hold onto her frail frame as she cries for hours or minutes; I don't know. Sloane is a complete time blob. "Mama?"

She sniffles. "He's not doing well, baby."

Amy pats my back and excuses herself to get Hyla and the bags out of the car.

"Come on. Let's head inside. We don't need a busybody seeing us out here and adding whatever they please to the rumor mill."

She sniffles again and walks us to the front door. Stepping foot into the living room brings back a carousel of memories: the back of the big, gray sectional in front of me, ready for company. The twice recycled coffee table, where Nana swindled us in rounds of Rummy. The thirty-two-inch TV, as dusty as it was six years ago, and the same old area rug we rolled in one cool, fall day, and the carpeted wraparound staircase off to the side, leading to rooms full of secrets and pain. Six years away doesn't ease the sting of heartbreak or make the wounds any less deep.

"Kate." Mama's brows furrow as she looks around the room and back at me. "Would you like some tea?"

Mama's sweet tea is unlike anything else around. I gather my thoughts and follow her into the kitchen.

The 90's checkered tile floor is sparkling, the faint scent of lemons still lingering in the air.

Mama fills three glasses and gestures for Amy and me to sit at the old oak table.

Amy pulls out the captain's chair, and Mama and I both scream, "Not that one!" right as the front left leg crashes onto the floor.

"What the hell?" Amy jumps back in the nick of time.

"It needs to get fixed," Mama offers, tilting her head off to the side.

I pull out the other end chair as Amy slides into the table's side bench. "It's been needing to get fixed for fifteen years, Mama."

She waves her arm in my direction. *Hush.*

"Mama, what happened?"

She cries again.

I rub circles into her back. "It's okay, take your time."

"I don't know what happened. Your daddy collapsed, sweetie. He was lying on the kitchen floor when I found him. He says he got dizzy, but when he sat down, he missed the chair."

"What happened next?"

Her breath slows. "He went to the hospital, and they found the tumor."

"How bad is it?"

"I don't know. I kind of blocked everything out after they said—" She breaks off into more tears. "The 'c' word."

Shifting my chair closer to hers, I pull Mama into my arms and close my eyes to brace for the tears. We stay like this for a matter of minutes before the front door swings open, jolting us apart.

"Lizzie! Katie girl! Ame!" Nana calls our names one by one, then heads into the kitchen, squinting. "Oh, there y'all are. Len, they're in here!" she shouts back at Pop as he steps foot in the house, paper bags in hand.

He follows Nana into the kitchen, sets the groceries down, and extends his arms as his face lights up.

I jump into my grandpop's warm embrace and squeeze.

He holds on for a moment before patting my back twice and pulling back to study me. "Well, look at you."

"Look at *you*," I counter. "Have you gotten stronger since your visit this summer?"

Pop's smile reaches his eyes. "I've been trying but had a little help ... but you—you're as pretty as ever, Katie girl."

"Thanks, Pop."

"Hey, Kate, why don't you and Amy go unpack and wash up upstairs, and we can let you know when it's time for dinner," Mama offers.

"Oh, Mrs. Dailey, we can help with dinner," Amy counters.

Mama puts her hand up in objection, and we silently agree and take our luggage upstairs.

THIS KIND OF LOVE

After showing Amy to the guest room at the end of the hall, I tiptoe to my old bedroom out of habit. Closing my eyes, I take a deep breath before turning the brass knob.

Nothing's moved since I left, except the overturned dresser that's made its way upright again. The queen bed my parents put in here when I turned sixteen still sits in the middle of the room, a fluffy, green comforter not a bit out of place. Four pillows rest on the bed, two on each side. The small closet is inches away, with a floor-length mirror hanging over the doorway, and my desk is to the side of it, followed by a bench at the bedroom window. The wooden window frame holds hundreds of scrape marks, years of pebble-throwing leaving their mark. The same ol' Magnolia tree is still standing tall in the sideyard, waiting for me to climb down her on my way to meet up with the boy next door. The boy who changed everything.

I wish I could blink away the memories, but instead of fading away, they get stronger and stronger, until they're all I see.

Until *he's* all I see.

Chapter 4
Then: Eighteen Years Ago

The moving trucks pull away from the house next door when Nana shouts up the stairs, "Katie girl, come on! I don't want to miss the funnel cake."

I drag myself off the window seat after spending hours staring at a new family carrying boxes into the old Craftsman house next door. It was empty for one month before the sign read: SOLD. I glance over one last time before barreling down the banister, my long blonde hair flying behind me like a cape.

This elicits a scold from Mama. "Careful, Kate."

"Are you coming with us?" I run into her arms for a hug.

She smiles down at me. "Not this time, sweetie. Go with Nana and Pop and be good."

"I'm always good." I squeeze before letting go.

Mama's face wrinkles in disagreement, but she doesn't argue.

Daddy's already snoring in a kitchen chair. Mama hums to herself as she selects a large pan from the cabinet. The oven beeps after it preheats, but Daddy never stirs.

Nana opens the front door, which regains my attention. "Which ride are you most excited about, Katie girl?"

"The slide! Ooh and the spinney one!"

"Which spinney one?" Pop whispers to Nana.

She rolls her eyes and mumbles, "Gravitron."

"Oh, yes, the Gravitron." Pop grins. "I think you're still a little small for that one, angel girl, but we could do the Tilt-A-Whirl if you want?"

I shrug. "Okay."

The annual carnival falls on the second week of July without fail. It's a few days before my birthday, and Nana and Pop come down from Nashville to make a week of it. It's one of the only times I get to see them over the summer, but this year, the trips have been more frequent. Sometimes, they help Mama, or they talk to Daddy. If I'm lucky, they take me out for the day.

As we approach the church, the air is consumed with fresh, fried desserts that'll be covered in layers of powdered sugar soon enough. The lights are blinding, almost like there's a mini city in a parking lot begging for adventure in a way a small town *doesn't*.

Despite the unbearable heat, the carnival hums to life with people folding balloons into animals, gathering by the pie stand, throwing at the dunk tank, and waiting in line for rides.

Nana gets a book of tickets and rubs her hands together. "Okay, what's up first?"

I study the options. "Can we do the castle?"

Her gaze doesn't meet mine. Stretching on my tiptoes, I glance around.

Pop's in the funnel cake line. Nana gives him a look, and he smiles.

She laughs. "Sure … after dessert."

The funnel cake is gone in a matter of minutes, and Pop and I are in the castle while Nana cheers for us on the ground. We make it past the silver bars and over the bridge before sliding down to the ball pit. A couple of kids are in the ball pit when we get there.

"Hey! I know you," a girl says to me.

I look at the dark-haired, green-eyed beauty in front of me. She seems like she's a couple of years older than me. I'm trying to place how I know her, but then I see *him:* the same copper skin, same dark hair, but green eyes a little more piercing. My stomach drops.

He smiles. "You're the girl next door. I saw you—watching us at your window earlier."

I retreat. "I don't think so."

"I'm positive it's you," he calls back.

I gulp and twist my head again. *No.*

Pop put his hand on my shoulder. "Katie girl, want to keep going?"

I nod, voiceless.

The girl lifts her hand to wave goodbye, and I wave back, looking past her to him.

We're no sooner out of the castle when Pop asks me, "Where to next?"

"Tilt-A-Whirl?"

Pop's eyes sparkle. "Race you there."

We must spend hours riding rides, playing games, and eating junk food. I'm in a daze when we leave, holding hands with Pop and skipping the second half of the way home. Then, a scream from a few doors down breaks through our happiness.

Smash.

THIS KIND OF LOVE

Shouting.

"Len," Nana warns Pop.

"I know, Mags." He rubs my hand as our skipping slows.

Three kids are running around playing tag, unaware of the chaos ensuing right next door.

Pop nudges my shoulder. "Hey, Katie girl, aren't those the kids from the Castle?"

"Yeah, they just moved here."

What is it like having siblings? People you can play with when the screams start or hide with when it gets scary. People who *get you* in a way your parents never could.

"Why don't you go play with them?" Pop pokes.

"Really?" I don't take my gaze off the scene in front of me.

He pushes me along.

I hug him before running next door.

"Oh, hey!" the girl from the ball pit calls me over, still dressed in a T-shirt and jean shorts. She pulls her braids over her right shoulder. "Do you want to play tag with us?"

"Sure," I reply.

"Oh good, the boys like to gang up on me, but I don't think they will with another girl here. I'm Jade."

"I'm Kate."

"That's Jack." She points to her younger brother. "Jase is over there." She shifts her attention to her youngest brother. Both boys are wearing basketball shorts and matching soccer jerseys.

"*You.*" Jase approaches me.

You, I think back, but answer, "Hi."

"Jase, leave her alone." Jade rolls her eyes. "Ignore him. He forgot how to make friends when we moved."

"It's ... okay." My feet awkwardly shift from side to side.

"How old are you?" Jade studies my face.

"I'll be six next week."

"Jase turned six last month, too. Jack's seven, and I'm ten-and-a-half."

Jack stomps his foot. "Can we play already?"

Jade transfers her hand to her hip and flips around, giving her younger brother a *look*. Turning back to me, she explains, "Okay, so, the boys are 'it.' Our base is the treehouse out back."

"Treehouse?"

"Go!" Jase shouts, and we all take off.

Jade is faster than I am, and she scales the ladder with ease. I'm close to the steps when there's a push on my left shoulder, almost knocking me over.

"Tag, you're it."

I turn around, out of breath, and come face-to-face with Jase.

He has a wide grin and is missing his top right tooth. "You're it," he repeats.

"Go, Kate!" Jade screams. "Go get him."

I bolt but miss the branch sticking out of the ground from the Magnolia tree in the side yard, right between our houses. Given it's the one I can see outside my bedroom window that I've spent enough time looking at, I should know where it is by heart. I trip and fall, letting out a huff as I grab hold of my red knee.

"Kate!" Jase comes running over. "Are you okay?"

"Ow!" A sting comes from a small cut on my left knee.

"Jade! Jack!" Jase calls.

Jade comes running from the treehouse and Jack from the front yard. Jade crouches down. "What happened?"

"She tripped," Jase says.

"Did you push her?" Jade counters.

"What? No. She fell."

"I think he pushed her," Jack interjects.

"No, I didn't," Jase cries.

I sniffle. "He didn't do it. I fell, but I'm okay."

"Maybe we should get you home." Jade helps me stand.

But instead of walking home, I squint in the distance. "Are there ... ?"

"Fireflies." Jase's smile widens.

"I'll go get the jars." Jade runs indoors.

Jack doesn't wait for her to get back before he takes off and catches them one by one in his hands before letting them go.

"Come on." Jase takes my hand.

"Where are we going?" I follow him back toward the treehouse and beyond the house into the woods before I realize how late it must be. Mama's probably worried. "I should go home."

"Kay, wait—look."

"Kate." I correct, but as my eyes trace his arm and pointer finger, I smile. Fireflies. Everywhere.

The light above the kitchen side door blinks three times in a row. It's the last call to come home. "Sorry, I've gotta go." I spin toward home.

"Kay, wait, you didn't get any fireflies," Jase objects.

"Next time," I call back, surprising myself with the promise.

I hustle inside and see Mama, Nana, and Pop enjoying a glass of Mama's sweet tea at the kitchen table.

Mama yawns. "Have fun, sweetie?"

"They were cool." I wash my hands in the sink.

There's a light knock on the side door followed by a quiet, "Ex-cuse me?"

We all turn around, facing the little voice. Mama stands.

Jase.

"Hello, and who do we have here?" Mama leans down.

"This is for Kay." Jase pulls a jar out from behind his back. He sets it on the kitchen floor and backs away.

Four dandelions stick out from the top of the jar with several holes in it, like Daddy taught me to do. His daddy must have taught him, too. The jar lights up. *Fireflies.*

Mama shakes her head. "Oh man, not even six years old and she's already got a boyfriend. I'm in trouble, huh?"

Nan and Pop laugh as Mama lifts the container onto the countertop.

As she tucks me into bed, her word echoes in my mind:

Flowers.

Fireflies.

Jase.

Trouble.

Chapter 5

Now

I lace up my old, black running shoes and reach for Hyla's leash, ready to sneak out into the darkness before the rest of the house—and the sun—wake up. We slink out the kitchen door, and the cool breeze hits my back as I stretch. I steal a glance at the house next door: there's a minivan in the driveway and a new swing set in the backyard where the old treehouse used to be. I didn't expect the wood to last forever, but the sight of the new plastic one doesn't sit right.

Hyla and I take off into a slow jog, absorbing Sloane—much like the neighbor's house, it's familiar but not the same as when I left. The decorative lights at the start of every driveway, kids running around, and the leaves, as bright and brilliant as they can be in the fall, are as I left them. There are Jack-O'-Lanterns on porches, fried cooking on the air, even early in the morning, and the score of the latest home game is shown on the marquee at the high school. The Farmers Market is still held every Wednesday through Saturday, festivals once a month, and exactly one of everything. The church across from the elementary school still has the same sign it's had for the last twenty years. There's a lot that remains the same, but it feels distant now like it doesn't belong to me anymore. Like *I* don't belong *here* anymore.

We make a left on Main Street and run right by Firefly Lounge. The lights are off, but I don't want to stop. Jase had dreams of being an artist, and he was a damn good one. Now, he works at a bar of all places. What happened? Would he have told me if I'd made a trip back down?

The front door opens, and Hyla and I pick up the pace, staring straight ahead, hoping if it is Jase, he doesn't see me, yet still kind of hoping he does. What's wrong with me? I turn up the volume on my earbuds to try and drown out the thoughts in my head, but it doesn't work. All I can think about is him.

When we get back to Mama's house, I open the side kitchen door, pour crunchies for Hyla and a glass of water for myself, and gulp it down in three sips. Putting my hands on each side of the sink, I gaze out the side window. Four kids run around the old Magnolia tree between our yards, screaming and playing like we used to do. Dandelions are growing, waiting to be trampled on by a stampede of young feet or plucked by me. I used to twist their stems in between my fingers when there were door slams, screeches, and glass that shattered into a million pieces on the hardwood floor. I'd cringe and flinch and tremble, and Jase would wrap his long limbs around me to keep me safe and warm. He'd rock with me, back and forth, back and forth, until the noise would plummet into a deafening silence we couldn't ignore.

"Thinking about the boy next door?" Nana enters the kitchen behind me.

I snap out of the haunted memory and turn around. "What in the hell are you wearing?"

Nana is in a bright pink, fluffy prom dress. *My* prom dress, frills and all.

"I found this in the attic. Isn't it great?" She twirls.

"It's *something*." I try to keep my shock in check.

With this, Amy comes trotting into the kitchen in a tight, yellow, floor-length number I wore to freshman formal.

I check my watch. "Did I miss last call for prom, or what is going on here?"

"Oh, we thought it would be fun to spend the day like this."

"Are you kidding? You're going to end up in Matilda's column faster than you can click your clunky heels together."

Amy shrugs. "So? From what I hear, she's a gossip columnist who will write about us anyway. Might as well be for something fun."

I cough. "Something fun is relative."

Amy puts her right hand on mine. "Relax, it's for a quick photo shoot to fill in the New Year's issue before I meet up with Reese's team on Monday."

Nana tries to sit, but the chiffon does not cooperate. She gives up and leans against the kitchen counter. "Do you want to come with us, Katie girl? I think I saw another dress up there."

I shake my head. "No. Thank you, though."

"Suit yourself," Nana replies, heading out of the kitchen as quickly as she swished in.

Amy kneels to give Hyla ear scratches. "Hey, ever hear anything from Nick?"

I sigh. "No, but not exactly surprising, I guess."

"Maybe he's waiting a few days."

"Maybe. What's going on with your work flirtmance?" I counter.

Her eyes narrow. "We're not talking about me and Leo."

"Oh, so there is you and Leo?" My phone buzzes. *iMessage from Nick.* "When did you get a crystal ball?"

45

She stands. "What?"

I hold up my phone. "He texted me."

"Maybe I should play the lottery. What did he say?"

> NICK SCOTT: "Good morning, beautiful. Is the three-day rule still a thing? It seemed like forever. Can we rule it out next time?"

Amy squeals. "See, I told you he was probably waiting it out. The rule *is* outdated."

I can't help grinning. "He seems pretty old-fashioned."

"Kind of cute. He did say next time. I think it's worth a reply."

Pacing my fingers across the screen, I pause. "And say what? I'd love for there to be a next time ... at some point, when my life isn't falling apart, states away?"

"Come on, Ame," Nana calls from the other room. "We should get going!"

My best friend shifts. "I mean, maybe start with what's going on."

"Would you stick around waiting for someone you went on one date with?"

She puts her hands up in surrender. "He may surprise you. Are you sure you don't want to come with us?"

"Definitely not on a town photo shoot, but I could use some coffee."

Amy points in my direction. "Deal. But go shower first."

An hour later, we're in line outside Java House, enjoying the brisk fall breeze and watching the candy apple leaves sway on the trees. There are six people ahead of us, but with each order, the door opens, and I can catch a whiff of rich espresso brewing a few feet away.

Amy is explaining the difference between a caramel latte and a caramel macchiato to Nana when a familiar, deep voice calls out, "I hear the maple latte is pretty good here."

My breath catches in my throat, but I don't turn around. I act like I don't hear him. When the next group moves forward, we do, too.

Amy and Nana are too deep in their conversation about all the things caramel to notice Jase's presence.

"Although, it *is* Pumpkin Spice season," Jase whispers, his breath cool near my ear.

I close my eyes and try not to inhale his husky cologne. *Go away.*

"Unless you want to go with old faithful."

I grit my teeth. "What do you want, Jase?"

"A vanilla latte, then? Borrrr-ing. You should at least go with something apple cidery." I open my eyes and turn to find his smile as annoyingly perfect as I remember.

Don't let him break you down, Kate. "Were you always this obnoxious? Or is this a new thing?"

"Oh, come on, Kay. You used to find me endearing." He's teasing, but he's right: I did.

I scoff. "*Used to* is the key phrase there."

Our former elementary gym teacher taps his foot behind Jase, as impatient as he's always been.

When I turn back around, there's an open space in line. Okay, maybe the foot tap was warranted. We inch forward.

"Katie girl, what're you gonna get?" Nana's attention shifts. "Oh, hello, Jason. Isn't there anywhere else you could be this morning?"

"Nana ..." I warn.

She doubles down. "Well, isn't there?"

"Wasn't there another bar *y'all* could've visited yesterday? It's the charm of a small town." He shrugs, unbothered.

The door opens, and we walk inside. A brief break from Jase.

Before I know it, he's inside behind us. "Kay, can we talk a sec?"

"No." I refuse to look his way.

The barista asks for our order, and Nana and Amy order caramel macchiatos while I ask for a vanilla latte, even though the voice in my head is screaming at me that it's boring. I don't care. 'Boring' is exactly what I need right now.

"Here, I've got this." Jase holds his card out to the barista. I push his hand into his chest.

"No, thank you." I tap Apple Pay at the register. His quickened pulse reminds me my left hand is still holding Jase's, and I recoil. The loss hits me as soon as I let go.

Jase stares at the floor. "You know, you can hold my hand. It doesn't have to mean something."

My heart pangs. "Not in this town. I hold your hand once, and everyone will be talking about it." I mumble, but it's loud enough for him and me.

He winces, and we look around, seeing the patrons staring and pointing at us.

"Oh, great. Matilda," I groan.

"Screw her. Screw all of them." He raises his voice.

The barista calls our order. Nana and Amy grab the coffees and wave me over.

"I have to go." I brush past him.

"I miss you!" Jase all but shouts as I near the door.

The entire world freezes for a moment.

Matilda is staring at me, phone in hand, ready to print this entire interaction in her weekly column and spread it to any and everyone who will listen ... which, for a town this small, is still somehow a lot.

"Good." I turn my back and walk out of the door.

"Ooh, girl, I am proud of you!" Amy says. "How do you feel?"

The adrenaline from the moment is still going strong. "Energized, but I have more to say." I backstep to the coffeehouse.

Amy yanks my arm.

"Oh no. If you go in there, it's going to minimize the power of the whole interaction."

"But..."

"I know." Amy pats my back.

We walk past a few businesses and further into town before stopping at the outdoor Farmer's Market between Main and Broad streets to pick up fresh produce and surprise Mama with dinner.

"This is ... busy." Amy steps back as a postal worker comes rushing by.

"It is." I take in the crowd of people throughout the lot.

"Of course it is; it's gorgeous out," Nana acknowledges and takes off for the jam stand in the middle of the setup.

"The jam booth looks popular."

"Oh, you have no idea." I roll my eyes. "Jam is probably the thing people in this town fight over the most."

"I don't ..." Amy trails off as Nana and another older woman grab hold of a jar of Apple Pie spread, each pulling, refusing to give in. "Okkkkkkay. I'm gonna turn around and pretend I don't see the whole thing happening." She moves her hand in the air, gesturing to the scene about to go down.

"Told ya," I say. "Come on, let's go pick out some fresh bread."

Amy's eyes light up. "Now you're speaking my language."

We're a few feet away from Jackie's Bread Stand when there's a tap on my shoulder.

I all but jump. "Jase, I thought I told you—" My voice drops as I turn around and stare into the daunting, chocolate brown eyes of the fiery, sixty-year-old, ice blonde in front of me. "Oh Matilda, hi."

"Hello, Kate. Welcome back." Her shrill voice hasn't changed in the years I've been away.

My grin freezes in place.

"I'm sorry to hear about your daddy."

"Thank you." Despite her genuine tone, I can't help a chill from running up my spine. She wants something.

Amy must sense trouble because she puts on her professional editor face, complete with a soft smile, and extends her hand. "Hi there, I'm Amy Park, a friend of Kate's."

Matilda's right eye twitches for a brief second before she recovers and shakes Amy's hand. "Matilda Grey, it's nice to meet you."

"Nice to meet you, too."

The two women are stuck in a staring contest, trying to out-smile each other.

I interrupt, "Lovely of you to come over, Matilda, but we should get back to shopping for dinner."

"Oh, sure." She blinks. "Just a reminder about the Annual Pumpkin Festival tomorrow night."

"Right ... the second Friday in October."

"Every year," Matilda sings. "And as you know, everyone ... and I mean *everyone* will be there, if you catch my drift." She winks.

I sneak away. "Yes, I hear you. Well, as I said, we should get our groceries."

A scream rings out from the jam stand, causing Matilda to put her right hand to her heart. "Oh, is that Maggie? Bless her heart. See y'all tomorrow." She princess waves and walks away.

The smile I forgot I was holding drops from my face when I hear her fake-ass *bless her heart*.

Nana runs over, face flushed. She puts her hands on her knees and leans over to try and catch her breath. "We have to go."

There's an older woman with gray hair, small wire glasses, an embroidered scarf, and a leaf-patterned dress hot on our tails. "Maggie Dailey, get your ass back here with my jam."

Nana spins around to stick her tongue out and blow a raspberry at the woman before picking up speed. "Come on, girls, make a right down this alley."

We pick up our pace to match Nana and dart down the alley in question. We hide behind a big, blue dumpster and wait for the woman chasing Nana to pass. She steps into the backstreet, and I peek behind the dumpster to see this poor woman who has been chasing us in a dress and heels. What did Nana do? The woman scrutinizes her surroundings, but she doesn't seem to see us. Her heels click as she runs past us. We collapse on the ground in relief.

Amy grabs hold of her nose. "What died?"

I pat the dumpster. "This."

Nana laughs erratically.

Amy and I catch each other's gaze above Nana's head. She raises her eyebrows, and I roll my eyes *all* the way back.

"What's so funny?" I don't hide the snark in my voice.

"I won." Nana cackles. "I can't believe I won."

"Nan, did you steal the jam?"

"Oh, hell no. I threw a twenty down on the table at the same time Thea did, but the poor girl behind the table said it's up to us to decide who gets it since it was her last jar. Thea always looks put together, no matter the day, time, or place, and it's *annoying*. Plus, we needed a win, so I ran like hell."

My head sinks into my hands.

Amy's laughter roars.

I tilt my head a full forty-five degrees.

"Seventy-year-old Mags ran down Main Street like she stole jam when she probably overpaid for it."

"It was worth it," Nana counters.

Amy chuckles. "Seriously, Kate, chicken legs over here ran down the street ... for *jam*."

I can't help my belly laugh. Okay, she's right. Nana, who makes fun of me for running for fun, flew down the street like her life depended on it "for jam." I say the last part out loud, which starts a new laugh cycle between the three of us.

The Emergency Exit door next to us flings open. Jase exits with an empty keg over his shoulder. He sets it down when he clocks us and puts both arms on his waist. His blue jeans and dark Firefly Lounge tee are both snug in all the right places, and my mind goes a mile a minute. Did his arms get more toned since the coffee house?

He catches me staring and plants his hands on his hips. "See something you like, Kay?"

I fake gag. "Do you always come barreling out of doors like a hurricane?"

He smiles, slow and knowing. "Sweet girl, if I knew it was you on the other side of this door, I may have come *barreling out* a bit faster."

I growl.

Nana mumbles, "Hot damn."

"Amy, Maggie. If not to gawk at the town bartender, is there any other reason you're hiding behind a dumpster on this fine day?"

Nana stands, straightening her sundress. "This was a pit stop."

"To?" Jase holds out his hand.

I say, "We were just leaving."

But Nana counters with, "Panty shopping."

Jase raises his eyebrows, clearly not expecting Nan's answer. "Oh, really?"

"Katie needed some hot lingerie for her new fella."

Jase coughs as my cheeks suddenly feel warm, "Well, all right then." He moves around us to dispose of the keg. "Y'all let me know when my alley is clear again. I don't want people thinking they can hide out here instead of coming into the bar."

Jase's hand connects with the handle, and he turns the knob. The door creaks open, and I think he's going to go back to work without another word, but he turns around, his green eyes on fire. "Hey, Kay ... good luck finding that lingerie." He winks and disappears into the building.

Jase's snarky laugh and wink break into my thoughts. When did he become a guy who winks? Nick's a guy who winks, not Jase.

"Okay ... I know it was a joke at first, but I really could use some panties. Your pop and I have had a long, successful marriage, thanks to that store." Nana points to the Victoria's Secret knock-off a few doors down.

Even Amy cringes at that one. "I can't believe Sloane doesn't have a Target but has an entire store in the middle of town dedicated to lingerie."

"We've got priorities," Nana quips.

Amy pulls my hand along. "Come on, who knows what Nana has up her sleeve for Pantyland."

I wince. "Oh, God, can we not call it that?"

"No promises." She smirks.

While Amy swears by "no promises" when she doesn't want to break her word, my gaze drifts back to the bar's back door, to a time and a man who promised everything—and then took it away. I know I've needed to let him go for far too long, but what if I can't? What if I'm incapable of it, because he never let go of his hold on me? First loves aren't meant to be your last ... are they?

Chapter 6
Then: Fifteen Years Ago

"Jase, slow down!"

"We're almost there, Kay. Keep your eyes closed." Jase guides me along.

My right foot hits the stump between our side yards, and I almost fall. He catches me and helps me back up to walk a few more feet on steady ground.

"Are you okay?"

"Mhm, thanks."

Jase removes my hands from my eyes. "Okay, we're here."

I blink them open. "The treehouse?"

"Well, the real surprise is up there, but I didn't think you should climb it without being able to see." He kicks the ground, a small blush rising to his cheeks.

Reaching for the ladder, I place one foot in front of the other and climb up with him right behind me.

There's a child-size table with two chairs pulled out right in the middle of the house. A tiny plate sits on top of the table with a Funfetti cupcake and a smattering of icing next to a glass jar full of dandelions and a hand-drawn card of us chasing fireflies.

"What's all this?" I turn to Jase.

His forest green eyes are full of something I can't quite put my finger on, but when he smiles, my whole world stops. "Happy Birthday, Kay."

"This is ... this is—"

"Kate! Come in and wash up, you can help me make supper!" Mama shouts from the kitchen window.

"I have to go home, but this is ..."

His lips curve into a frown. "It's okay."

"Jase—"

He sticks his hands into the pockets of his basketball shorts. "I'll be right next door if you need me."

"Kate, come on in, sweetie!" Mama calls again.

I climb down the treehouse steps and run through the kitchen door. "Hey, Mama."

"Hey, birthday girl! How's Jason doing?"

"He's good. He made me a cupcake and a card."

"A cupcake *and* a card, huh?" She washes her hands but gives me a wink over her shoulder. "He must like you."

"Yeah." I giggle. "Are Nana and Pop coming for dinner?"

"Pop got stuck at work. They're going to come by for cake and coffee in a bit." She takes the biscuits out of the fridge while I wash my hands. "Here, can you help me roll these guys out on the tray?"

I pull the tin toward me. Helping with the biscuits is the best part—you get to make sure they have the right amount of fluff and buttery goodness.

Mama cuts an onion. "Want to measure out the milk?"

I grab the gallon of whole milk and pour four cups into a large measuring cup when Daddy stumbles in the kitchen, nearly collapsing in the chair.

"What're you girls making?" he slurs.

"Biscuits and gravy," Mama answers.

"Mmm, my favorite meal, and my favorite girls." He tries to stand but can't find his balance and falls back down. His face is beet red, and his mahogany eyes are bloodshot; he blinks to try and stay awake.

The snores start while the gravy starts to sizzle in the pan. I peek over at Daddy. His head is leaning back against the stripped wallpaper, hair like it hasn't been brushed in months, ripped jean shorts falling off his waist, his tank top torn, and his mouth wide open.

Mama rolls her eyes and stirs the gravy. She whispers, asking me to put the milk back in the fridge and set the table.

"How can he live like this, Mama? How can we? He didn't even remember it's my birthday."

She shivers, and I can't tell if she's cold or crying.

I put my right hand on her shoulder.

She mumbles, "I'm sorry, baby."

Daddy snores himself awake and asks what's going on.

"Supper is about ready," she says.

I set three water glasses on the table while Mama takes the biscuits out of the oven.

Daddy pushes his water glass away and stammers, "Beer." His angry eyes look like they're looking through me to Mama. "Beer," he repeats, louder.

Heat rises to my cheeks. Trying to keep the tears in check, I open the fridge and take out a can of beer, bringing it to Daddy.

Mama portions out each of our plates and places them on the table, avoiding eye contact with me.

The rain starts to fall as Mama and I sit down. It trickles at first, followed by more steady drops. Soon, it is all-out pouring. Rain splatters echo on the roof, drowning out Daddy's attempts at fighting with Mama. He doesn't have a reason to fight with her. He never does, but it doesn't stop him from trying. She's ignoring him and focusing on me instead.

"How's your summer reading coming along, sweetie?" She takes a bite of the biscuits and gravy.

I gulp. "I'm about halfway through."

"What did you start with?"

"The *Magic Treehouse* one." I reach for my water.

Daddy extends his arm and whacks the cup out of my hand. It falls to the floor and the glass shatters everywhere right as thunder booms and a flash of lightning briefly lights up the room.

"Enough!" he shouts. "Enough of this bullshit."

"Kate, go to your room," Mama directs, voice even keel.

Don't cry, Kate. Stay strong. "Mama ..."

"Now, Kate." She points to the banister.

I back away and run up the stairs.

Between the thunder and the shouting, I want to run to the Coles' house, but it'll be worse if I don't stay in my room. I hide behind the other side of my bed, gripping my knees in my hands, close my eyes, and rock myself back and forth. I don't know when the tears start, but they're everywhere, wetting my face, ricocheting onto my hands and running down my legs.

Clink.

What was that?

Clink.

What the—?

Clink.

I unroll myself and cautiously approach the window: Jase. I open the window a smidge and a burst of wind and rain hits the left side of my face. Jase stands in his all-black hoodie and Adidas sweatpants, feet sinking in the wet grass as he leans his arm back, ready to throw another pebble.

"What're you doing?!" I shout down.

"I thought you could use a friend."

"I—I can't leave my room right now."

"Okay." He takes a deep breath, "I'll come up there." He climbs the Magnolia tree between our yards.

"What are you doing, Jase? You're going to hurt yourself," I cry.

"I am not." He reaches from the tree to the terrace on the side of my house and shifts over to climb the last bit to my roof. "Open the window."

I lift it open, and he climbs in, tripping over the leg of my desk chair. "And he sticks the landing," he jokes.

"What are you doing here? I can't believe you climbed up here in the middle of a storm."

Jase reaches his hands out, and I put mine in his. He pulls me into a hug, and he holds me tight. "I promised I would be here, and I meant it." Jase takes the creased card and plastic-wrapped cupcake from his hoodie. "I know this isn't how you want to spend your birthday but pretend the candle's lit and make a wish."

I sniffle and close my eyes. *I wish Daddy would stop drinking.* With an exhale, I let the silent wish escape into the ether before clinging onto Jase like the lifeline he is. "Thank you."

"You're welcome, Kay." He holds me tightly and lets me fall apart.

And then he puts me back together.

Chapter 7

Now

Mama walks through the front door as the kitchen timer goes off. The second she looks at me, I zero in on the dried tears on her face that she tries to mask behind a smile.

"Hey, Mama." I extend my hands and pull her into a deep hug, noticing for the first time how frail her frame has become. When did it happen? Why wasn't I here for it? Here for her ...

"Hey, sweetie." She collapses into me. Separating, she sniffs the air intently. "Is that biscuits and gravy I smell?"

"It sure is. Hoping some good ol' comfort food will help make your day a little better."

She smiles and holds my hand. "You always make my day better."

"I love you, too, Mama."

"He loves you, too, you know." She whispers and pulls plates out of the cupboard.

My shoulder blades tighten, and I freeze. *Dad.* I shake my head. No, he doesn't.

"I'll get the parmesan out if you want to call the girls in for dinner."

"Kate," she calls.

I lower my head. *I hear you.* I just know better than to believe in a delusion like that.

Amy and Nana walk in, grab a plate, and fill it with hot, gooey meat and cheesy biscuits.

Gray dots form in front of my eyes, and the room spins. Taking a deep breath in and out, I clear the fuzz. Mama puts her hand on my shoulder, radiating calm energy. I tell her I'm okay, but all I can think about is *he loves you, too, you know.* And I act like everything's fine, but I am not okay.

Not even a little bit.

Not at all.

My levee broke last night. I sobbed until my eyes dried out and my muscles convulsed, eventually shifting into a restless state of tossing, turning, thinking, and rethinking.

He loves you, too, you know.

He doesn't. He never did.

I play those three sentences over and over in my mind until I can think of nothing else.

"I need to write it out," I mumble to myself.

Hyla lifts her head off the bed long enough to watch me grab my laptop and slip back under the covers.

My fingers feel like lightning typing a blog post that'll never see the light of day, and when I'm done, I feel like I can breathe for the first time in twenty-four hours.

THIS KIND OF LOVE

"What time are we leaving for the Pumpkin Festival, Katie girl?" Nana shouts down the hallway. "I've got to change into my new outfit."

I lay out a pair of dark blue jeans and a maroon, off-the-shoulder sweater. "Soon after Mama and Pop get back."

Ten minutes later, Mama walks in and collapses on the sofa. "Went that well, huh?"

She groans. "Just tiring, that's all."

"I bet." I step into my shoes. "Where's Pop?"

"Staying at the hospital a bit longer."

Her words set off an alarm bell. Is it serious enough that Pop had to stay so he's not alone if he ... "How's Dad doing?"

Mama sighs. "He's ... okay. Not his best day but there have been a few like this."

I sit next to Mama on the couch and notice the dark circles around her eyes, the burden she's bearing, and how much I'm probably adding to it by coming all this way and not easing her load. Not seeing my dad. Not giving Mama a break. I put my hand on hers and squeeze. "He'll be all right, Mama."

"I hope so." She sniffles and looks away. "In other news, I finished my book."

I close my eyes in relief. Saved by Steven King. "How was it?"

She pinches her fingers and kisses them. "King never gets old. Anyway, I better get ready to go." She points to my sweater. "That color looks nice on you."

"Thanks, Mama." I smile.

Minutes later, we're all on our way to Sloane's Annual Pumpkin Festival. Amy and Nana are walking ahead while Mama asks me about work and the latest *Case of the Mondays* post.

Amy stops walking a few houses before the church and cocks her head over her shoulder. "Okay, what should I expect here?"

"Oh, I'm sure we'll be asked at least a dozen times why we didn't bring our scarecrows and pumpkins," Mama guesses.

"What for?" Amy asks. "I kind of assumed you buy pumpkins here?"

Mama laughs. "Well, yes, you can buy pumpkins here."

"And any other pumpkin-flavored thing you can think of," Nana adds.

"Oh really?" Amy's eyes light up.

Mama answers, "Yes, but by far, the biggest part of the festival is the weighted pumpkin challenge. The bigger the pumpkin, the bigger the prize. Even though we never enter, Matilda asks me where our pumpkin is every year."

Amy's eyes dart toward me. "Do you guys even grow pumpkins?"

"No." Mama lowers her voice. "Most people search nearby towns for 'em, but shh, little town secret."

"It's a sham?" Amy all but shouts.

Nana covers Amy's mouth with her right hand. "Talking like that could get you banned."

Amy sighs, and Nana drops her hand.

We enter the festival right as the band plays "Home Is Where the Heart Is."

"This is one of my favorite Lady A songs." Nana spins around.

"Hello, Dailey family." Matilda waves a map of the church grounds in the air, but before she can approach, someone taps her on the shoulder and steals her attention.

Mama visibly exhales. "Come on, let's get dessert."

"Man, you guys weren't kidding with how serious this is." Amy takes in the sight of various pumpkin activities across the church lot and in the wide-open field behind the lot. "I get the scarecrow judging contest, but what is pumpkin chucking?"

Mama laughs. "Exactly what it sounds like. The catapults out in the field get a lot of action today."

"How about the corn maze?" Nana suggests.

Mama and I give her a stern look.

"You know, after pie," she amends, and we all calm down. My mama always told me dessert is its own food group, and who am I to argue with my mama?

Amy stares at the pie stand in amazement.

I can't help but indulge in a long inhale, taking in the fresh pumpkin, apples, and pecans permeating the air. "It smells like your kitchen, Mama."

She winks. "I knew I raised you right."

"Ugh, the line is long this year," Nana caws as we get to the end of the pie line.

I nearly salivate at the thought of gooey pumpkin pie. "It's always worth it, though."

"Kate Dailey? Is it really you?" I hear from the direction of the pie.

Putting a hand to my forehead, my eyes narrow at the sound. "Oh my God, Jade?" I screech.

"I knew it!" she exclaims, hopping over the pie stand and running toward me, throwing out various "excuse me's" and "coming through's" until she reaches me. We simultaneously grab each other's hands and jump up and down. She stops and studies me. "My mama told me she bumped into you but I can't believe you're really here. Girl, look at your hair; it's red!"

"It's red," I echo and move up as the line does.

"It's short," she says.

"It is."

"You look great." She smiles.

"So do you." I reach for her long, dark hair. "Did you curl this?"

Jade shrugs. "Well, you know, I had to take out the braids at some point."

"You didn't," I reply. "You're beautiful no matter how you wear your hair."

She blows me a kiss. "Thanks, babe." Then, she pulls Mama and Nana into a group hug while telling them how much she's missed them.

"You've always been a good hugger, Jade-a-licious," Nana shares before letting go.

"Ame, you look incredible."

"Right back atcha, smoke show." My two besties embrace, and a sense of pride swells in me that my old life and new life have integrated in some way, even if it's just through the trips Jade religiously takes to visit me in New York each summer.

"Where's Rick?" I look around for Jade's long-term boyfriend.

"Oh, he um ... it didn't work out." She shrugs and changes the subject. "Have you seen you-know-who yet?"

"I always forget you're Jase's sister," Amy says.

Jade raises her hands. "Please don't hold it against me. I got all the brains in the family ... and beauty."

The sound of sweet laughter fills the line for a second before I look at her. "Hey now, Jack's pretty good-looking, too."

"True. I bet you haven't seen him lately?" She wiggles her eyebrows.

I shake my head. "Not since I left, but you know, Insta."

Jade's eyes light up, "Speaking of which, it looks like we have a lot to catch up on since the summer."

My feet shift, but Jade catches it. "Everything okay?"

"Everything's great." My voice is a little too high.

Jade's eyes narrow.

"Next!" the cashier calls, and it's our turn to place our order.

"I'll let you go, but text me." Jade sneaks back under the pie stand to help.

We pay for a pie with whip and pick a table to sit at. We each grab a fork and dig in. "Mhm," Amy moans. "This is really good."

"It's homemade." I wink.

"Really homemade or another of those we-get-pumpkins-brought-in things?"

I shrug. "Small town secrets."

Taking another bite of pie, I linger on the creaminess and light taste of cinnamon, savoring the taste and the feeling of being back in my hometown after all this time. A lot has changed, but this pie has remained the same.

My eyes drift to the busy lot. There are a lot of familiar faces bustling around, dressed in bright colors, trying to get to the rides or the corn maze, standing in line for pumpkin pie or pumpkin chucking. The one face I don't see is Jase. For a festival *everyone* in town goes to every year without fail, it seems like an event Jase wouldn't want to miss. At least, it didn't used to be.

Nana stands, pulling me out of my fog. "All right, girls, where to next?"

"Scarecrow Judging?" Mama offers.

I elbow Amy. "It's Mama's favorite part."

"How could it not be? They're always creative." Mama's face lights up as we get closer.

As if on cue, Matilda shimmies over. "Liz, did I hear you're heading over to the Scarecrows?"

Mama just blinks.

Matilda's left eyebrow lifts in a diagonal on her forehead and she smirks in a way that I find slapable. "No entry again this year?"

Mama takes an audible breath in and out but, otherwise, she doesn't flinch. Never let 'em see you sweat.

"No, Matilda. With my husband in the hospital, I didn't happen to find the time to create a scarecrow for the Sloane Pumpkin Festival."

Matilda's smile is frozen in place. "Oh, Liz, bless your heart. How is Andy anyhow?"

Mama softens slightly. "He has good days and bad days. Thank you for asking." Mama grabs ahold of my hand and squeezes. "Well, it was nice chatting with you, but we really should get on about our night."

"Oh sure," Matilda says. "I don't want to hold you up. Perhaps next year, you'll have a scarecrow, then."

Mama's eyes roll all the way back into her head, which she somehow makes effortless as she shoos Matilda.

"Damn, Mama, that was the closest I think you've ever come to telling her off." I pat her on the shoulder. "I'm proud of you."

She comes to, and her shoulders sink slightly. "I was rude, wasn't I? Maybe I should apologize."

"Don't you dare." Nana pulls her along, "Matilda is the scum of the Earth, and trust me, what you did wasn't even close to all she deserves."

Mama shrugs. "Maybe you're right."

Amy leans in and whispers, "Now I see where you get it from."

Nana rushes to the scarecrows. "Hey, look, someone made Jack and Sally!"

Mama gives a nod of approval and then finds her favorite. "Oh, there's Moira Rose!"

I turn around and see the hay Mama's pointing to. Sure enough, it's in the shape of Catherine O'Hara, looking fresh off *The Crows Have Eyes III: The Crowening*. "You're right. The attention to detail on this one is kind of insane. Even the feathers look real."

Looking around for Amy, I find her inspecting a set of scarecrows based on *The Wizard of Oz*. Mama's moved on to a *Shrek* lookalike, and Nana's eyeing the Sanderson sisters. For a second, everything seems right in the world. Almost all my favorite people are at one of my favorite events, enjoying the creativity and artistry of my small town.

My perfect bubble pops when I turn around and finally see him. *Jase*—at the pie stand, leaning on the post, talking to his sister, and making everyone behind the booth laugh. Looking fine as hell in old, ratty blue jeans with muscles filling out an old T-shirt in *all the right places*—damn him.

When he turns around, I'm ready to make a run for it, but I can't look away. Placing my hand on my forehead, I look toward the stand and strain to get a better view. Wait, it isn't Jase. *Jack*. His eyes find mine at the same moment I find his.

He smiles and holds his hand up to wave. "Kate?!" he shouts.

Several people within earshot turn around to see what the commotion's all about. Jack's long legs carry him in a short stride, and he's in front of me before I know it. Picking me up, Jack gives me a squeeze. "Kate, Kate, Kate, man, am I excited to see you."

I smile as he holds me. "Hey, Jacky."

He puts me down and holds his arms out to me. "Shh," he whispers. "The girls around here don't know me as Jacky anymore. I'd like to keep it between us if you don't mind."

I laugh. "Of course, the secret's safe with me."

"How are you? How's your daddy?" His blue eyes search mine for an answer.

"I'm doing all right. Think Dad's okay, too."

He knows full well how I feel about my father. "How long are you in town for?"

"I ... don't really know yet."

"Understood." He looks around covertly. "Hey, have you run into my super obnoxious, less good-looking brother around here?"

I can't help giving him a once-over. It may have been six years since I've seen Jack, but it looks like time's been good to him. The once lanky kid has filled out into a built twenty-five-year-old.

Catching me in the act, he tips his ball cap. "Gonna guess no, then?"

"Not today." I shake my head. "Though I haven't been as fortunate earlier in the week."

He smirks. "Same here. He's having me help at Firefly, which is why you see me like this instead of in my sweeping-women-off-their-feet clothes."

"Is that so?"

"Sure is." His voice dips low, seductively.

"Jack Cole! What has gotten into you?" I flick his arm.

He laughs and takes a slow step backward. "You're right, you're right. Jase would be mad if he knew I was hitting on his girl, anyways."

I hold a warning finger out, and my voice feels an octave higher than normal when I say, "I am not his girl." *Anymore.*

"Hey, hey now, I come in peace." Jack holds up two fingers, forming a peace sign.

"Yeah, that's what I thought, Mr. Peace Corp."

"So, you've been keeping up with me?" His eyebrows raise, but my head tilts, causing him to stop. "Listen, I'd hate to keep you away from your family any longer than I have, but it was good to see you. Hopefully, I'll see you around before you head back up north." Jack leans in and gives me a kiss on my right cheek.

I close my eyes. Wrong brother.

Jack backs away but throws up his hand to Mama and Nana. "Hi, Liz, Maggie."

"Hey, Jack!" Mama shouts back.

Nana waves.

Amy waits for Jack to disappear before she heads over. "I thought you were talking to Jase for a minute and was this close to coming over, but then Mags stopped me. Soooo, he's the hot brother?"

I catch Amy's head tilt as she watches him walk away and roll my eyes. "Yes, he's the hot brother. Jack." Amy's mind works a mile a minute, and I can see the gears turning. "And yep, it would be weird for you to go after him."

She sighs. "Okay, okay. He's cute, is all I'm saying."

"Yeah." I exhale. "He's cute."

"See? You're still wrapped up with the other brother. Why can't I have this one?" She pouts.

"I'm not *still wrapped up* with Jase. Besides, aren't you into Leo?"

"We are not discussing Mr. Steal-My-Job. But hey, isn't that Jase?" Amy points to the pie stand.

My eyes betray me as they glance toward the pie stand—and then droop when I realize he's not there …

"Mhm, you're totally over him."

Totally. Over. Him … but where is he?

I stretch my arms out. "Hey, you know what, y'all? I think I'm going to head home. I forgot how overwhelming a night in Sloane can be."

Mama pulls me into her grasp, holding me and touching her head to mine. "Are you okay?"

"Miserable as usual, thanks for asking."

She kisses the top of my head. "Want me to come with you?" Her voice is raspy.

"Or me?" Amy counters.

"Hell, we can all go home," Nana offers.

I put up my left hand. "No. Thank you, though. I could use some alone time until Pop comes home and beats me at Rummy."

"Hey now, that's my job," Nana interjects.

"Kate," Amy objects.

Mama puts her arm out to stop Amy.

"No, really, I'm fine," I say, but I don't even convince myself.

Mama tilts her head, her gaze studying me.

"I'll *be* fine," I amend.

She pats my hand. "There's my girl. There's Ben and Jerry's in the freezer."

Bless her.

Mama ushers Amy and Nana to the start of the maze as I back away. I don't remember the walk home. I don't know if I see anyone or if I run into anything. I don't know if the sun has set or if it's cold outside. All I know is I need to get home, snuggle with Hyla, and decompress more than I need anything else right now. The relief is real when I walk in the front door and call out for Hyla. Her collar jingles as she runs over. "Hey, baby girl."

Hyla makes her way onto my lap and snuggles into my arms. A forty-five-pound mutt shouldn't be a lapdog, not logically, anyway. I know it. She does too. But somehow, she always knows exactly what I need, and sometimes I need to have my dog as close to me as possible. For all that's wrong in the world, Hyla helps me keep it (mostly) together.

"What do you say, girl? Ice cream in bed?"

Hyla leans her head back and gives me a big lick across my cheek.

"All right, let's go." I stand and grab a treat for Hyla and a pint of Half-Baked from the freezer. "Oh, Mama, you knew," I murmur to myself. Mamas always do.

We settle into bed, pint in hand, *Friends* on TV, when my phone lights up with an incoming call. Expecting it to be Mama checking in on me, I answer. "Hey, I mean it. I'm okay."

"Everything alright?" the deep voice on the other end of the phone asks, concerned.

"What? Who is—Nick?"

"Yes," he answers. "Sorry, I knew I should have waited for you to text back. I thought maybe you were mad, so I waited a few days to reach out. I knew I shouldn't have followed that dumb rule."

I put the rest of the Half-Baked carton on the nightstand and sit up straighter, "Hey, Nick?"

"Yes?" He pauses.

"Let's start over."

He sighs. "I would like that. Hi, Kate, it's Nick Scott."

"Hey, Nick. It's nice to hear from you. I had a great time the other night," I say, unable to hide my smile, even though there's still a deep ache in my soul.

"Me, too." His laugh is sweet through the phone. "I'd love to do it again if you're interested?"

Touching my right thumb to my lip, I can feel my cheeks warming. "Kate?"

"I would like to, too," I say. "But there's something I should tell you."

"Oh no, the 'but' doesn't sound good."

I take a deep breath and spit it out. "I'd like to go out again, but I'm not in town right now."

He exhales audibly. "Oh! Okay. When do you come back?"

"I—It could be up to a month." The second the words woosh out of me, I feel their impact. It could be *up to a month* before I'm back to my normal life. And if something happens with my dad, it could be longer. The thought almost drowns me. "I'm sorry," I say to Nick. "That's not fair. It's true, but it's not fair. I don't expect you to wait for me. I'm sure there are plenty of girls you could go out with, girls you *should* go out with instead."

"Maybe," Nick says, and I wince. He continues, "But I want to go out with you."

The tears well before I know they're there. "But you don't know me, not really."

"Sure, but I want to get to know you. I'm happy to wait until you're back in town."

"Really?" I can hear the hopefulness in my own voice.

"I mean, we're not talking years down the road, right?"

I laugh. "I hope not."

"I hope not, too. So, what brings you out of town, anyway? A crazy mission for Lucy?"

I shake my head, even though he can't see me. "I wish. No, I'm ... visiting family."

"Down south, right? You're from ..." He snaps his fingers. "Outside of Nashville?"

"Yes. I'm surprised you remember."

"I remember that accent of yours came out when talking about your Mama's cooking."

"You're right," I say. My accent is probably strong on nights like tonight when I'm back in my childhood room at my mama's house.

"So, tell me, Kate Dailey, what do the stars look like there tonight?"

"Hmm, the stars, you say," I repeat as I hop out of my bed and head toward the window seat. "Well, it's a clear night here, so there are too many to count. They're brilliant, bright white and a tinge of yellow by the moon."

"Mhm. It's the one thing I'd change about the city if I could. My parents moved to New Jersey a few years ago, and I can see the stars from their back porch, but not here ..."

"I know what you mean. Turns out I really missed the stars and fireflies," I say wistfully. I missed them more than I'd like to admit.

"I always forget lightning bugs are around when I'm home."

"What? What do you mean, you 'kind of forget' they're around?"

"I don't know. I think I chased them once, maybe. I was an adult by the time I was able to. My sister was far more interested in it than I was ... which come to think of it, could be what influenced her biology career."

"Could be. I love seeing them light up in a jar. I've always thought it's breathtaking." I yawn and lean my head against the wall behind me.

"I did like seeing them light up." He yawns back. "Now see what you started."

"Well, good, if you didn't yawn, you'd be a psychopath, and you'd need to lose this number."

Chuckling, he concedes. "I believe I heard that somewhere, too. Glad to know you're not a psychopath either. On that note, we should probably call it a night."

I sigh. "Maybe you're right. This is nice."

"It is. Can I call you again tomorrow?"

"Tomorrow?" I ponder, waiting for any knee-jerk reaction to run. But it doesn't come. "I'd like that."

"Goodnight, Kate."

"Goodnight, Nick."

His voice is the last thing I hear before I fade off to sleep with a promise of tomorrow and a smile that stays through the night.

Chapter 8
Then: Thirteen Years Ago

A big, yellow bus parks at Sloane Middle School. The doors swing open, and Jase jumps on board in his blue jeans and Pokémon tee. He looks over his shoulder at me. "Where are you thinking?"

"Third to last row," I reply.

Jase takes a pack of fruit snacks out of his backpack as we slide in. "Want some?"

"Sure." I unzip my backpack to take out my iPod and headphones. "Who do you want to listen to today?"

His eyes crinkle, and we both laugh. "Taylor," we say together.

I put on "Our Song," extend an earbud to Jase, and lean back in the seat. He places his right hand on his lap, and I intertwine my fingers with his. This, right here, is my favorite part of every day. Just Taylor, Jase, and I.

"Eww, get a room." Jack throws his backpack onto the seat in front of us.

Jase sticks his tongue out.

"Hey, Jacky." I take my earbud out and extend it to him. "Want to listen?"

He shakes his head. "No thanks, I know what you guys listen to: *love stuff*."

I close my eyes, expecting Jase to deny it, but he doesn't. Instead, he looks his big brother right in the eyes. "What of it?"

"Nothing." Jack plops down and pulls a book out of his bag.

I plug my earbud back in, and Jase squeezes my hand. I don't mind listening to love stuff. Not at all.

The bus turns onto our block before I'm ready. The sky has shifted into a deep navy, and the leaves turn inside out one by one. The wind picks up when we follow Jack off the bus. He runs ahead to the house as Jade's bus pulls up from the high school. She flies off, waves, and runs inside. Tonight feels like it's gonna be one of *those* nights. The kind that feels lonely beyond belief. The kind I'd rather live without.

Jase stays with me. "It's going to be okay. I promise."

"You don't know that." I choke back tears.

"I'm right next door."

"Andy! Andy, don't you dare go out the door!" Mama screams at Daddy, begging him to stay in the house.

His chestnut eyes darken, and his jaw stiffens in defiance. "Too fucking late!" he bellows, slamming the front door.

Jase and I shift to the side of the house by the kitchen, hiding from Daddy and trying to get to Mama. I open the door, and Mama falls onto the tile floor, weeping.

When she sees me hiding in the shadow of the door, she straightens, wipes her eyes with the sleeve of her favorite cardigan, and reaches out to me. "Come here, sweetie."

I run for her arms and cry as soon as I reach them.

"It's okay. Let it out." While she stands there holding me, letting me full-on sob, she stays there, stoic as an ox, shouldering the pain, the burden, the fear—all of it.

Mama urges Jase to go home as Daddy's truck starts in the drive. She closes her eyes tightly, while mine go wide in panic.

"Mama, we can't let him drive."

She shakes her head. "I tried, baby. I tried to keep him here."

"Mama, we have to go get him. We need to stop him." I squirm out of her arms.

"Kate, no!" she calls after me.

I shove the door open and run down the driveway. I lock eyes with Daddy through the dashboard window and scream incoherently ... but it doesn't matter. His Cheshire smile haunts me as he pulls his truck into reverse.

I sprint back to Mama. We should have done more. We should have stopped him from driving. We should have done *something*. It takes me a while to realize she's plugged one ear to hear the other end of the phone over me.

She hangs up and sighs. "Nana and Pop are on their way. Nana will stay with you, and Pop and I will go look for your daddy."

"I want to go, Mama."

She holds up her hand. Not going to happen.

"Can I try calling him? Maybe I can talk him into pulling over, and we can go get him." I plead with her.

She shakes her head. "It's not safe, sweetie. Nana and Pop will be here soon."

"Nashville's thirty minutes away. He could hurt somebody," I cry.

Her head hangs low. "Enough, okay? I'm not happy he's out there, either, but I am going to do everything in my power to bring him back safely. Right now, I need you to understand there are things you don't know. Let me handle this, okay?"

"Okay." I put my hands on hers. She puts her other hand on top of mine, and we sit there in the kitchen in complete silence. Mama taps her left foot, slow at first, then quicker. It's causing a vibration on the tile floor, but I let it be, let her be. I lose track of how long we're at the table before the front door swings open. I nearly jump out of my skin thinking Daddy's back home—but it's not him.

Nana dashes into the house. "Kate, Liz, where are you?"

Letting go of Mama's hands, I stand and walk into the living room. "Over here, Nana."

"Oh, Katie girl." She pulls me into a big bear hug.

Pop comes in shortly after, more 'business' than I'd ever seen him. He's always been the person I could count on the most to make me laugh, but he's not laughing now. None of us are.

"Hey, sweetie." Pop pats my head before stepping in front of Mama. With a hand on either shoulder, he eyes her. "Are you ready?"

Mama crouches down to talk to me. "Be good for your nana. We'll be back soon, okay?"

I sniffle.

The front door closes like a gust of wind came through. Nana and I peek out the side window in time to see Mama and Pop head off in Pop's blue pickup truck, Old Blue.

"Are they going to be okay?"

She pulls me in for a side hold. "They're all gonna be fine, sweetie."

"Promise?" I hold out my pinkie. I know a pinkie promise doesn't mean everything's okay or things will be okay forever, but somehow, when Nana clips her finger in mine and gives it a kiss, I cling to the hope it gives me.

"So ..." Nana pastes a smile on her face. "What do you want to do tonight?"

I glance toward the window. I want to help find Daddy.

Nana tugs my arm and leads me to the living room. "Let me rephrase: what do you want to do to take our minds off this?"

I shrug. "I have a deck of cards in my room?"

"Sure. Why don't you get the deck, and I can teach you how to play Rummy?" She wiggles her eyebrows.

I take the stairs two at a time, excited to spend time with Nana and anxious to know if they've found Daddy yet. The second I flip the light switch I see a pebble hit my window. *Jase.* I open the window.

"What took you so long?" He wraps himself around the tree as he climbs up.

"Had to deal with some stuff."

"I heard," he says solemnly. "Move over. I'm coming in."

"I don't know, Jase."

"About what?" He sits on the branch by my room.

"My nana's over. We're going to play cards." I hold up the deck. "And I don't think she'd like you crawling in the window or me going out to play tonight."

He hangs his head. "I watched him leave .... are you okay?"

"I don't know." I shake my head and try not to cry.

"Kay, let me in. Please."

I step aside. He pulls me into his arms in no time, holding me and rubbing my back, telling me it's okay to cry. I shake my head. Never let 'em see you cry. I glance at my bedroom door. "Thank you for coming over, but you really should go. I need to go downstairs."

"I'd like to stay. Please, Kay. You can play with your nana, and I'll sit here quiet as a church mouse until you come back."

I want him to stay, but I don't want Nana to know he's here and give my grandparents and Mama something more to worry about. They have enough going on right now. Jase's hands are folded into a prayer, and ugh, he's right. I need him.

"Okay," I whisper. "But you have to be quiet."

He holds up three fingers. "Scout's honor."

"You're not a scout."

"Still mean it." He settles on the floor.

I crack the door and bump into Nana. "Oof," I exclaim.

"Everything okay up here?" She cranes her neck around me.

I stretch. "Great! Got the cards; we can go downstairs and play."

Nana's face has *yeah, right,* written all over it. "Where are these cards?"

"Um," I look at both hands. "Oops, must have put them down after all. I'll be right down. Meet you there, Nan."

She rolls her eyes and turns around to go down the stairs. "Tell Jason he's welcome to play, too."

"Uh, what? Jase isn't—Jase isn't here, Nana." I stumble around my words, knowing full well how unbelievable it sounds.

"Lying gets better with age," Nana quips on her way down the banister.

Sneaking back into my room and leaning against the closed door, I mumble, "How did she know?"

"Know what?" Jase stands.

"She knows you're here." I narrow my eyes.

He puts his hands up in surrender. "Hey, don't be mad at me. You're the one who lied. We all know you're a terrible liar."

"Am not," I argue.

"Kay," he states plainly.

"Okay, fine, what do you want from me? I didn't get the lying gene."

He takes my hand and urges my chin upward with his pointer finger. "Hey, look at me."

I stare into his sea-green eyes as he stares into mine.

"It's a *good* thing you're a bad liar."

"Really?"

"Yes." He moves a piece of hair out of my face. "It means you, Kay Dailey, have a good heart."

It skips a beat as he moves his face closer to mine. I shift my gaze from his eyes to his lips.

Right as we close our eyes, Nana calls up the stairs. "You guys coming? I'm gonna put in a delivery order for burgers and fries while we play."

The moment fades as quickly as it began. I pick up the cards from my nightstand. "Guess we should get down there."

Jase puts his hand on my cheek and whispers, "To be continued."

My breathing slows as I think about his comment on the way down the stairs, through Nana explaining the game, and after several rounds of Rummy. *To be continued.* My mind continues to wander until a few hours go by, and the door opens unexpectedly.

Mama comes in staggering. "Mama?"

She extends her arms, and I run into them. She squeezes me tight.

A few minutes later, Pop comes in the front door, two sets of car keys in hand.

They found him.

"Pop!" I run into his arms. "Where's Daddy?"

"Shh," he mouths to me. "Let's let him sleep a bit."

I look around Pop for him, but he blocks the doorway.

"Speaking of sleep—shouldn't you be in bed by now?"

Mama points to the stairs. "She absolutely should."

Nana comes to my rescue. "We were playing Rummy—my idea."

"I see," Mama says, right as Pop says, "Of course it was."

"Jase, you should probably head home before your parents have my head for you being out late, weekend or not," Mama says.

"Yes, ma'am. Kate, can I see you tomorrow?"

"Mama?"

She yawns. "I'm sure you can."

"Okay. Goodnight, everyone." He waves on his way out the door.

"Kate," Mama says, "bed, please."

I nod and climb the stairs two at a time. After throwing myself in bed, I pull the covers up past my face and listen intently for any sign of Mama. When her footsteps patter down the hall, I fling the comforter off the bed and tiptoe to her room.

The sobs are so foreign, I almost think it's the TV. I sit in the hallway and hold my knees while Mama's heart aches. I want to knock on the door and crawl into her bed more than anything in the world. But Mama wouldn't want that. She wouldn't want me to know she's breaking down.

I lean my head against the door as Pop comes upstairs.

He waves his hand to call me over.

I avoid each of the creaky spots on the hardwood floor on my way to Pop.

"Come on, girl," he urges. "Let's get you to bed, for real this time."

"Yes, sir." I sulk back to my bedroom. "What happened? Where's Daddy?"

Pop tucks me in and kisses my forehead. "You shouldn't have to worry about all of this. It's adult stuff. You should focus on being a kid, learning how to play Rummy, playing with your friends."

"I do worry about it, though. His actions affect all of us, especially Mama," I cry.

"I know." He sighs. "Everything's okay for now, right in this moment. Your mama's having a tough night, but she'll be okay, and your daddy will be okay." His eyebrow lifts in waiting.

"I love you, Pop."

"I love you. Get some sleep."

In the morning, it's like nothing ever happened. Mama, Nana, Pop, and Daddy are all in the kitchen, eating waffles and drinking coffee.

Did I imagine the whole night?

I run to hug Daddy, and he clings to me like he's excited to see me. He smells like his cucumber body wash, and he's dressed in a new pair of jeans and a polo shirt. He pours a glass of orange juice and directs me to take a seat.

My eyebrows smoosh together. Was it all a dream? In scanning the room, my gaze lands on Pop's.

He puts a finger to his lips.

Maybe it did happen.

There's a light knocking on the kitchen door.

Jase.

Mama waves him in.

"Good morning." Jase surveys the room. He remembers it too.

My dad stands and shakes Jase's eleven-year-old hand. "Good morning, Jason."

"Mr. Dailey," he replies. "How are you feeling this morning?"

Mama, Nana, and Pop's faces each drop as they look at Jase, but Daddy doesn't notice.

Instead, he looks him straight in the eyes and shrugs. "Miserable as usual, thanks for asking."

"Great!" Jase's voice is a little too high. "Is Kay able to come out and play with us?" He cocks his thumb over his shoulder at Jade and Jack waving in our shared side yard.

"Sure," Mama says.

"Why doesn't she meet you out there after she finishes her waffles?" Daddy adds.

"Okay." Jase walks to the kitchen door.

I shove the waffles in my mouth while everyone's deep in a conversation about Matilda's latest musings. Putting my dish in the sink, I give a brief hug to each adult and run out the kitchen door. As I step foot outside, Jase pulls me into Mama's burgundy hydrangea bush.

"What the!" I scream.

"Shh." Jase places his hand over my mouth.

I slap away Jase's hand and turn around to face him. "What the hell?"

"Yeah, exactly. What happened?"

I shake my head. "I don't know."

"What do you mean you don't know? What happened last night and this morning?"

I lift my arms. "Jase, I really don't know. Mama cried herself to sleep. Pop tucked me in, and I went to bed. I woke up to whatever *that* was." I gesture to the kitchen.

"Your daddy slept in Old Blue last night." Jase points to Pop's truck in the driveway.

"Wh ... what?"

"I was up early. I was walking to your window when he snored. I got scared he was gonna wake up."

I trot to the Old Blue before Jase finishes his thought.

He chases after me. "Where are you going?" Jase puts his hand on my left shoulder as I reach the truck.

"I have to know," I stammer.

"You don't," he replies. "You're a kid. Come on, let's go play."

Looking down the way, I can see Jade and Jack running around, but I shake my head. I have to know the truth. I rip open the driver's side door, which creaks with every inch it opens. Empty beer cans come crashing out.

"Oh my God!" I shriek, losing my balance. "Is this all from after Pop picked him up?"

Jase takes a step toward me and pulls me back into a hug.

"I can't believe this ... what was he thinking? He's in the kitchen eating waffles and smiling ... and they're humoring him?"

Jase stays silent.

"Seriously, what the fuck?" I scream, the f-word feeling strange on my lips. There's a first time for everything and a time like this calls for it.

"Woah," Jade calls from her front yard. "What's going on over there?"

I spin around to Jase and lower my voice. "Do they know?"

He snaps his head toward his siblings. "No."

"Nothing!" I shout back at Jade.

Her lifted eyebrow says she doesn't believe me, but I don't care. There are bigger things I need to figure out. If the adults are in the kitchen acting like last night didn't happen, what kind of hope do I have to prevent it from happening again?

"This is bullshit," I mumble, just loud enough for Jase.

"Come on, sailor, let's get you out of here." He takes hold of my hand and pulls me toward his siblings.

I tug the sleeve of his sweatshirt twice. "Wait, Jase, I can't. I don't want to talk to anybody."

His eyes twinkle. "I know."

We speed by Jade and Jack, picking up the pace into a full-blown run.

"Where are you going?!" Jack yells after us.

"Don't worry about it," Jase calls back. We run into the woodlot behind our houses, feet crunching on the leaves under our feet. Jase's focus is straight ahead, but I'm watching the ground, trying not to step on any animals and especially trying to avoid any snakes.

"Slow down a little," I say.

"Keep up. We're close now." Jase looks back at me with a sly smile.

"Close to *what*?" I drop my hands on my hips and plant my feet firmly in the mud.

"You'll see," Jase sings.

"Jason Everett Cole! Where are we going?" I retort choppier than intended.

He sighs but marches over, mud splattering with each step. He grabs my hands in his. "Trust me."

I toss the thought over in my mind for a few seconds, eventually nodding. Okay.

Jase lifts his pinkie up to mine. "I promise it's nothing bad."

I link my pinkie with his and agree to keep moving. Not long after, streams of sunlight emerge from behind the trees.

"We're here." Jase beams as we stop at a secret oasis.

My eyes take in the wide, open field in front of us; ankle-high grass sways in the slight breeze. There's a beautiful cerulean lake with calm, relaxing water. The sunlight glistens on top of it like it never wants to leave. Tall, shady trees on one side lead my gaze to an old wooden dock with rusty planks that barely look safe to walk on and two oversized rocks at the edge for steps.

"What is all this?" How can a place like this be so close to home?

"Right? Isn't it amazing?" Jase's green eyes shine.

"How did you find this? How come there's no one else around? This can't *exist* in the middle of nowhere."

He shrugs. "I went exploring the other night. I haven't seen anyone ... but it's real."

I arch my hand firmly on my hip. "How do you know?"

Jase outstretches his right arm. "For one, I see it."

"People see mirages all the time."

"In the desert," Jase exclaims. "But you see this, too."

"Yeah, I see it, too, but you and I are the only ones who remember what happened last night. Maybe we're in this dream or something, where everything seems real but it's not."

His laugh is sharp. "And two, I've been swimming in the lake."

"What do you mean you've been swimming in the lake?"

He takes off his shirt in one quick maneuver. "I mean, I've been in it. Swimming." Jase wiggles his hips as he walks near the water. "Are you coming or what?"

"Or what." I sit on the cold grass. "There is no way I am swimming in an unknown body of water."

"Suit yourself." He steps foot on the dock, avoiding a brief hole between planks, and reaches up blindly.

I shift my head to the right to see what he's doing.

"If you're curious, why don't you come over here?" He reaches up, and something whips down like a snake.

I scream.

Jase drops it for a second and walks to me. "Hey, it's okay. It's a rope."

I exhale and take his hand to pull myself up on the dock.

He picks the rope back up, places my hands on it, and his hands on mine. "Hold on, okay?"

"Okay." I gulp.

"You'll be fine," he whispers, his breath hot on my neck. "Let go when I tell you to."

I close my eyes, trying to remember to breathe. I let Jase pull us back and run when he tells me to.

"Let go, Kay."

I do as he says, and we both go flying in the air before crashing into the water, me in my sundress and cardigan, him in his basketball shorts. The crisp water hits cooler than I thought it would, but it's somehow refreshing and not as unwelcome as I imagined.

"Woo!" Jase screams, adrenaline high. He swims over to me. "So, what do you think?"

I laugh. "Okay, that was fun."

"I told you. Come on, let's do it again."

My heart skips a beat as I follow him out of the water. Jase makes me feel safe and wild and free and … completely me. I feel more at home with him than I have in a long time. Maybe ever.

Chapter 9

Now

"Vanilla latte for Kate!" The Java House barista sets the cup on the counter.

I mouth my thanks and settle into a comfy chair in the back corner of the café with my latte and Kindle while I wait for Jade. I check the time as my phone lights up with a new text. *Nick*. It's been four days since our call, and we've spent every night studying the stars from two different places, learning about them and each other, too.

> NICK SCOTT: Good morning, beautiful.

> KATE DAILEY: Oh hey there.

> NICK SCOTT: How's your day going?

> KATE DAILEY: Better now.

I bite my lip and close the cover of my kindle.

> NICK SCOTT: Oh? I haven't even said anything interesting yet. 😉

More winky face texts, huh?

> **KATE DAILEY:** Oh, did you think I meant your text? I've got a latte and the new Lauren Layne book.

> **NICK SCOTT:** Sounds like your perfect day.

> **KATE DAILEY:** You know me already.

Hovering over the emojis, I add a playful face for good measure.

"Hey, babe!"

I look around in a love-drunk haze, and my eyes land on Jade and her waving hand.

"Oh, hey!" I stand to give her a hug.

"Sorry I'm late ... and interrupting an important chat." Her lips break out into a sly smile.

"What? I, uh, it's nothing ..." I look down to hide my burning cheeks.

Jade's finger air swipes from my feet to my forehead. "Want to try again?"

Shaking my head, I put my phone in the back pocket of my jeans.

"You're lucky I can keep a secret." Lowering her voice she adds, "Unlike anyone else in this town."

"I can hear you." Ms. Truly, the town librarian, scoffs from her chair halfway across the café. Her gray hair is in a tight bun at the top of her head, wireframed glasses rest on the bridge of her nose, and her lips are tilted up in disapproval at us talking in a coffee shop.

"Hi, Ms. Truly." Jade waves across the room.

She narrows her eyes at us before getting back to her magazine.

Jade flops into the chair adjacent to mine. "So, who's the guy?"

"Do y'all mind?" Ms. Truly snaps.

Jade rises and squints her dark green eyes, and I know we're one shush away from Jade handing me her purse and marching over to our eighty-year-old-should've-retired-years-ago librarian.

Pulling on Jade's sleeve, I gesture toward the door. "Maybe we should go?"

Her eyes dance when she realizes it means more time together in a place where we don't have to worry about being too loud for an old biddy. Her words, not mine.

Oh, God, did she say it out loud? I grab Jade's hand and rush out of the café. "Pleasure seeing you, Ms. Truly."

The door clicks shut. Jade flails her pointer finger at the coffee shop. "People like that is why I wish I could stay out of this one-horse town. It's such bullshit."

"Hey, now." I rub her forearm. "You're getting hangry."

She pulls me into a hug. "I've missed you. You get me, you know?"

"Same. Where to?"

"You're not gonna like it." She bats her eyes. "They have the best burgers in town."

I close my eyes. "No. Not happening."

"Oh, come on, please, I'm starving," she begs.

"Jade, I can't. Please. Anywhere but there ... unless you can promise me your brother isn't working today."

She turns her back to me. "Which one?"

I shake my head adamantly. "No way."

"But I've been waiting forever to catch up with you."

"Why can't we catch up over ice cream later?"

Her face lights up. Jade Cole loves ice cream ... almost as much as her youngest brother does. *Almost.* Her stomach growls.

"I'll walk you there," I volunteer. Then, I'll go home, alone, and take a nice hot bubble bath before anyone else gets home.

"Kate, you can't avoid him forever." She skips down the street.

I give her a pointed look. "Why not? I've done a pretty good job this week."

For some reason, my feet follow hers down the block, into Firefly Lounge, and straight to a corner booth. Peeking behind the bar, I relax my shoulders when I don't see Jase.

His sister snickers and says a little louder than necessary, "Girl, you have never learned how to be discreet, have you?"

I tilt my head and raise my eyebrow at Jade. "Oh, really, Miss I'm-gonna-shout-your-business-all-across-the-bar?"

She has the decency to close her lips together and blush. Leaning in, Jade lowers her voice, "Is this better?"

I roll my eyes, and she falls into the booth cushion.

"I mean, to be fair, all of Sloane will probably know every intimate detail of this lunch before we leave, no matter what I say." Jade cocks her head.

She's right. Matilda's not here, but her spies are everywhere. It's only a matter of time before the coffee shop tiff with Ms. Truly, and our lunch, end up as the whole town's business.

Grabbing a menu from the stand behind the ketchup at the wall end of the booth, I place one in front of Jade before opening mine. "So, burgers, you say?"

"Mhm. He's not here."

Exhaling, my shoulders fall before I even realize they were tensed up. "Oh?"

"I don't think so, anyway," she amends. Her green eyes scan the menu. "What are you thinking?"

"I'm stuck between the Bacon Cheeseburger and Black and Blue Burger."

"I'd go with the Cowboy Burger." Jade's voice is much deeper than it was seconds before.

I turn my head and see Jase standing by our table, bar towel over his shoulder, pen and notepad in his hand, eyes as striking as ever.

"Hi," he says, his voice breathy.

"Hi," I reply, just as breathless. It's only because I didn't expect to see him ... not because I care he's here.

"Okay, well, I feel like I'm interrupting." Jade excuses herself to freshen up.

"Jade ..." I warn. "Are you sure it can't wait?"

"Oh no, it can, but I do not want to get in the middle of whatever is happening here." She waves her hands between her brother and me.

I squeeze my eyes shut, yearning to be transported anywhere but here.

"Sorry, Dorothy, you're still in my bar." Jase's southern drawl stops me in my thoughts.

I sigh. He's right. *I* came *here*. I knew where Jade was headed, that there was a chance he'd be here, and I came, anyway, despite him. *Because* of him.

"So, what'll it be?" His drawl is as thick as it's ever been.

"I—I um, I've gotta go." I reach for my jacket. "Please apologize to your sister for me."

He puts his hand on my shoulder. "Kay."

Stay.

Everything in me is telling me to run—but I don't. If I run, it'll cause a scene ... again. The last thing Mama needs is another reason for the town to talk about her twenty-four-year-old runaway daughter who came back but didn't come home.

He clears his throat. "I'll put two burgers in and get you another server. You can stay here and have lunch with my sister, who's missed you and talked about you non-stop since you've been back."

I swallow. "Okay."

"Okay." He's silent for a long minute, his eyes overcast. "Maybe we can meet at our spot later, though? We need to talk."

I try to process the idea of meeting Jase at our spot, after all this time, but I can't do it. "I don't ... I don't think I can."

"Think about it, Kay. Please." He backs his hand away and heads over to the bar to unload a rack of newly washed wine glasses.

Jade turns the corner slowly, hand on her purse. "So, how'd it all go?" When she scans the room and hears a few whispers, she shakes her head. "Never mind."

We step back into the booth, and my head collapses into my hands. I scream inaudibly, and Jade pets my hair. "It's okay, babe. You'll be okay."

When I lift my head, I see a glass of water for Jade and a Chamomile tea for me. Jase is already out of sight, but the tea makes my stomach flutter. *He remembered.*

A server flies out of the kitchen, the door swinging behind him. He places the burgers on the table and disappears.

"So." Jade cuts her burger in half. "Tell me all about what's happening now at your fancy magazine?" She practically sings the end of the sentence, and I feel all the tension wash away and catch up with my childhood friend on the last few months of work, New York, and how strange it feels being home.

She tells me about her recent promotion as a hot shot bank executive, how she travels often but can't leave-leave because of her mama, and maybe cause of the fling she's got going on with Jimmy, a bartender at Firefly and a former high school quarterback.

We talk about almost everything there is to talk about, but we don't bring up her ex or mine. Despite it all, my mind circles around how much I missed this town and her.

And *him*.

The hours feel like minutes, and before I know it, the wait staff is setting up for dinner. My phone starts to buzz as group chat messages fly in like torpedoes.

> MAMA: Kate, what time are you coming home? We're thinking pizza tonight.

> NANA: Bring Jade with you!

> AMY PARK: We're making it a girls' night.

I swing my phone over to Jade, and she smiles. "I'll bring the wine."

We giggle and walk the half mile home, still deep in conversation. I'm trying to focus on what she's asking about the upcoming issue of *Q*, but my mind keeps flipping back to Jase's bright but troubled eyes. I want to know what's behind them, what he's thinking, feeling, everything, but my heart aches. *He* did this. He lost me. He lost *us*.

"Kate?"

Jade's voice brings me back to the present.

"Hmm?"

She tilts her head. "Are you okay?"

"Oh, yeah, just zoned out there for a minute."

She narrows her eyes and studies me. "Alright, I'll grab the wine and be over in a few minutes. You sure you're okay?"

I nod. "All good. See you soon!"

I walk into the house, head to the kitchen, and open the fridge. Even though I pick up the water pitcher, I can't help searching for beer cans.

"They're not in there," Mama says from behind me.

I almost jump out of my skin but somehow keep the pitcher steady. "Geez, Mama, sneaking up on people can cause heart attacks."

She shakes her head. "Not when you're perfectly young and healthy."

"Where did you hear such nonsense?" I skeptically close the fridge. "Water, Mama?"

"Sure, sweetie." Mama takes a seat at the table, "I know what you were looking for, and I can assure you, it's not there."

"Oh, I ... Mama."

"Sweetie, it's fine. I get it. I know it's hard to believe. I didn't believe it at first either, but in the last few years, he's really been sober." She lifts her hand to the sky.

"When ... when did he stop drinking? Why?"

Her shoulders move up to her ears. "I'm sure he had a reason. I'm sure there was a day of some significance." Her eyes well up. "I didn't notice right away." A few tears land on her T-shirt.

I close the distance between the counter and the kitchen table and put my hand on her shoulder, letting her know she can tell me what she needs to say.

Mama sniffles. "I'm ashamed."

"For what?" I sit next to her and scootch closer.

"I didn't notice. He was proud of himself for quitting after struggling for all those years, and I ... didn't notice."

"Oh, Mama, Dad's been a drinker for as long as I can remember. Hell, as long as anybody in this town can remember. I'm sure when he quit, it took everyone a while to notice."

Her tears fall a little freer now. "Yes, but I'm his wife. I'm his person. I was supposed to notice, supposed to care. I feel like I wasn't there when he needed me."

My blood boils, and I stand, knocking my chair out from under me. "Mama, are you serious? You stayed with this man. You were his rock *for years*, despite addiction and bad decisions, the hate he spewed, or driving your only daughter away ... you are not to blame here. For a man to drink every day for twenty-five years to up and quit, of course, you didn't see it right away. Who would?"

"Kate," she interrupts, eyes still watery.

"Mama, I mean it, you're a good woman. *Too* good a woman." *He doesn't deserve you.* I don't finish my sentence, but she hears it, anyway. Of all the things I could've said or thought about saying to my mama, this was one of the worst. She needs someone to listen to her and tell her what she's feeling is valid. Instead of doing that, I piled on.

She blinks the hurt away, but it's too late. The damage is done. Maybe I'm my father's daughter, after all.

Nana and Amy come running in the side door, fanning themselves.

"Man, it's hot out there today." Nana whistles.

Amy steps back. "Woah. Apparently, it's uncomfortable in here."

Jade breaks the tension without trying, entering with wine and movie snacks. "I don't know about y'all, but I'm ready for a girls' night to end all girls' nights."

Nana rubs her hands together. "Then what are we waiting for?" She pulls a deck of cards out of her pocket.

I shift my gaze to Nana's and shoot an eyebrow up to the sky. "Oh, really?"

"What?" Nana asks as if the last time I played Rummy with my Nana wasn't at my apartment in New York last summer when we played with some friends for money, and Nana didn't kick every one of our asses. Handedly.

"You know, Mags, Kate's right, it may be a little unfair," Mama agrees. "Let's see if we can find something else to play."

Nana sighs. "Y'all are scared ... fine, how about Twister?"

"That's a four-player game, Nan," I say.

Mama lifts her hands. "Why don't I be the designated spinner, and all you coordinated, balanced people can play." She's always insisted she's been a klutz, but I've yet to see it.

"Jade-a-licious and I can set it up." Nana runs to the living room.

"I'll call for a pizza," Amy offers.

"I'll feed my dog." I click my tongue for Hyla.

"Hey, Kate," Mama calls after me.

I turn around.

"No matter what, I love you. You know that, right?"

My heart clenches. "I love you too, Mama."

Thirty minutes later, Domino's rings the bell, and Amy squeals because she can "get the good stuff, even down south." Mama whips up a pitcher of tea. Equally sweet laughter fills the room as we dig in and talk about the hijinks surrounding Nana's day.

Mama puts the pizza box on the coffee table and gives the wheel a spin. "Right foot yellow."

Nana maneuvers on the mat and almost slips right off.

"I gotta admit, Mags, I thought you were a goner there." Amy laughs.

"Now come on, girls, have a little faith in me. I don't ever go down without a fight."

"Can confirm." Mama flicks the next spin.

My phone buzzes with an incoming FaceTime. *Nick.* I flip it to silent and set the phone down on the coffee table, but evidently, I'm not as discrete as I thought, as I look up to four pairs of eyes on me. Guess Jade was right. "What?"

"You gonna answer it?" Nana points to my cell and takes a long sip of her tea.

"Oh, I can get it later. Amy, it looks like you're up."

Amy crosses her arms. "I can wait."

"Go ahead and answer it." Mama encourages me.

"Oh, no, really, I can get it later." I rub my hands together. "Okay, I can go if Amy needs a minute."

"We know you've been talking to your man-friend every night," Nana says pointedly.

Amy and Jade snicker.

"What? I don't know what you're talking about." My voice drops by the end of the sentence, and when I see even Hyla wake up from her slumber on the floor to give me a judgy face, I shrug and give it up. "Okay, what do you want to know?"

"How long have you been talking to this guy?" Nana skips my and Amy's turn and moves her right hand to red.

"Only a few days. It's still new and Nick and I ... well, we're figuring out what it is."

"Is Nick who you two were talking about at lunch?" Mama tilts her head.

"Oh, it made it all the way back already, huh?" *Fucking Sloane.*

"All I heard is you guys had a lunch date, you had major sparks with Jase, and then y'all spent the rest of the time whispering." Mama shrugs. "I feel like the town can't help it. Matilda's trained her minions well. I don't think they would know what to do if they didn't do a full check-in on the daily."

"You're kidding, right?" Amy asks Mama. "I mean, I know small towns talk. I guess I've seen it in the time we've been here, but in New York, no one cares. Like I'm an editor of a gossip magazine, and we don't even care that much. We have to *dig* for half the scoops we get."

"*Q*'s a reputable magazine," I counter.

"Sure, but we still have gossip, and Sloane puts us to shame."

"I'm sure if you hire Matilda, she'd be happy to find dirt on anyone you need," Jade spouts.

"Are we officially done with this then?" I gesture to the Twister board.

Amy nods. "Go ahead and call Nick back."

"FaceTime." I correct, then regret it.

"Hold up—it's FaceTime serious?" Jade lifts her tea. "Spill."

I shake my head and feel my ponytail swipe the back of my shoulder blades. "Nope, wouldn't call it serious. Wouldn't call it anything."

"FaceTime him back. I want to have a looksie at your fella," Nana teases.

"Don't you have plans with Pop? Where is he, anyway?" I peak around Nana for my grandfather.

"He won't be home for a while, but we have all the time in the world." Nana's eyebrow raises in a slight challenge.

I pick up my phone and debate running to my room, but there's no point. As soon as I leave the room, they'll all tiptoe up the stairs and hold a cup to the door to hear what's happening. Might as well take it here. "Okay." I take a deep breath and FaceTime him back.

He answers after the second ring. "Hey, beautiful." His megawatt smile is on point.

I wave.

"Katie girl, let us see!" Nana shouts.

I cringe.

Nick laughs. "Who's that?"

Before I can answer the question, Nana gets up from the Twister board and rushes over behind the couch to wave through the phone at him. "Oh, hello, handsome." She blushes.

"Hi there," he replies.

"Nick, this is my nana. Nana, Nick."

"Hello, Nana," he amends.

"Hello, Nick." She enunciates every syllable and practically salivates.

"Oh kay, Nana, maybe you should go take a spin," I suggest.

"I'm good," she answers, walking to the front of the couch and taking a seat next to me.

"Sorry I missed your call. We started a game night." I flip the camera around so he can see the Twister set up and pizza box.

Amy, Jade, and Mama wave, and Nick waves back, saying hello. He apologizes for interrupting and asks me to call him later if I'm up for it.

I tell him I will and beg him not to hold Nana's cougar advances against me.

"Speak for yourself," she says. "I am who I am, and I'm proud of it."

Nick chuckles and waves.

I no sooner hang up and see everyone's eyes lifted, staring at me.

"What?"

"You're a lucky girl." Nana sighs and leans into me.

"He's hot." Jade fans herself. "I feel like you've left out how hot he is."

"I have not. I told you he's hot."

"You left out that he's hotter live than on his socials, though." Amy sides with Jade.

"He seems like a good sport to put up with all of us in one video chat," Mama says.

I put my head in my hands. "Oh, you're right. The call must have been annoying. Did I blow it?"

"No," they all say in unison.

"He *likes* you," Amy adds. "You know, I say go for it. It'll be good to have a hot boy toy in the city when we get back."

I shake my head. Amy's always encouraging having a boy toy. My eyes flick to Mama, and if I'd have looked a half-second later, I would have missed her flinch, but I don't.

I redirect the conversation. "My turn?"

"'bout time." Nana takes her place back on the mat.

We play several rounds of Twister before Mama and Nana retreat upstairs. Jade pops open a bag of Twizzlers and a pack of M&Ms and tosses them my way. "Catch."

I extend my arm and snag them mid-air. I'm half a Twizzler deep before the quasi-intervention begins.

"So …" Amy folds her hands in front of her.

"So?" I arch my eyebrow.

"So …" Jade echoes.

I blink at them. "Use your words, ladies."

Jade flings a Twizzler around her finger. "What's going on with you and Jase?"

I shrug. "I don't know ... nothing. You know."

Amy wrinkles her nose. "Okay, so that's a whole lot of gibberish. You've been giving off a vibe, and we just want to know what's happening. Is this a bang it out and move on?"

"Ew ..." Jade covers her eyes.

Amy continues, "Or a falling back in love situation?"

Popping a pile of M&Ms in my mouth, I chew slowly and consider what they're asking. I shake my head. "I wish I knew what was going on. I can't be near him, but I can't be away from him ... not when I'm here and he's *everywhere*."

"You can't even be away from him in New York," Amy mumbles.

"What does that mean?"

"You haven't been in a long-term relationship since I've known you. The closest was Flannel Jim, and we all know that hardly counts as any sort of 'ship.'"

I grimace. She's not wrong.

"Can I plead the fifth?"

Jade picks up a bottle of red. "Do you need more wine?"

I nod and take a long sip after she fills my glass. "I think it's time for you two to dish on your love lives."

"What love lives?" they ask, again in unison.

I tilt my head. "What's going on with Leo? What happened with Rick?"

Jade collects our glasses and pours with a heavy hand.

Amy sighs and rests her butt on her feet. "Okay, fine. Alexis and I ended things a few weeks ago, and I was feeling a little lonely, so I downloaded Tinder."

"I knew it!" I point at her. "Amy Park, you *are* on dating apps."

"App," she corrects. "One app ... one time. I swiped right, and this guy did too. We met at The Saloon, hit it off, did seven too many tequila shots, and hooked up ... only to find out two days later he's the new guy who's vying for my new promotion."

I grip her hand. "Oh my God, why didn't you tell me?"

"It's embarrassing as hell, that's why. I deleted that app right after. To hell with dating."

"Here, here." Jade clinks Amy's glass with her own.

"Now, now, Ms. Cole ..."

Jade gulps. "Now, now?"

"What happened with Rick?" I nudge.

She averts her gaze and pulls her sleeves down. "Let's just say some people aren't who you think they are. He showed his true colors one too many times, and if it weren't for my brothers, I wouldn't be here today. I wish this town wasn't so *involved*, if you know what I mean, but to some extent, I'm grateful, because everyone, even Matilda, for all her faults, has my back if he comes to look for me. One day, he got a little too close, and Jimmy stepped up. He's been incredible, and we've kind of been fooling around ... but it's still so new, so keep that between us, will you?"

We pinkie promise.

"Oh, Jade, I'm so sorry you've been dealing with all that."

"We're here for you," Amy promises. "You're not alone."

"I love you guys," Jade gushes.

We pull each other into a group hug, and Hyla wiggles her way in to give puppy kisses. We cackle and resolve that it's time for bed.

I let Hyla out, hug the girls goodnight, and walk to my room. Hyla lifts her head as I fold back my sheets, but she refuses to get in and instead stares at the bedroom window.

Clink.

I shake my head.

Clink.

No.

Ignoring the pebbles, I flip my light switch off and wait. The clinking doesn't stop. Hyla stretches, and I know it's useless. I amble to the window and open it, watching for any incoming objects. "What the hell, Jase?"

"Kay," he says softly.

"Go away, Jase."

"Kay ..."

"What?"

"Look!" He points to lightning bugs illuminating the side yard between where our houses used to connect. He holds up an empty jar and shakes it.

I shove my hand into my hair and look up to the ceiling. "I don't want to talk to you."

"You don't have to talk to me. We don't have to talk at all. Promise." He holds up three fingers.

I don't know what makes me go, but before I can think twice about it, I sling my arm out the window and onto the nearby tree branch. I climb down in my ripped jeans and T-shirt, belatedly thinking I should have changed—or at least put shoes on. My bare feet hit the ground with a slight splash in a muddy spot of grass. "Great," I mutter.

Jase hands me the jar and takes off running. "Come on."

Maybe it's the way his eyes light up. Maybe it's the fireflies taking me back to simpler times. Maybe it's the way Mama's face keeps replaying in my mind when she realized I'll have to go back home to New York eventually. Maybe it's all the girl talk and wine. Maybe it's that Jase said we don't have to talk about us, what we had, what we were, what we lost.

Without even realizing it, I let myself let go. I let myself enjoy this moment for what it is:

Him.

Me.

Us.

For now, but not forever.

Chapter 10

Then: Ten Years Ago

In Sloane, Tennessee, Fall Friday nights are spoken for. At seven-o'clock sharp, the town cascades onto the bleachers of Sloane High, waiting for kick-off to start. Tonight, we are running late. I keep checking the clock as if it will freeze time, but it doesn't.

"Maggie, it's six-fifty, we have to go." Mama taps her foot at the landing of the front staircase.

"Coming, coming." Nana hustles down the stairs, dressed head to toe in cherry red and navy blue, with *Sloane Spartans* pom poms in toe.

"Jesus, Mom, don't you think you're taking school spirit too far?" Daddy hangs his head in embarrassment.

Her gaze meets his in defiance. "Nope."

She reaches for my hand as we leave the house. It's been a month since Nana and Pop moved in with us. Mama says it's to help around the house while she picks up more shifts at work, but I have my own theories. Daddy's been sneaking a few extra cans. The fighting's escalated. Pop's the only one able to calm him down and keep him company when he's writhing in pain from a one-day detox here and there. Pop's also the only one he'll let near him when he inevitably picks the bottle back up again.

Nana claps her hands together as we walk down the block to the high school. "Ooh! This is exciting. It's Len's first game coaching since you were a tot, Andy."

Daddy purses his lips. He's hardly tolerant of her musings on a good day, and today's not a good day.

Nana squeezes my hand. "Want to race?"

"You hate running."

"On my own," she replies.

I glance at Mama, silently asking for permission and begging her to come with us so she's not stuck with *him*.

Mama lets out a light laugh. "Go ahead, girls, we'll meet you there."

"Okay." Nana puts her hands on her knees and lowers down. "Are you ready?"

I stretch my hamstring.

"On your mark, get set, go!"

Nana's off to a fast start, but my legs are longer, and I catch her in a few strides.

"Hey now," she calls. "You're supposed to let your nana win on account of I'm old, and I get tired."

I face her but don't stop running toward the school. "You're not old, Nana, and we both know you could smoke me if you wanted to."

"As long as you know it. Now stop showing off and run forward; you're creeping me out."

I laugh and do as I'm told.

Nana sneaks up behind me and slips in the stadium gate before me by half an inch.

"Nana!" I shout.

"Track and field champ, Katie Girl. You've gotta have a strong start and finish." She huffs, transitioning to a walk to catch her breath.

"I thought it was 'slow and steady wins the race?'"

"Well, I think we just learned that wasn't true. Come on." She pats my stomach with the back of her hand. "Let's find some seats."

Hundreds are bundled in the stands with various face paint and glitter signs to hold. I don't have a sign, but I have some stickers Jade passed me in fifth-period study hall.

"Kate! Over here!" Jade waves from the second to last bleacher by the thirty-yard line.

"Oh!" I hold up a pointer finger, letting her know we'll need a minute. Mama and Daddy come in a few seconds later and ask where we're sitting. I point to the Coles.

Mama leads the way up the bleachers.

Daddy stumbles on the metal stands but manages to get to the spot without too much of an incident. It doesn't matter though. Whether or not he came tonight, he'd still be a part of Matilda's big news on Sunday. *The witch.*

"Here, Mama packed some hot cocoa." Jade passes a tall, gray thermos my way.

I take a long swig, and the heat warms my insides and my anxiety. Even though we've been going to Spartans games my entire life, this one's different. Tonight, Jase is playing, his daddy's coaching, and Pop is assistant coaching. Tonight, the neighborly "how y'all doin's" and "whatcha grilling's" are becoming bonds, even friendships, over a love of football and small-town togetherness.

It's the first home game of the season, so the LED stadium lighting is on full display, and the scoreboard is set to zero-zero. The snack stand has a line five-deep, and the music is hopping with Flo Rida blasting through the speakers.

"He looks ready." I pass the thermos back to Jade.

Carrie and Mama are deep in conversation. Daddy's passed out next to them.

"He really does," she agrees.

Jase's uniform looks *good:* blue pants and bright red jersey with blue accents and a white 11 right in the middle. The black grease under his eyes makes the storminess in them wilder than ever. He waves his finger at me, causing my heart to skip a beat. He's so ... hot. When did he get so hot?

I finger wave back, unable to hide my grin.

Jade bumps her shoulder into mine. "All right, lover girl, you'll see him after the game."

My cheeks burn, but I roll my eyes at her remark, trying to hide the shift in our relationship. It's too new to share with other people, even Jade. The wind blows by, and a shiver runs up my spine. "It is much colder than I thought it would be."

"Oh, hell yeah. I'm bundled in this winter coat, unlike your hoodie. I do not have time to catch a cold before midterms."

Jade's dark hair is pulled back, or a full-on hair flip could've been coming.

"Trying to show Spartan pride here."

She laughs with a perfect smile in place and her teeth not chattering in the least. "Trying to show Jason Cole pride is more like it."

I shrug. Okay, maybe I'm not the best at hiding our relationship after all.

The whistle blows, and the game kicks off. The first quarter goes by in the blink of an eye. Nana and Jack disappear.

I turn to Jade. "Where'd they go?"

She signals to the bottom of the bleachers. "Over there."

They're at the fence, and Nana's yelling at the ref for our zero-to-seven start.

"Oh no, I should go get her." I frantically work to stand on a leg that's fallen asleep.

"Oh no, you don't." Jade pulls me back down. "She's a feisty lady. You do not need to get in the middle of it."

"I'm pretty sure I can lure her away with walking tacos."

"Hell, for walking tacos, you can lure *me* away." Jade pulls her puffy coat down as she gets up. What's not to love about seasoned meat and taco toppings mixed up in a bag of chips?

The snack stand is one hundred and eighty degrees from us, near the opposing team's bleachers. We tap Nana and Jack on their shoulders on the way, and sure enough, tacos can unite. Without Nana annoying the refs, they start the second quarter.

I swear I can hear the ref whisper his thanks as we back away, but Nana's too busy raving about extra guac, which is all that matters. The walking tacos are *that* good here. Cheering erupts from the home team bleachers, and I whip around to see what all the commotion is about. Our seasoned quarterback threw a forty-yard pass to our wide receiver.

"First down, Spartans," echoes loud and clear over the speaker.

"Atta boys!" Nana shouts. "Don't let them refs cheat you out of this game."

Audible groans come from the away stand next to us, with a few, "Go home, Grandma" and "Shut up, lady!"

Nana takes this in stride and throws her fist in the air. "Give 'em hell, kids."

I shake my head but continue moving—the line's only going to get longer the closer we get to halftime, but a breeze blows by, and my eyes are glued to the ball the second it leaves the quarterback's hand ... and right into Jase's hands. *Jase. Ohmygod.*

"Run, Jase!" I scream, but he's already long gone. Running yard after yard, seemingly picking up the pace the closer he gets to the endzone. He's in, and the rest of the team is in and lifting him up.

"He did it." I gasp, still playing the run over in my mind.

"He did it," Jade repeats.

"Yeah, he did." Jack puts two fingers in his mouth and lets out a loud whistle.

"Woot! Turning this game around." Nana moves closer to the fence, trying to taunt the ref again.

As the team puts Jase down, he spots me in the crowd and offers a megawatt smile.

My grin matches his.

"All right, let's get some tacos before you jump my brother in the middle of the game," Jade says a little too loud, resulting in some unwelcome gawking from moms walking by with their littles.

But it doesn't matter.

They don't matter.

He's all that matters.

The rest of the game is a blur. It's a mix of screams, shouts, jumping up and down, hugging Jade every time we score, and looking for Jase and finding him looking for me too. The butterflies flap in my stomach before I even notice they're there, and when the final whistle is called, I can hardly hear the final score over them.

"Hey, did we win?" I rest my left hand on Jade's right shoulder.

Her eyebrow arches. "Yes, weirdo, forty-two to fourteen."

"Oh." I exhale. "Great." But my tone doesn't match my words.

Jade turns her knees toward me and plants her hand on my forehead. "Are you okay?"

I can't find the words to answer her—not since Jase's finger wave sent a shockwave through my system. All I can think about is him, and she knows it.

"Come on, Juliet."

I follow Jade's lead out of the stadium, leaving the adults behind.

It doesn't take long for the clock to expire and for the players, coaches, and townspeople to make their way to the open field behind the stadium and down a large, grassy hill for a big bonfire, and everyone lets loose.

Typically, parents will usher smaller children home around midnight, but the rest of us stay until the early morning hours, eventually walking home and retrieving our cars on Saturday. Grandparents stay the longest, in lawn chairs, drinking local brews and reminiscing about the good ol' days—the days back when they used to play and cheer. Friday nights are a longstanding tradition in Sloane. One of my favorites.

By the time Jade and I get down the hill, the bonfire's spark is picking up. We run to get hot apple cider before the line gets out of hand and eye up a good spot when a pair of arms wrap themselves around my waist and pull me tightly into a set of stiff pads. My smile grows as I turn around and see a sweaty, dirty Jase standing in front of me, his grin wide.

The mud on his face and the orange glow behind him make his eyes look emerald. "I did it, baby," he says. He's proud as hell to have scored in his first home game.

I'm proud as hell, too. "Never doubted you."

Jade turns around and all but shoves a cup of cider into her brother's ribs.

He yelps. "What the hell is that for?"

"Stop making 'do me' eyes at my girl in public." She cocks her head and passes cider over to me without taking her eyes off her brother.

My cheeks get warmer by the second. "Wow, Jade." I throw *knock it off eyebrows* her way.

Jase rolls his eyes and studies his cider. "What, are they out of cocoa?"

"You get what you get, and you're grateful," Jade replies.

Nana skips over. "Do I smell cider?" she asks like she didn't grow up on Sloane's brew.

"Sure is." Jade grabs another cup off the table to hand it to Nana, "and it is *good* tonight."

Nan sips, and a smile spreads across her face. "Alright, I'll take it from here. You kids run along and enjoy the bonfire."

Looping my pointer finger in the top of Jase's jersey, I turn toward the bonfire and pull him along behind me.

"Where are we going?"

"You'll see," I tease, aware of my hips swaying as I continue to lead him.

"Kate, Jase, over here!" Jack waves us over to a blanket he's planted on. Letting go of Jase's jersey, I skip over and plop down, careful not to lose any cider. I take a long sip, looking over my shoulder, my blue eyes locking with his wild ones. My breath catches in my throat, but I glance back at the company on the blanket before anyone notices. "Hey," I say. "Great seats."

Jade approaches and agrees.

"Looks like it's about time for some s'mores." Jack checks out the bonfire.

I whistle. "Ooh yeah, look at the flame go."

"I'm glad it's warm. Finally," Jade replies.

I extend my cup to hers for a cheers. "Here, here."

Jack stands, wiping loose leaves off his jeans. "All right, I'm gonna go get some sticks; everyone roasting tonight?"

We all raise our hands, and Jack promises to be back in a few minutes.

"You know, that's one less person we have to hide in front of." Jase wiggles himself closer to me.

"Gross! You two know you are not a secret, and I'm still here." Jade covers her eyes with her hands as she speaks.

"Oh, Jade. He's messing with you. We're just friends," I lie. But it isn't Jade I'm looking at. It's Jase, and his eyes flashing an unfamiliar sight ... hurt, maybe?

"Yeah, big sis, relax. Nothing's happening here."

My heart is in my throat, but I can't drop the façade. Not now. If Jade knows, then the Coles all know, and Carrie will mention it to Mama, who doesn't keep secrets from Daddy. If Daddy knows, it's as good as dead—and I can't lose Jase. Not yet.

"Uh huh." She sips her cider. "Neither of you are good liars, nor are you even fooling yourselves."

Sweat beads on my forehead from the fire. Yeah, it's from the fire, not the heat on the blanket. Not at all.

Jack comes around the corner with four s'mores sticks in hand, but his smile fades as he approaches. "Okay, what did I walk up on?"

"Nothing," Jase and I say at the same time as I wipe the sweat off my brow.

He studies us. "Uh huh."

Jade's staring a hole into her fingernails. She's silent for enough time for me to think she's not going to say anything, but she does, "These two say they're just friends."

Jack looks between Jase and me and almost drops his sticks from laughing so hard.

"Sure, and I passed my driver's test on the first try," he jokes.

"What? It's true." When I look for validation on Jase's face, he won't even look at me.

"Excuse us a minute." Jase grabs my hand and pulls me up. It causes my cup to fall, spilling on the grass next to the blanket. We don't turn back for it.

"Where are we going?"

He doesn't answer. The music blasts through the field.

"Jase!" I shout.

"Kay!" he calls back, voice echoing in the darkness.

"Where are we going?"

"You'll see." He shakes his hips like I did earlier, but with far more attitude.

He pulls me past the table of drinks, the baby bonfire set up for little kids, and a bunch of grandparents, sitting and talking, waiting for their time to get close to the fire, and straight into the woods. The same woods that run behind our houses. He surprises me when he stops walking and spins around.

I huff. "What is this all about?"

"I don't know, Kay. What was *that* all about?" His voice is gruff.

"What?" I catch my breath.

He points back to the picnic blanket. "Saying we're just friends?"

I look down at the ground, avoiding his gaze and the question.

"Kay."

"I don't know. It's new ... I wasn't sure if we were telling people."

He lets out a laugh, but it doesn't sound like his normal soft laughter. This is harsher, a bit higher. "Oh my God."

"What?"

"Are you embarrassed to be my girlfriend?"

I shake my head. "Are you kidding? No. I ... if we say it out loud, it makes it real, and if it's real, it could end. I can't lose you, Jase, please ..." My voice shakes.

He scowls at me. It feels like there's nowhere to hide. "How is it possible that after all these years, you think you'd lose me?"

"We're ... best friends," I choke out.

"Damn it, Kay. I'm not grabbing other people by the waist or calling them 'baby.' I'm not asking other people out on dates. I *like* you, just you. Always you. The flowers. Climbing your tree. Catching fireflies. Our spot. You're *more* than my best friend—you're everything to me, and you're never, ever going to lose me."

I can hardly hear what he's saying over my heart beating a mile a minute. I've been waiting years for this.

"You're ..." I close my eyes and take a deep breath. "You're everything to me, too."

Jase puts his hand under my chin. "Hey," he whispers. "Kay, look at me."

When our eyes meet, it's like electricity runs through my veins. I don't know who reaches for whom first, but I'm in his arms, and he's in mine. He starts slowly and gives me a few sweet pecks. When my lips open, his lips match mine. Our teeth clink, and I shake my head, not expecting that to happen. *Ow.* He shifts his head to the side and sticks his tongue in my mouth.

I pull back, laughing. "What are you doing?"

His exhale is heavy, and his cheeks are flushed. "I don't—I don't really know."

"Me either." I shift closer. "Let's slow it down." I take control, slowly biting his lip, and then take his lips in mine. The second time's the charm. It's like I've been kissing him my whole life.

The fire crackles in the background, and we break apart. We're not at home, not alone. If anyone sees us, they'll *talk*. But it doesn't matter; all that matters is Jase ... and that kiss.

For the first time in a long time, I feel like I don't need to run or hide. I close my eyes and reach for him, doing any and everything to stay right here, in this moment, forever.

Chapter 11

Now

There is something about a pair of ripped jeans that fit just right. The perfect hug to your curves, the right amount of stretch without falling into the *mom jean* category, and most importantly the confidence they give when you feel your best. But as I stare at my reflection in my floor-length mirror, it's not the fit that pulls me in ... it's the dirt lingering on the bottom third of my legs. The mud continues to cake the denim the further down I look. Cringing, I will my favorite jeans to clean themselves for the umpteenth time in two days. If they were clean, I could undo sneaking out the other night and meeting *him*. I keep trying them on and expecting a different result, but they're still grimy, and the other night still happened. Sticking the jeans in the hamper or washer before Mama sees and asks where I've been seems impossible. She's stealthier than a spy. There's no way.

"What do you think, Hy? Can we sneak out?" I shift to the side, and a glob of mud falls to the floor.

Hyla stares as if she's considering her next move. She rolls over.

"Thanks for the support." I groan.

The door creeks open. "Want me to throw those in the washer?"

My hand flies to my chest as I exhale quickly. "Jesus, Mama, are you trying to give me a heart attack?"

"Ha!" She laughs out loud, eyebrows raised. "Says the girl with a bucket of mud on her pants. This isn't exactly what I expected to see when I came in here."

"Oh, I ... this isn't what it looks like," I say. Staring at my mismatched socks, I compare the state of my life with my outfit.

Unlike me, Mama has her life together. She's in her favorite blue maxi dress, her dark hair in a bun at the top of her head, her makeup done, and her purse and car keys in her hand. "Uh huh."

I gulp.

Mama walks further into the room and takes a seat on my childhood bed. It bounces slightly as she sits. "You didn't sneak out with Jase?"

I turn back to my reflection in the mirror and lower my voice. "I don't know what you mean."

She puts her hands on her hips faster than I expect. Her keys jingle as she drops her purse on the floor. "Bullshit."

"What?" My head whips around. Mama doesn't curse ... not like this, anyway. "What did you say?"

"Bullshit."

I blink at my mother.

She waves her hand at me. "Kate, come on. I know you'd sneak out every night when you were a kid. I just thought it changed when you guys broke up."

"It did change," I argue. Another glob of mud falls on the floor.

She cocks her head to the right.

"And it wasn't *every* night," I say.

"Give me some credit. My poor Magnolia tree had hundreds of scuff marks—not to mention the dent in the window from all the rocks. Neither one of you could bother covering your tracks, especially during the rain."

I want to fight it, but she's right. Back then, I didn't care what the consequences were. I wanted to be with Jase. He was all that mattered. *We* were all that mattered. But now he shouldn't get to throw a rock or shake a firefly jar to get me to run off with him. There are more important things happening here than Jase.

Mama stands and points at the dirt pile forming on the ground. "Clean the mess up before it sets."

"Yes, ma'am." Her hand is on the doorknob when I call after her.

"Hey, Mama?"

"Hmm?"

I fidget. "Are you going to see Dad?"

She's quiet for a long minute. I can't tell if she can hear me. When she looks up, her expression is guarded. "I am."

"Can I go with you?"

"Really?" Her shoulders relax. "I would love for you to come. Maybe shower first."

I stretch my arms around her, careful not to get my legs too close to hers.

She pulls me in.

"I'll bring up a spray for the stain." Mama gestures to the dirt I've drug through the room. "Take those pants off and leave them by the washer. They need some work."

"Thanks, Mama. For what it's worth, I'm sorry for sneaking out."

She shakes her head. "Oh, sweetie, I know why you did it, and I don't blame you."

I slump my head.

She takes my hand. "Kate, your dad's alcoholism was enough to handle as an adult. I can't imagine what it did to you as a child. None of what happened—the drinking, fighting, aftermath, none of it was your fault in any way."

I stifle tears. I witnessed firsthand how much being a parent destroyed my dad, how it caused him to drink more and more. He wasn't happy ... because of me, and I wasn't happy because of him—how poetic.

Mama pulls me in. "I'm glad you had someone here for you. I wish *I* could have been more present with you, but I was selfish and wrapped up in my reactions. I didn't realize the damage it was doing to you until you left, and it was too late."

Her admission is like a punch in the gut, and my breath hitches. "You weren't selfish, Mama. You did everything you could do to protect me from him. Me leaving you alone with him was selfish." It's the first time I've allowed myself to think about it, let alone say it all out loud, but the weight it lifts is temporary.

She sniffles, and there's a cut in her voice. "I'm not making excuses. You were a kid. I should have been there for you. You should have been able to lean on me instead of having me push you away to New York."

It's not the full story. I can't look at her. I've never been able to handle it when mama cries. It wrecks me in a way I can't explain. My mama's always been a superhero fighting Dad's disease and outbursts, dealing with me acting out, and keeping the house in line, all while holding down a full-time job to keep us afloat.

"Mama," I murmur.

"No, sweetie, please. The way I handled this was a mistake, Kate. I'm sorry. I promise I'll make it up to you." She wipes her tears onto her sleeve and steps out of my room. "I'll give you some time. We can go whenever you're ready."

"The way I dealt with it was a mistake, too. We all made mistakes ..."

She's already gone. It's just me, my muddy jeans, and my aching heart. When I left, I never considered the damage it would do to Mama. I didn't consider anything. I just had to get out of Sloane.

Hyla jumps up on the bed. She sniffs my leg before curling her nose up and spinning herself into a ball right by my pillow. Even though she seems to disapprove of the smell coming off me, and I disapprove of a lot more than that, the one thing moving away taught me is how much getting Hyla helped fill the holes in my heart. And how much moving back here picked at them again.

Running down the stairs, I toss my wet hair into a messy bun and slip on a pair of strappy sandals.

Mama shakes her head when she sees me. "How many times have I told you not to go outside with a wet head? You're going to catch a cold."

I roll my eyes. "Oh, Mama."

She grips the door handle. "You know ... if you're not ready to see him or don't want to go, it's okay. Having you home over the last week has been nice."

I put my hand on her arm and study the crease in her brow. "It's okay. I want to go with you."

Her inhale is longer than normal. "Okay. I should warn you, he's not ... you're not—he doesn't look like you remember."

I cross my arms, and my lips turn over in a frown. "What do you mean?"

She shifts her nails to her mouth and bites down. A nervous habit she's always had and one she passed down to me.

"What is it?"

"He's *different,* is all. He's ... fragile now."

Fragile? The word cements me in place. What does it even mean? Dad's always been larger than life. Too big, perhaps. He's loomed over any and everything as the tough, drunk guy, who some days would say things to push me away, and other days be calm and gentle, forgetting how terrible the bad days were for me, Mama, our family. I've barely been able to process the idea of seeing *that guy*. To see someone frail ...

Mama seems to recognize the anguish on my face. "Hey, like I said, you don't have to see him. It's okay if you're not ready."

I focus on the clock over the door, on the breeze blowing the leaves on the trees outside, and the creaking of the hardwood in the upstairs hallway as Nana wakes up. I focus on anything but Mama and the heartbreak all over her face, but I can't. It's right there. *She's* right there. As much as I've dodged coming down here, seeing him, for *years*, I know time is up.

"I don't know if I'll ever be ready." I bite down on my lip. "But I'm tired of avoiding him."

She squeezes my hand. "You're going to be fine, but if not, I'll be right next to you."

The ride to the hospital has always been a ten-minute drive from home, but today, it seems like two, maybe three minutes. While Mama looks for parking, various questions and scenarios consume my mind. What will it be like seeing my dad after all these years? Will he yell? Cry? Refuse to see me? Maybe he still holds a grudge, like I do. Maybe he knows I'm in town. Maybe he doesn't. Maybe he does and doesn't care.

Mama puts the car in park and faces me. "Ready?"

Ready to be sick.

"Kate?" She places a hand on my shoulder, centering me.

I fake a smile and unclick my seatbelt, wiping sweat from my palms onto the bottom of my yellow sundress.

The automatic door slides open, and my eyes strain to adjust to the harsh, fluorescent panels in the ceiling. There's a page over the loudspeaker calling for doctors and nurses to prep for an incoming ambulance with someone in critical condition. A man dressed in a white coat curses and straightens from where he is leaning on the reception desk, flirting with the coordinator. He dashes off toward the Emergency Room down the hall, and I stop moving, reaching for Mama's arm. It's a cruel reminder that life is fleeting and that Dad may or may not pull through.

My feet are planted in the doorway of Sloane Memorial while I steady my breathing.

"This way." Mama leads. "He's out of the ICU."

THIS KIND OF LOVE

"Oh." I run the thought through my mind to see if Mama's mentioned this over the last few days and if I had been paying enough attention or if I blocked it out.

"I didn't tell anyone," she answers my silent question. "It's looking good, but he's not out of the woods yet. I don't want to either worry anyone or give them false hope."

Mama turns down the hallway with ease, leading me from one area to another, to an elevator, followed by another hallway, and finally through big, wooden doors, announcing the Sloan Memorial Cancer Center in bold, black letters. My breath wooshes out of my chest. Something about seeing it in print—CANCER—seems definite. Part of me didn't believe it when Mama told me. Part of me blocked out the words, the meaning. It's hard to do when the word's right there, taking up *space*.

For something quite common, it hits a lot harder when it's close to home, even with someone I haven't spoken to in a long time. Especially then. What if it's too late? Would I be grateful? Relieved? Should I have come sooner? I can't help the tears from falling or the deep remorse in the pit of my stomach for spending all this time being angry ... but I can't help being furious, still.

We approach his room before I know it, and I take a step back. Before any interaction with my father, I would always wait and listen for a minute to see what mood he was in and what I would be getting myself into.

Mama heads in and crashes Pop's time with him.

"Liz! You look pretty today." My dad's voice booms with excitement at seeing his high school sweetheart standing there, like every day before. To me, his voice sounds like a stranger's.

I can't see them, but I can imagine a smile spreading across her face. "You say that every day," she replies.

"Doesn't ... make it any less ... true," he stutters.

He sounds more vulnerable than I expected. There's pain in his voice as he tries to talk, and Mama's words from this morning come back to me: *He's fragile now.*

My feet nearly give out. Now I know what she means. Any one thing could change everything. I can't be responsible for setting his health back. She'd never forgive me. My feet backpedal until I knock into a heart monitor and trip.

A nurse extends her hand to me. "Hey, are you okay?"

"Yeah, I'm great." I lie, ignoring her kindness.

I run out of the Cancer Center as fast as I can. The world feels like it's spinning all around me. My hand reaches out to find a wall, and I crouch down. My fingers find my temples and massage them. The stars come before I can stop them, and everything goes fuzzy before my eyes.

I sit, grip my knees, and start to rock slowly, steadily. I inhale for four seconds, hold for seven, and exhale for eight, repeating until I can peel my eyes open and find a thick, wooden hospital chair to focus on. The green plastic is stiff yet worn, with three small tears on the right side. I breathe in again, hold, then exhale.

"Kate? What happened?" Pop sits next to me and holds my hand, squeezing three times to help me come-to.

"I just ..." I shift my hands to either side of my legs and push my weight up onto them.

"Woah, woah, Katie girl, take it easy."

I blink to adjust to the hospital hallway I'm lying in. And there it is again, CANCER CENTER, as big as can be.

Pop leans down, eyebrows drawn in concern. "What's going on, babe?"

I shake my head. "I don't know, one second I was waiting for Mama to let me know it was okay to come in and see Dad, and the next, I—I don't think I can handle it if he doesn't want to see me, or if me being here makes his health worse."

I look away, but Pop puts his hand under my chin and lifts my gaze to his. "Hey, Katie girl, you listen to me. There is nothing you could do to disappoint your daddy or make him not want to see you. Do you hear me?"

I blink but don't reply.

"Kate?" he pleads.

"Okay," I say, but I know for a fact he's wrong. There *is* something that would disappoint him. There already *was*. Something disappointed him enough that I couldn't stand to see his face full of disgust anymore. Something made me leave and made him cut me out of his life for over half a decade. Something could change everything if Mama knew, too.

"Ready to go?" Mama strolls out of the hospital room but stops when she sees me. "Oh sweetie, what happened?"

"Nothing, Mama; everything's okay." I take the help she's offering and stand slowly. "What about Dad?"

She waves her hand in the direction of his room. "He's having a good day and found a Gordon Ramsey marathon on TV—he won't miss us until tomorrow." She makes it sound casual, but I know this can't be easy for her or Pop, and my causing a scene makes it a lot worse.

She gives me a warning look, and I follow her down the hallway to the elevator and through the rest of the hospital maze. I know better than to argue with Mama when she's made up her mind and she's decided—we're out of here.

Mama reverses out of the parking garage spot, checks her mirrors, and turns to me. "You know, you don't have to go to the Homecoming game tonight."

I bring my palm to my forehead, cursing. "Fuck. It's tonight?"

"Language." She puts the car into drive. "If you aren't feeling up to it, stay home in bed and rest."

I pull out my cell phone, scroll Snap stories, and sure enough, several people in town have already posted about Homecoming. I sigh. "The only thing worse about going to Homecoming would be not going and seeing what Matilda has to say about it in her next column."

She pulls a pair of sunglasses from the middle console. "You're not wrong."

I wish I was. I'd love nothing more than to stay in bed watching *Friends* reruns, avoiding a big-town event where all eyes will be on me. And Jase.

I hear the unmistakable sashaying of pom-poms before I see them. Nana's running down the hardwood stairs, shaking the poms back and forth wildly as we step into the living room. "Hey, look at what I found!"

"You look festive, Mags!" Amy takes in Nana's Spartans jersey and cherry red corduroy pants. Her signature Firetruck Red lipstick is well on display.

THIS KIND OF LOVE

"Thanks." Nana spins, showing off the French braid she made with some pom-pom strings threaded throughout. Nana's nothing if not on-brand.

"Well, look at all of you; you have to change." Nana shakes her finger between the rest of us, gesturing for us to get ready for the Homecoming game.

Amy leans in. "Oh, I, um, what should I wear? This is my first time at a high school football game."

"Is it now?" Nana's eyes light up: *project!*

"Hurry up. We don't want to be late!" Mama shouts.

"Be there in a minute," Nana calls back. "Besides, we haven't been late in years."

"We were late to the last home game," Mama mumbles. It's no good fighting with Nana. Out loud, anyway.

Pop sits on the arm of the sofa to wait.

A few minutes later, Amy emerges in my old cut-off Spartans emblem T-shirt, jean jacket, and pair of ripped dark blue jeans. She holds her hands out to the side. "So ... what do you think?"

"Gorgeous. Now come on, let's go." I grab Amy's hand and rush out the door.

"What the heck?" Amy asks.

"You'll see." I glance over my shoulder.

"Why do you look like you're trying to keep tabs on a stalker?"

I turn and face my best friend, right hand on her hip, eyebrows arched.

Nana and her pom-poms start lunging out the front door, and Amy does a double take. "Um, Mags, what is happening here, exactly?"

Nana's breathing is a little staggered. "Have. To. Stretch."

Amy purses her lips. "Okay, but we're going to a high school football game—not the Olympics."

"You'd be surprised." Mama locks the front door. "They do this all the time."

"Do what?"

Nana straightens. "All right, girlfriend, are you ready or what?"

I crack my knuckles. "Ready."

"On your mark, get set, go!" Nana shouts. She takes off before she finishes saying go.

I give Nana time to set her pace before I let my legs carry me down the sidewalk, catching up to her in a few strides. I nod as I pass and hear Amy whisper, *what the hell?* But Nana's *dammit* is loud and clear.

The band is playing the fight song as the pep rally wraps up. Nana, Pop, Mama, and Amy are still a while back when I approach the gate. I take a moment to catch my breath and study the scene in front of me: gray stands packed with nearly everyone in town, the brass section of the band echoing through the stadium, scoreboards lit up: set to zero-zero, cheerleaders huddling, the home team in their red and blue, eye black painted on, putting on their helmets, chanting and getting ready to go. It's enchanting.

"Wow," Amy says behind me. "This is really something."

My gaze meets hers. Trying to see things through her eyes, I can see the wonder, the spark. My first home game made me feel that way, too. Hell, *most* of the home games made me feel the same way.

Nana coughs behind me, almost dropping pom-poms at the call for the National Anthem. Instead, she moves them both to her left hand and puts her right across her chest.

"This *is* serious, huh?" Amy breathes.

I place my hand over my heart.

The singer approaches the mic. The way she belts out the Anthem is even better than I remember.

"You know," Mama says. "I hear her sing each week, and I always forget just how talented she is."

"Me, too." Nana sniffles.

Pop mumbles he's going to go see if the coaches need any backup. They probably don't, but will welcome him, anyway. After four state championships, Len Dailey is a coaching legend in Sloane.

Needing a distraction from *who* he helped coach, I eye up the snack stand, "Nana, why don't you and Amy find some seats, and Mama and I can grab the snacks."

Nana shakes her poms and grabs Amy's hand as if she's five and not twenty-six. "Come on," Nana says to Amy. She winks and lowers her voice to me. "Hey, Katie girl, grab me some of the good stuff, okay?"

I laugh. "Walking Tacos with nacho cheese, side of Reese's?"

Nana smiles. "That's the stuff."

"Sounds amazing," Amy agrees.

"I'm gonna get a full round, y'all," I call back.

The walking tacos are the best thing on the menu by far, and according to Nana, anything salty *must* be accompanied by something sweet at major events. Make no mistake about it: in Sloane, Tennessee, the Homecoming Game is a major event.

It's halfway through the first quarter when we get back into the stands.

"What took you so long?" Amy smacks Nana's hand out of her taco.

Nana huffs. "This is nothing. The line can get long, but it's *so* worth it."

"What's the score?" Mama squints to see the scoreboard in the distance.

"Mmm," Amy exclaims, salivating over her first bite of what I'm assuming is her first real walking taco.

Mama cranes her neck. "Does the board say fourteen-nothing? It was hard to pay attention in line."

"It does. Been an awful start, girls," Nana replies.

"It doesn't look like it's about to get any better," Amy mumbles. She ducks, focusing on her taco and her taco alone.

I bump her shoulder. "What?"

She avoids eye contact.

Mama taps me on my shoulder. "Over there."

I follow the direction of her head tilt and see Jase standing at the bottom of the bleachers, his eyes lost, searching the stands.

When his gaze finds mine, the world around me freezes. He's the last person I want to see, but after today, he's also all I want to see. I shouldn't have snuck out the other night and put six years of building a wall around my heart at risk for Jase and catching fucking fireflies. It was stupid.

Jase's lips curl up in a smile, and he walks by the bleachers and around the fence.

My breath quickens, and I watch him as he backs away.

"Go," Mama says, loud enough for only me to hear.

I rush down the bleachers but focus on each step, trying not to trip and be the center of Matilda's next column. Maybe she'll assume I need to use the Ladies' Room. One can hope, anyway.

Turning the corner around the bleachers, I run straight into a firm six-pack with an old wide receiver's jersey over it.

"Guess the fireflies were a better move than I thought." Jase laughs.

I cock my head and place my hands on his chest, trying to distance myself from him, but I only end up pulling him closer.

His smirk stays in place as his gaze drifts to the sideline, where members of the Homecoming Court fuss over their dresses and tuxes. The matching hues are perfectly on-point, corsages straightened, and anxious smiles frozen on their faces. It's almost time. "Remember when that was us?"

I sigh, lost in the memory of us *then*, being crowned King and Queen at eighteen in our matching emerald green, smiles brighter than the stars in the sky ... I clear my throat. "Looking back, I don't know how we won."

Jase turns his attention to me. He moves a stray strand of hair away from my face and tucks it behind my ear. "We won because this town loves a good love story."

Goosebumps prick my skin. "Were we, though—a good love story?" I blink away the tears, and the strain in his left eye tells me he knows exactly what I'm asking and why.

"We were the best love story this town has ever seen." He rests his hands on either side of my face and leans down, slowly moving closer to me.

I'm drawn to him like a moth to a flame. Always have been ... and maybe I always will be.

My phone buzzes, jolting us away from each other. I pick it up without looking and gesture *one second* to Jase. "Hello?"

"Kate!" Nick's voice booms loud over the line, loud enough to hear over the announcer sharing the five-minute countdown until it's time to announce the King and Queen.

Turning my back to Jase, I lower my voice, "Nick? Is everything okay?"

He laughs awkwardly through the receiver. "Depends on how you feel about my news."

My stomach drops. What news?

"We have a trial coming up, and some witnesses need to be deposed ... in Nashville."

"My Nashville?" I ask. Nashville is thirty minutes away from my hometown. He'll be thirty minutes away from me ... and Jase.

"Your Nashville, huh? You never mentioned owning the whole metropolitan area."

"Oh, you know me, just a city princess."

"It tracks." His laugh is infectious, and I'm so distracted by it that I almost miss the rest of what he says. "So, my boss asked me to come down to take care of the case, and if you are up for it, I'd love to take you out for a nice fancy dinner while I'm there. But, you know, as I say it out loud, it could be adding too much to your plate right now."

I don't answer right away, not sure what to say.

"Kate?"

"Um. I mean, yes, of course, I'd love to see you." I'm physically talking to Nick, but I can't focus on anything he's saying until he ends the call with *see you tomorrow.*

"Wait, see me when?"

The call drops, and "out of service" flashes on the screen. I turn around to talk to Jase, but he's nowhere in sight. *Where did he go? Why did he leave?*

"Hey, there you are! Come on, they're about to crown the King and Queen." Amy waves her hands. "Kate, are you okay? Why do you look like you've seen a ghost?"

"Ni—Nick's coming to Sloane," I mumble. *Nick is New York. Jase is Sloane. Where is Jase?*

"Kate? Really, you don't look good; maybe you should sit down." Amy places her hands on my shoulders, and while I feel her there, I'm lost in the nostalgia of King and Queen, of clinging to Jase like he's the one person who can save me while he simultaneously breaks me ... and why did he disappear? The world starts to fade before my eyes, and I hyperventilate for the second time in one day.

So much for avoiding Matilda's column.

Chapter 12
Then: Nine Years Ago

"No, no, no, what are you doing?" From the passenger seat, Jase throws his hand onto the worn dashboard of my old Plymouth Sundance.

"Stopping at the stop sign." I take my right hand off the wheel to gesture to the bright red hexagon we're approaching.

"You can't stop in second gear. Shift to neutral."

"It's stopping."

He sighs. "You're going to stall."

"No, I'm not." But sure enough, the car stalls, and I can't get it to move at all. "What's happening?"

"You stalled." He brings his hands to his face. "Okay. Okay, foot on the clutch, and move the car into neutral."

"It shut off?" I bring my ear down to the dash to see if I can hear anything.

"Mhmm."

Panic floods my mind. "Is it safe? Oak's kind of busy for there to be cars hanging out in the middle of the road."

Jase runs his left hand through his buzzcut. "Trust me, Kay, no one's gonna miss you in this."

My jaw drops open. "I knew you had a problem with teal! Why do you hate it so much?"

"I don't 'hate it,'" he says with air quotes. "I just think this particular color belongs on a Peacock and not a car."

"Rude!" I swat at his basketball shorts.

"Kay ... can you please put your car in neutral?"

"Lily," I reply.

Jase twists to face me. "What?"

"Her name is Lily."

The back of Jase's head hits the seat rest. "Okay. Can you please put *Lily* in neutral?"

I reach my left foot over the clutch pedal and adjust the shifter to neutral. "Okay."

"Keep your left foot on the clutch, move your right foot to the break, and turn the key."

"Okay."

"Put it back into first." He shakes his head. "Why did we think you were ready for the road?"

"Um, *you* thought. I was ready to go to bed, but you insisted I 'was ready for the road.'"

"Are you kidding me? Are you messing with me right now?" he scolds me.

I tilt my head ninety degrees. "What?"

"I'm the one who pushed you on the road? You haven't been asking me for the last week?"

I turn the car off and cross my arms, anger seeping from my pores. "Fuck you!"

Jase blinks three times rapidly. "What?"

141

I arch my brow and hold my ground. "You heard me. You're not the only one who can be a dick."

"You're frustrating. I'm trying to help you."

"Please take me home, Jase. If I'm going to be hollered at, I'd rather be at home." Where I can hide and be alone.

These words nullify his anger instantly, like rain to a flame.

Jase reaches his hand out, but I ignore it. "Come on, Kay. You don't mean it. I'm sorry—I'm tired."

I open the driver's side door and storm to the passenger's side. "Switch with me. Please. I want to go home."

He locks his door and shakes his head. "Can we try again?"

I turn away from him, not entertaining his pleading green eyes.

"Okay. We can go home, but you can drive."

"No. Switch with me."

"Kay," he begs.

It's too late for soft. There's heat rushing through my body, and I'd rather be anywhere but here. "Jase, get in the driver's seat."

Rain seems to come out of nowhere, cascading to the ground and bouncing back up. A late summer storm. Cursing, I stomp down the road.

Jase hops out of the passenger seat and slams the door closed. "Where are you going?"

"Home."

"What? Kay, come on, get back here."

I turn around, sure that the mascara on my face is running with the rain. "No."

"Come on, don't be ridiculous."

"Oh, now I'm ridiculous? Got it."

THIS KIND OF LOVE

He waves his arms in the air. "Kay."

I keep walking, but Jase runs to catch up to me and pulls my arm back. "Hey, please talk to me."

I blink to hide the tears.

"Kay, I'm sorry. Come on, let's go home."

I study the raindrops. "And you'll drive?"

"Yes. I'm sorry I got frustrated. I know you're learning, and the weather sucks."

I nod.

He pets my hand. "I really didn't mean to hurt you. I never want to do that again." Jase pulls me in close. He holds me while it rains. The tears fall, and I can feel the hollow ache in my heart and the simultaneous beating.

Clink. Clink.

By the time the second pebble hits my bedroom window, I almost have it open.

Jase is standing by the base of the Magnolia tree, holding a handful of dandelions out toward me, his grin wide, even in the pouring rain.

"Please don't think cheesin' it down there with a pile of wilting weeds is gonna get me to climb down this tree again today."

"Oh, come on, Kay," he calls up. "I said I was sorry. Let me make it up to you."

"How?" I cross my arms.

"I have ways." He wiggles his eyebrows up at me.

"No, thanks." I pull at the window.

"Would you rather I go around front and ask your parents to see you?"

Nope. I push my legs out the window and grab the nearest branch to help wrap my body around the tree on my way down. "Now, why would you go and involve them?"

Jase extends his arms. "If you want to drop, I can catch you."

I roll my eyes, but in the rain, my footing isn't as stable as it normally is. "I might drop."

"I've got you."

And he does. He catches me with ease and pauses for a few seconds before helping me put my feet on the cold, wet ground.

"It's a little muddy." Jase's eyes look a little wilder with every flash of lightning. He's soaking wet, but he doesn't seem to mind. He smiles, and I feel my anger fade. "What?"

You're perfect, I want to say, but I shake it off.

He tilts his head to the side. "Really, what?"

"I—um, nothing."

The light switch outside my kitchen door flips open, and Mama brings out an old bag of trash. We stay still, feeling every pulse as we try not to get caught. Mama doesn't seem to notice, and she's back inside quickly.

"So…" Jase extends his arm and spins me. "I have big plans for us tonight."

"Cause the first plan turned out so well?"

"I've revised a bit."

I plant my hand on my hip. "In the last couple of hours?"

"Mhmm." He pulls me close as he moves us into a slow dance, and my anger dissolves like sugar in water. As much as I want to go inside, away from the rain, I don't want to leave this either. I've always thought things like dancing in the August rain were tacky in the movies, but somehow, when I'm with him, nothing seems tacky. Everything feels *right*.

I rest my head on his chest, which is getting noticeably more muscular from playing football but is still soft enough for me to lean on.

I lose track of time dancing with him, my clothes sticking to my skin more and more by the minute, but when the rain lets up a bit, I pull away and wring out my hair. I sling it up into a bun at the top of my head. When I catch him staring at my lips, I tilt them into a smile.

"You're beautiful, Kay." He steps closer.

His magnetic field pulls me in, and I can't help reaching for him. My arms wrap around his neck, and he lifts me. I wrap my legs around his waist.

Jase backs up until he bumps into the old Magnolia behind him, holding us. "I love you." He tucks a strand of hair behind my ear and rests his palm on my cheek.

"I love you, too," I reply.

Jase moves his head down to mine and grabs my lips with his. The kiss starts sweet. Then, I can't get enough. I move my hands to either side of his face and pull him closer; the kiss deepens. I moan and hear him curse under his breath when he pulls away for a brief second before kissing me again.

There's a quick flash of light in front of me, causing my eyes to blink open.

"Police! Hands where I can see 'em!" a deep voice bellows out of the woods. The light becomes steadier as it gets closer, and Jase puts me on the ground. We put our hands up in the air right as the officer approaches. Instead of arresting us, he laughs.

"Son of a—Jack." Jase throws his arm right into Jack's crotch.

Jack doubles over and exhales. "I really had you two going there for a minute." He points back and forth between us.

Jase glares at his brother. "You know damn well Dad would beat the crap out of us if we were arrested."

Jack chuckles. "Yeah, if you guys were dumb enough to start humping by a wet tree when there are two houses you could go into to be warm and have privacy, then it'd be your fault."

Shifting my left hand to Jase's mouth, I stick my right pointer finger at Jack. "Okay, first, we weren't 'humping.'" I raise my middle finger to join in and continue, "Second, please don't ever say humping again."

He snorts.

I flip him the bird.

Jack raises his hands in mock surrender. "Okay, fine. All I'm saying is you guys should probably move inside before it's more than me walking up on you."

I roll my eyes and remove my hand from Jase's mouth, but Jack has a point. I'd go to my grave before telling him that, though.

Jase shoves his hands into his jeans. "Do you want to come inside?"

I should head home before they notice I'm gone … but then the fighting starts inside. By the quick escalation, I can tell Dad's in one of his moods. Mama's gonna give him a run for his money before he ends up falling asleep, and he won't remember it in the morning … but I will.

Jase gestures to my kitchen. "Are Nana and Pop home?"

I shake my head. "Not yet."

He tugs at my hand. "Come on."

"Jade left a ton of clothes this semester. I'm sure she wouldn't mind loaning you something dry," Jack suggests.

"Thank you." I follow the brothers inside.

THIS KIND OF LOVE

I expect to see their parents in the living room when we walk in, but to my surprise, they're not home. Jack runs upstairs. I twirl to inhale the scent of vanilla. It doesn't matter if anything's in the oven; the Cole household always smells like vanilla. Handmade artwork decorates the sky-blue walls—artwork their kids made growing up—the kind most parents hide after their kids get to high school. Hand turkeys and house sketches adorn the room, like they always do. I admire them like I always do. The space feels so ... loving. I turn and smack Jase in the stomach.

"Ugh." He doubles over when I connect.

"Excuse you—your parents aren't even home, and we were outside in the rain?"

He shrugs. "Like you didn't like it?"

The blush rises to my face.

He points at my cheeks. "See, I knew it."

"Oh yeah, I'm sure your parents are gonna love it when I leave a trail of water through the house." I walk around the steps to the downstairs bedrooms, turning right to head into Jade's room.

"How many times have you heard my mama say she'd rather the house be lived in than clean?"

I bite my lip. "At least a dozen ... but I still don't want your parents to come home to a mess."

Jase catches me in a few quick strides and twirls me around, pinning me against the bedroom door. "I don't want to talk about them. I want to talk about *us*." His voice is low and slow.

I spin out of his grasp and step into Jade's room. "I'm getting some dry clothes."

His hand caresses the door. "Oh, Kay Dailey, you're in trouble."

After I find a button-down flannel shirt and pair of leggings to replace my wet clothes, I open the door to Jase leaning against the wall. "What was it you said about trouble?" I bat my eyelashes.

"You *are* trouble." He swats my butt as I walk past.

"Now, now," I tsk. "That's not the way to get what you want."

"I want *you*," he says.

"I want dinner," I counter.

"Happy wife, happy life." He says it so casually I almost miss it.

I pause on my way to the bright yellow kitchen, full of joy and sunshine—when there isn't a storm outside, anyway. "Happy what?"

He shrugs. "Something my dad always says, 'Happy wife, happy life.' It means if you're happy, I'm happy."

Wife. It's intoxicating and leaves me breathless.

Jase opens the pantry and pulls out a box of pasta. He shakes it toward me like he didn't just say the most romantic thing I've ever heard. "How about mac and cheese?"

"Are those spirals?" I strain my neck to read the box.

"Nope. Shells."

"Do you have spirals?"

"What, are you five?" He pulls out a pot and fills it with water.

I dance around the counter and sit on the tall stool at the kitchen bar, but his comment almost stops me in my tracks more than the *wife* comment. "Um, no. Spirals are the best."

"Are you kidding?" He whips around, pot in hand. "Shells are *the* pasta for mac and cheese. The shape holds little pockets of cheese."

"Shells are okay, but spirals are the best, hands down."

"Okay, I take back 'happy wife, happy life.'"

"No." I put my hands on the counter in front of me. "You can't take it back."

"Oh yes, I can. Spirals over shells is a deal breaker." He salts the water and reads the cooking time on the box of noodles. "I can't believe I didn't know this about you after all these years."

I shrug. "It's not new."

"Yeah, but mac and cheese is your favorite. How did I not know you despise the perfect shell when it's done nothing to you?"

"Okay, I never said I 'despise' shells. I think they're *fine*. They're just not better than spirals."

"Uh huh, well, tonight dinner will be served with shells. You're welcome."

I roll my eyes. Hard. But when the mac is done, and we sit back on his familiar, comfy couch and take a bite, I stifle a moan. I shove another bite in my mouth before he notices. Maybe the shells weren't bad after all.

"What do you think?" He reaches for the remote and loads Netflix.

"It's ... all right." I hold my pride close. "What're you putting on?"

Jase sighs and hands the remote over. "What do *you* want to watch, Kay?"

Smiling, I put on my favorite Nicholas Sparks adaptation, *The Longest Ride*, and lean into him, the bowl of mac in my lap. "Happy wife, happy life, right?"

He places a sweet kiss on the top of my head and holds me close with his left arm, reaching for his mac with his right. "Someday."

While we watch one of my favorite movies, eating my favorite meal with my favorite guy, all I can think about is: *Someday*.

Chapter 13

Now

"Remind me why the 5K is the morning after the Homecoming Game again?" I check behind me for bystanders before stretching my hamstrings. The street's starting to fill with runners and observers for what's sure to be a long 3.1 miles on a dreary mid-October day.

Mama shakes her head and points up to the greying sky. "At least it looks like the weather may hold out for a while."

I shift into arm swings and take a few deep breaths.

Mama hands me a sixteen-ounce thermos. "Energy boost?"

I take a long swig of French vanilla coffee, steamed like Mama likes it. "Thanks." The wind brushes my shoulder, and I shiver. "I guess I just regret agreeing to this one on …" I wince, looking at my smartwatch, "five hours of sleep and a Tennessee chill I've yet to miss."

"It's better than the humidity we've been seein', and you've survived colder in New York," she encourages me.

"That's not the chill, I mean."

Matilda jogs over in lime green spandex, her hair pulled back by a matching headband, and there's a neon clipboard in her hand.

"Ah." Mama takes a deep breath. "Matilda, hi." Her voice drops when she greets her.

"Hi, Dailey family." Matilda consults a piece of paper fastened on her board. "Weren't three of you going to participate in the run today?"

Mama shakes her head.

Matilda double-checks her list. "I definitely have three."

"Check again." Mama lets a little 'tude slip in.

My hand finds Mama's, and my thumb starts massaging the top of her hand. "It'll just be me, Matilda. Mama's helping with refreshments, though."

The whispers from the crowd must have started some time back, but my ears didn't catch them right away. Now, the hiss from the crowd is deafening. "Maggie. Running. What's she wearing?"

"What on God's green earth?" Matilda says, her tone snide.

I bend to see Nana, all but huffing up the hill. Amy's right beside her, holding her hand, helping her along. The closer Nana gets, the more blinding her outfit becomes. "You know, Matilda, your pre-race email did say dress to be seen." I stifle my laughter.

"This is *not* what I meant." She sulks away.

"What do you think?" Nana spins, showcasing her traffic cone orange sweatsuit.

When Nana goes, she goes all out.

Mama tilts her head. "It's ... something, Maggie."

"Right? Exactly what I told her," Amy adds. To her credit, she doesn't cringe like I thought she would.

I study her black workout pants and sneakers. "Amy Park ... are you running in this race?"

Amy shrugs. "It's for the kids."

My smirk is instant. Well, I'll be damned. Maybe Sloane's growing on her.

"How hard is this gonna be?" Amy looks around to see most of the town in their running gear, with one or two tying their shoes.

Mama raises her hands. "Don't look at me; I'm here to give out the water."

Amy ponders this. "You know, I didn't realize my options. Maybe count me in for water, too. Runners need to stay hydrated, right?"

"You got all dressed up to run, Ame. You're running," I quip.

She sighs. "But I mean, how much would I be missed?"

"A lot." Nana sinks into a lunge.

Amy crosses her arms.

Nana has spoken, and that's the end of the conversation.

The three of us stroll to the balloon arch at the starting line, and Mama makes her way to the water station. We wish each other luck, but I know she'll need it more than we will. While we're busy running, Matilda will corner Mama at least half a dozen times with questions about Dad, how long I'll be in town, how long until Jase and I are back together, and so on. I'd rather run an ultra-marathon with double Charlie horses than talk about any of that.

Right as I'm in the middle of thinking about not thinking about Jase, I see him come up the hill.

Nana mumbles a "damn" right behind me.

I hush her, but *damn* is right.

How does he look more in shape than when he was playing football and working out every day for hours on end?

"Maybe he won't see us," Amy whispers.

It's like a jinx. The minute her words are out in the ether, his gaze finds mine. He smiles and sends a finger wave. I'm torn between wanting to burn down the ground he's standing on or rush to hug him. Jase takes a few strides toward us, testing the waters, but I can't move, react, or do anything but stare.

"It's okay to blink, you know." He grins.

I glance around, but I don't know why—*of course,* people heard him.

"It's also okay to not care about what people think, Kay."

I inspect the gravel beneath my feet. I've never been able to ignore the people-pleaser tendencies in me, and he knows it. It stings more than I'd like to admit that he knows me like that, still.

Jase lowers his voice. "Are you okay?"

"Y...es," I stammer. I kick a few pebbles loose.

"Jason," Nana says. It's only one word, but in her thick Tennessean accent and tough grandma 'tude, it comes out like "Asshole."

He ignores Nana's tone and tips his hat toward her. "Mags, nice to see you."

She snarls. "Hardly."

"Oh good, there are three people here from your house, after all." Matilda approaches and counts Amy, Nana, and I in the air: one-two-three.

In Sloane, your place in the race doesn't matter until Matilda counts you in.

"You know ..." Amy backs up. "I'm not really a runner. I was going to sub in for Len, but since Jase is here ... maybe I can give out water instead."

"Sure," Jase says.

Matilda's ever-present smile freezes in place. "Absolutely not. I mean, bless your heart, but everyone's been accounted for, so we can't make additional swaps. Jason is already running on his own." She wiggles her brow. "Unless you are now a group of four?"

"No." My voice is firm.

"All right." Matilda claps her prim and proper hands. "It's settled." She takes out three bibs and a handful of safety pins out of her pocket and hands them to me. "I trust you can divvy these out, Katherine."

"It's Kate," I call after her.

She's already walking away and waves her hand in dismissal.

Amy taps me on the shoulder. "You know I hate to agree with Matilda, but I can see her point; you two do look *matchy*." She wiggles her fingers toward Jase and me.

I rebut it. "So do you and I."

Amy's eyebrow arches. I glance over at Jase's outfit, which is entirely black, from his lace-less sneakers to his spandex to his zip-up runner's jacket.

It *is* like my outfit, sub the grey race T-shirt instead of the jacket. "Ugh," I sigh.

Amy purses her lips together. "Sorry."

Jase perks up. "For what?"

"Nothing. Don't you have somewhere to be?" My question comes out a little snarkier than I mean it.

His lips break out into a sly smile. "If I didn't know any better, Kay, I'd say you want me to be here."

"I don't," I spit out.

Jase moves his hand to his mouth, trying to laugh discreetly.

"It's not funny." I give his shoulder a small hit from the back of my hand.

"Oh yes, it is."

"Don't you have somewhere to be?" I repeat.

He shrugs. "Nope, seems like no one in my family wants to run with me. I guess I'll be running with you and yours."

"Well, I don't think my family wants to run with you, either."

When I turn around, the line moves up around us, and Amy and Nana are at the front of the line doing jumping jacks.

Jase's breath is hot on my neck. "Looks like it's just us."

I put my hands on his chest. "And everyone else in this town."

"I repeat, who cares?" He shifts his face down closer to mine.

The buzzer goes off, and I sprint to the start and down the trail.

"Kay."

I don't turn around. I keep running, focusing on my breathing. I see Nana's bright orange suit as I pass and hear Amy yell, "Go, Kate!" I see Mama clap as I pass the first water station without stopping, and I see the skyline in the distance, lighting up as Nashville starts to welcome tourists for the weekend. Tourists like Nick.

Nick.

Oh my God, Nick is coming in today and will meet me at the finish line. I squint to read the time on my watch and feel my shoulders tense. It'll be fine. Having the perfect man I'm talking to come see my mess of a life in the place it got set on fire will be fine. Just fine.

"Hey, slowpoke!" Jase passes me.

I exhale and pick up the pace. "You, son of a ..."

"Language!" A woman on the sidelines covers her young daughter's ears, and I wince and offer an apology as I jog by, but all I get is disappointing glares from other townspeople as they shake their heads.

Jase turns around and jogs backward. "If it helps anything, I don't think what you said was bad ... this town needs to grow up!" He shouts the last part over toward the crowd.

"I don't understand why there's a cheering section after all these years. Isn't there something better these people could be doing with their lives?"

Jase laughs. "Unfortunately, because the tradition has been to run, help, or spectate—this *is* the day. Everyone will be here for a few hours, and they'll all go to—"

"The diner," I say, right as Jase says, "Firefly Lounge."

"Oh?" My curiosity is piqued. "What happened to the diner anyhow?"

"You're looking at it." He fans himself with fake arrogance.

"Yeah." I roll my eyes. "I'm sure you serving at a bar for a few years really tops Fran working at the diner every day and night for the last sixty years."

"Fran passed away a few years ago," he mumbles.

"She what? Sweet Fran, with the dimples and fifties outfit and skates she wore religiously every day of her life?"

"That's the one."

"I really liked her. I wonder why Mama didn't tell me."

Jase shrugs. "She probably didn't want to bother you. She knows how busy you are in New York and how much coming home would be more stressful than not."

"How do you know?" I stop in the middle of the trail and put my hand on my hip.

The next closest group of runners is still far behind us.

Jase stops and regulates his breathing. "Everyone knows you love your big, busy job in New York and hate being back. You hate seeing me and are avoiding your dad."

I turn away. "That's not true." It's not wrong, either. I have been falling into old habits since I've been back—my attitude's been strong, my willingness to see family has been low, and my attraction to Jase has been unavoidable.

"Excuse us." A few runners approach, and Jase steps closer to me to let them pass.

There's a snap of a camera. I turn toward the onlookers, but after eyeing up the folks on the sidewalk, it could have come from anywhere. They're all happy to send dirt to Matilda to make the column and get a finder's fee if she decides to publish it.

I move my hand to my forehead. "This is too much."

"Come on, let's go. If we're moving, it's harder for them to capture something solid." Jase sprints again.

I take off after him, but I hear another snap shortly after.

He curses under his breath. "Guess I was wrong."

"Hey, it's all for the kids, right?" I quicken my pace, trying to separate myself from Jase.

He takes it as a challenge, like when we were kids, and before I know it, he's by my side again.

"We don't have to go, you know."

"Go where?" I look over my left shoulder at him.

"To Firefly. We could go somewhere else."

"Jase ..."

"I had fun the other night, Kay. It was like old times."

"That's the problem." I try blinking away tears from my eyes.

"I know I fucked up, but I really want to talk about what happened ..."

He slows, but I don't give him the satisfaction of messing up my pace for the second time today.

"Unless you can take back what happened with Lindsay, we don't have anything to talk about."

"Kay," he objects.

"Besides, I've moved on ... and my boyfriend's going to be touching down in Nash any minute." I don't stop, let him catch up, or explain. *Boyfriend* is a bit of a stretch, and the word feels foreign on my lips—but I can't process that now. Not when Jase could catch up and call me on it. Not when the whole town could see. Instead, I keep running and feel a burst of energy moving my feet forward, propelling me step by step. Sure enough, Nick's at the end arch, beaming and shouting my name. I run right for the finish line, the next chapter of my life, and straight into his strong arms. Without thinking, I jump up and wrap my legs around him.

He stumbles back, not expecting it, but recovers and smiles. "Hey there. Got your text about the run. Glad I didn't miss you."

"Kiss me," I say back.

He does, but when Nick's lips touch mine and pull me in, I'm not thinking about him, half of Sloane, or Nana howling from a distance. I'm thinking about the one person I don't want to think about, remembering my legs wrapped around him by that old magnolia tree. I'm wishing it was his arms holding me tight, like he said they always would, when he promised forever.

As I try to kiss the pain away, Nick holds me firmly and kisses me gently. It's like he knows I'm broken and holds me anyway.

Chapter 14
Then: Eight Years Ago

The chimes ring out from the steeple, and the eggshell white church doors peel open at the end of service. Neighbors take turns stepping out of pews, talking to the pastor, and walking past the windows of stained glass. Mamas and daddies step foot into the spring air with children hand-in-hand.

Mama and I usually sneak out the backdoor and wait for the Coles to join us for our walk home together. Today is no exception.

Carrie Cole departs first and winks at Mama. "No questions today."

Mama closes her eyes. "Thank you. It's embarrassing enough Andy doesn't come to Sunday service anymore, but to have to explain it ..." She shakes her head.

Carrie puts her hand on top of Mama's and squeezes.

Eric Cole strides onto the blacktop, grinning ear to ear. Jack and Jase are behind him, arguing about who gets their dad's car today.

Carrie rolls her eyes. "Boys, can we not fight on church grounds? And what's gotten into you?" she asks her husband, hand on her hip.

Eric chuckles and reaches for her hand, lifting it to his lips for a kiss. "It's a beautiful day, we had a great mass, and we're healthy—it's all I could ask for."

She sighs. "You're right."

"I could always hear it more," he teases.

She doesn't argue, just raises her gaze to Mama in a way only another wife could understand. *Men.*

Jase bumps his hip into mine and interlaces our fingers on the walk home. "Hey.'"

"Hey." I study him.

"What?"

My eyes narrow. "You're up to something."

Jase winks. "Maybe."

Mama and Carrie laugh up ahead while Jack and his dad discuss who's going to put new breaks on the family car.

I bump into him. "Well?"

He moves behind me and loops his arms around my chest. Lowering his voice down to a hushed tone, he says, "I don't know, it seems like everyone would be a little distracted if you get my drift." His lips lightly graze my neck and cause a shiver down my spine.

"I wanted to write today, but ..." I spin around and almost lose my breath when I see the heat in his eyes—and it's all for me.

"But what?" His brow arches.

A shiver runs down my spine, and it takes all my self-control not to jump into his arms right there.

"Are you kids coming?" Mama calls.

"Not *yet*," Jase mumbles, only loud enough for me to hear.

"Jason Cole!" I exclaim, but when everyone turns around to see what caused my outburst, Jase holds his arms up innocently. My cheeks burn. *Guilty.*

"All right, come on inside and wash up before lunch," Carrie says to her kids.

Jase turns around and smiles, causing a blush to rise to my cheeks.

Nana opens our side kitchen door and whistles for help getting the food outside.

Jack hustles over and picks up the breakfast casserole and fruit. Pop follows him outside with a thermos of coffee and an armful of cups and creamers. Mama and Nana set the table, and Carrie brings out banana bread.

Minutes later, everyone but Dad sits, and our picnic is underway.

Laughter fills the air. Jase runs his hand up my leg as he leans forward and picks up his glass of tea with his other hand. His musky and sweet cologne fills my lungs. Biting down on my lip, I come-to, but when he squeezes my thigh, I almost scream.

"Want to get out of here?"

I push my chair back.

Jase stands. "Can Kay and I be excused? We should practice for our group presentation tomorrow."

"What group pres—" Jack asks but stops when I shoot daggers in his direction. "Oh, right, the history thing you guys were talking about."

"Yes!" Jase and I say in unison.

"Can you help us clean up first, Kate?" Mama's voice drips in disappointment.

"I'll help you, Mrs. Dailey," Jack offers.

"Sure, thank you, Jack," she replies, satisfied.

I mouth. "Thanks, Jacky."

As Jase and I step foot in his house, his hands dive into my hair and he pulls me toward him.

"Jase, they could see—window. Upstairs," I say incoherently.

Taking my hand, he leads me up the stairs, into his back bedroom, and shuts the door with his leg.

When his lips crash over mine, a moan escapes my lips.

He curses under his breath. *Fuck.*

Jase moves in closer, minimizing the space between us. He dips his head, and his lips are at my ear. He nips it slowly, methodically, and I melt as my head tilts back. Stifling another moan, I whisper a curse.

He chuckles.

I run my fingers down his back, scratching enough to make him squirm.

"*Fuck, Kay.*"

I kiss the nape of his neck, the place that's meant just for me. I know what to do with it.

He groans and pushes my hands up, over my head, taking control once again. Moving us toward the bed, he sits me down and takes off his shirt before joining me.

There's a crash downstairs, and it jolts us apart. When everything quiets, Jase reaches for me again.

"Your mama could be downstairs," I object.

"Yeah ..." His voice is deeper than it was moments before. "She'll probably do the dishes and watch something on HGTV."

"Your dad and Jack?"

"Will be working on the car ... and we can be quiet, can't we?" His eyes dip to my chest, and my heart skips a beat.

"I mean, I can, but I don't think you can be," I tease and flip the lock on his bedroom door.

His mouth drops. "Me?"

"You." I double down.

"We'll see about that."

Turns out, we were both right. His Mama did watch HGTV—*loudly*—and neither of us was able to be quiet. Thank God for *Property Brothers*.

Lying naked in bed, snuggling Jase, I feel myself fading off to dreamland, but I can't let go completely. "I have to get home soon."

"You are home." Jase hangs on tight.

The pang in my heart grows stronger than I think is possible. I kiss his chest and snuggle into him.

"I love you." He pets my hair, and I close my eyes, savoring every second.

"I love *you*, Jason Cole."

"Goodnight, Kay."

"Good—It's still morning."

"Sweet dreams, angel."

I yawn. "I'll see you in dreamland."

And I do. In dreamland, all I see is him.

It feels like hours pass before I blink my eyes open and find Jase sitting at his wooden desk only wearing a pair of basketball shorts, sketching.

"Oh hey, Sleepyhead."

"Hey." I pull the covers up to my shoulders. "What're you working on over there?"

He flips it face down onto his desk. "Nothing."

I scootch out of bed and pull his sheet along to wrap around me. "Oh, nothing, huh?"

"Nope, nothing to see here."

I reach for his sketchbook, but Jase puts his hand over mine, stopping me.

My eyes narrow. "What is this secret you're keeping?"

He sighs. "It's not a secret. It's a surprise. You won't leave it, will you?"

"Not a chance." My hand calls it over.

Jase pats his lap for me to sit, and I do. He turns the pad, and I stare, mouth falling open.

"You drew this?"

"I am trying for art school, you know?" His voice cracks.

"No, no, Jase, I know you can draw. I meant you drew this for us?"

He bows his head.

I study the 3D house in front of me. It has big, open French doors and a prominent view of the sunset. The open-concept first floor has wide windows in the living room and kitchen, with beautifully shaded cabinets atop a detailed marble countertop. There's a kitchen bar off to the side, with two stools and a dog bowl right next to them.

"Jase, this is …"

He gulps. "You hate it."

I turn toward him, putting the picture in my lap. I place a hand on either side of his face. "I love it." I place a kiss on his forehead. "What does the upstairs look like?"

He turns the page and gently moves his fingers around, almost bringing the house to life. "The main bedroom is here, big enough for four to five dogs and space for the en suite bathroom."

"Four to five dogs, huh? You slipped that in casually."

"Oh yeah, I figured at least four, but six could be a lot. We'll have to draw the line somewhere." I chuckle, and he keeps going. "Kids' rooms here and here."

I raise my eyebrows. "Kids?"

He looks at me pointedly. "Can you let me finish?"

I wave him on.

"Guest room there, creative room down the hall—half art studio, half writing cave."

I lift his chin and stare into his blue-green eyes, mist coming out of my own. "It's perfect."

There's a tap on the door, followed by a loud bellow. "Yoo, bro, how's your history project coming?"

"*Shit.*" I climb off Jase and reach for my shorts and T-shirt by his nightstand.

"Yeah, one sec," Jase replies.

I toss him his shirt, which he throws over his head with ease before smoothing out his shortcut and opening the door a crack to peek an eye out. "What?"

"Mama is looking for you, and you're welcome for saving your asses," Jack argues.

"Whatever." Jase closes the door. He hustles around his room, making sure it's normal messy and not we-had-sex-under-our-parents'-noses messy, all the same.

"I should go..." I straighten to kiss his lips. "But I don't want to leave."

Jase reaches for my hand. "Stay."

I bow my head. "It'll be worse if I don't go home."

He shifts my chin up for his pleading eyes to look into mine. "I know, but the time we spend apart now is a drop in the bucket compared to our next chapter."

Closing my eyes, I breathe him in, slow and deep enough to get me through the next few hours. "I hate goodbyes."

"Our spot tonight?"

"Our spot tonight."

Carrie knocks on the bedroom door and twists the knob open. "Kate, are you staying for dinner?"

"Thank you, but I should head home."

She smiles and pulls me in for a hug goodbye, and I wish I could take her kindness with me to save me from the storm surely happening next door.

It doesn't work. The dark cloud is everywhere.

Mama's putting a casserole in the oven, and Dad's already on his big plans of screaming at her for who knows what.

I pop in my earbuds and turn Taylor on high, trying to block out the noise. Nana's reading in the living room, trying to block out the screams.

Pop's touching Dad on the shoulder and whispering, trying to get him to calm down, but he either doesn't hear him or doesn't care because he keeps ranting.

I thought after Nana and Pop moved in, it would calm down, and some days, it seems like it has, but on Sundays, when the bar closes early, he comes home and lets it out on Mama. I wish she would get up and leave, to learn her worth, and that she doesn't need him or this. Some days, I tell her. She never answers me, but she does pull me in close for a hug and holds on for dear life.

I look over again, and this time Pop's helping Dad sit down, which seems to lower his voice a bit.

Mama exhales as she sets the timer for dinner.

Removing my left earbud, I hear her humming, and I know music is how she's surviving this moment. Me too, Mama. Me too.

"Go on." Nana waves toward the stairs. "You better get in the shower before he escalates again."

I slip up the stairs, taking the quickest shower of my life. I'm nearly dressed before Mama knocks on my door and enters without waiting for an answer.

"Hey." She takes a seat on the edge of the bed.

"Hey ..." I pick up a pair of boots from my closet.

"Can we talk for a second?" Mama asks, then adds, "About earlier."

"Sure." I join her on the bed.

"I, uh, know you don't have a history report due tomorrow." She looks down at her hands.

I look away. This is as awkward for her as it is for me.

"Mama, I—"

"No," she interrupts. "I know why you go to the Coles." Mama's breath catches in her throat, and I turn to see her eyes blinking back tears. "I wanted to say I'm sorry. I'm sorry you don't feel safe here."

I want to disagree with her, but she's right. Even though it's not why I went today, it's why I didn't want to come home. I don't feel safe here. This house, this room, feels more like a prison than a home.

Mama sniffles.

I put my hand on hers. I'm sorry, too.

"I want you to feel safe, sweetie."

I want that, too, but more than that, I want Mama to be free. Dad hasn't hit her. He wouldn't because then he'd have to admit he's an abuser, and he thinks he's above all of it—like an abuser can only be someone who hits someone else. He refuses to acknowledge verbal, mental, and emotional abuse *is abuse*. The anger boils inside of me, and I can't help lashing out at Mama for helping prolong the pain.

"Why haven't you left him? Why don't you leave? Why don't *we* leave?"

"Your daddy's a good man, Kate."

I recoil as if her words physically burn through my skin. "That's something a victim would say."

This time, there's no holding back Mama's tears. "He's a good man with a drinking problem. He needs me. He needs *us* to get help getting sober, getting better."

"How would you know your leaving wouldn't be the push he needs?" I fire back.

She sighs through the tears. "I just know, okay? I'm going to help him get through this, like …" She shakes her head. "You know what? Never mind. It doesn't matter."

"What were you gonna say, Mama?"

"Nothing. I didn't come up here to fight with you. I want you to know I'm sorry, and I love you."

If you loved me, you would leave. I don't say it out loud this time, but from the way she squeezes her eyes shut, I know she hears it, anyway.

When she exits, I can't stop my jaw from tightening and fists from clenching. Why didn't I say something sooner? Maybe if I had said something more direct years ago, she would've left by now. Maybe not. I can't wait until something worse happens.

Tossing on my shoes, I throw my hair into a long ponytail and pull up the notes app on my phone. I scribble a quick list, letting my words come out as fragmented thoughts. I hear a familiar *clink* as I finish writing it out.

Plucking open my window, I lob my legs out and almost miss my footing.

"Woah, what's gotten into you?" Jase asks as I pull him from his spot by the Magnolia tree and move into the woods behind our houses.

"Don't ask." I brush him off.

"Kay, seriously, what's going on?"

I continue to drag him along behind me. "Want to run? I want to run."

"Kay." He yanks his arm back and dead stops in between a couple of trees that must have had their branches snapped during last night's storm.

"I can't do this anymore." I outstretch my arms.

"Do what?" He raises his eyebrows.

"This. Sloane. My parents. It's too much." My voice is squeaky and higher than I intend it to be. Feeling the weight of the world on my shoulders, I collapse onto the ground, still wet and muddy from the storm. "Ugh." I rest my head in my hands.

Jase walks over and sits down on the mud right beside me. "Do you want to talk about it?"

I look up, and my blue gaze locks with his bright green one. I do want to talk about it because he's the one person in the world who could understand. He's been here through all of it.

"I—sometimes it's too much. Dad's bad days are outnumbering the good ones. Mama puts up with it. Nana and Pop try to intervene, but it only stalls him—it doesn't stop him."

Jase nods, listening.

"Last night was scary, and I couldn't take what he was doing and Mama not saying anything. She raised me to be strong, and yet when it comes to him, she doesn't leave. I don't get it. This afternoon, she apologized for me not feeling safe, but even knowing all of it, she couldn't entertain the thought, not even for me."

I sniffle through the brain dump, and Jase lets me ramble, his hand holding mine, giving me the strength to let it out.

"She says it's his addiction, and I think it is, but do you know when he started drinking like this? Why he started drinking like this?"

Jase shakes his head.

"When I was born." My gaze drops to a shadow on my boot. I mentally trace the mud on the side of it as I vent. "Which is great to know, by the way. Highly recommend telling your teenage daughter her very existence caused you to go into a tailspin with fucking cheap ass beer. It's trash. This whole thing is trash."

Jase places a kiss on the top of my head.

I wipe my eyes with my shirt sleeve. "I'm sorry. I ..."

"Hey," he whispers. "Come here.." Jase places a finger under my chin and lifts it up. He adjusts his position to put a leg on either side of me and pulls me back into his chest. He wraps his arms around me, right under my chest. "You have nothing to apologize for. Okay?"

"I don't know."

"Do you want to keep talking?"

"Not about them." I shift my head from side to side, stretching out my neck.

He starts massaging my shoulders to help me relax. "Okay. You said you have a plan. Do you want to tell me about it?"

"Yes, but ... promise to hear me out." I extend my pinkie.

Jase loops his with mine. "Promise."

I open the notes app and clear my throat. "I want to move to New York."

Jase shifts his legs. "You want to what?"

"You promised to hear me out." I look over my shoulder at him, moving my own legs in closer, pushing my knees up with my feet pushing firmly into the wet ground.

"All right. What else is a part of this plan?"

I shrug. "I haven't thought it all through yet, but I know I can't be here much longer. New York has all these amazing opportunities for colleges and writing, it's the art capital of the world, and there's a lot of great running trails from what I've seen, and I ... could see us starting this great life there."

"Us?" Jase stirs.

"Yes, us." I rest my arms on his.

He shakes his head. "I, um, I don't know what I'd even do in New York City."

"Art."

He blinks at me. "You say it like it's easy. Moving states away without any money or a support system, to try and make it in two creative fields ... Kay, I ..."

I interject before he can fully turn me down. "Listen, I know it would be a shock, but you know I can't be here. I also don't want to be anywhere without you. It doesn't have to be New York. It could be somewhere else. We could do some*thing* else. Whatever you want, as long as it's you and me."

He's quiet for a long while, and I study him. Please say something.

"Oh, what the hell. Okay."

"Okay?" I sit up. "Really? Do you want to think about it?"

"I want to be with you. I want you to be happy, and if New York is going to make you happy, then I want to go, too."

"Ooohh!" I squeal and give him a fierce kiss on the lips. "I can't wait. It's going to be amazing. You can do anything in New York."

"We can do anything in New York. I can do anything with you." He smiles.

I grin back and place my hands on either side of his face. "Are we really doing this?"

"We're really doing this." He opens his arms, and I climb right back in.

Sitting there in his arms, I feel the lightest I've felt in months.

We're getting out.

Together.

Chapter 15

Now

CHAPTER FIFTEEN

"What do you think?" I twirl in high-waisted frayed jeans with a black long-sleeved crop top and boots.

"I think you need to change." Amy's never been one for sugarcoating. I look down. "Really? It's not bad."

"It's not bad for a girl's night or pizza at Nick's ... a few months down the road, but you need a first date 'do me' dress."

"I do not need a first date 'do me' dress. I think this is fine. Besides, it's our second date, and we've been talking every night for the last couple of weeks."

Amy crosses her arms. "Okay, you're further proving my point. You're on a second date by country standards, but by NYC standards, you're on *at least* your third or fourth date. You need a 'do me' dress."

"Ame, I didn't even pack anything nicer than this ... I chaotically threw clothes in a duffle bag."

THIS KIND OF LOVE

I can see the gears in her brain rotating. "Aha!" She snaps her fingers and runs out of the room. When she comes back, she's hiding her hands behind her.

I throw a warning glare and unplug my straightener.

"Okay, hear me out. If you don't like it, I promise I'll get on board with this." She waves her petite finger over my outfit.

I take a deep breath. "Fine. What do you have?"

Amy brings the mini dress she's holding around, and my mouth drops.

"You hate it."

"I love it." I lift my jaw back up as I walk to the dress. I feel the black, sparkly fabric beneath my hands. It's soft and smooth at the same time. The neckline plunges down to mid-chest. It's sexy and modest at the same time ... and exactly something I would wear at home, out at Encore.

Amy's face lights up. "Ooh, goody! I have heels to match!"

"I'll definitely ask to borrow this beautiful dress, but I draw the line at heels." Amy's gaze is off in the distance, and I point a finger in her direction. "I mean it, Ame."

She sighs. "Okay, fine."

"Why'd you even pack something like this?" My fingers keep tracing the material, as I'm giddy about getting to wear something comfy and pretty for the first time in a while.

"You never know what the day is going to bring."

I roll my eyes. Of course.

The doorbell rings, and I jump. "Right on time."

Nana whistles downstairs. "I knew I liked him."

"Here we go." I take a deep breath and stroll down the stairs. "Why do I feel like I'm heading to prom?"

"Is it the corsage?" Amy bops my nose.

"Or lack thereof? I don't think my prom date got me a corsage either." Unless you count a pile of dandelions he pinned together before they fell apart.

Nana cuts us off to open the door. "Hi, Nick. Nice of you to come pick Katie girl up."

"It's my pleasure." His face lights up when he spots me. "You look amazing."

I smile. "Thank you." Taking in the full-fledged gray, pinstriped suit, brilliant blue tie, and navy dress shoes, I have to stop myself from drooling. He catches me staring and grins—his perfect white teeth. His short brown hair compliments his chestnut-brown eyes, which are full of fire. "You look great, yourself."

"What's the plan?" Nana grabs her purse.

Does she think she's coming?

Nick straightens his jacket. "I was thinking dinner, drinks, and dancing if you're up for it?"

"That's perfect." The butterflies in my stomach can't wait to get out of here.

He shifts his attention to Nana. "Should I have her back at a particular time?"

Nana rubs her hands together. "The later, the better, if you know what I mean." She winks.

My palm finds my face for what is certainly not the first time today. Good Lord, Nana.

"All right, well, you two should get going." Amy pushes us out the door. "Have a great time!"

"Ooh, a minivan," I giggle.

THIS KIND OF LOVE

Nick opens the van door for me to get in and then climbs in himself while laughing loudly. "Sexy, I know, but this is all the rental company had on short notice. Please don't dump me for it." He holds his hands up in surrender.

"I mean, that's going to be tough. I only date guys with Bentleys or greater," I tease.

He laughs. "What's greater than a Bentley?"

I shake my head. "Evidently a minivan."

"How do you feel about Hondas? I still have one parked at my parents' place because I don't have a use for it, but I can't bear to get rid of it."

"A Honda's good, and I've been there for sure."

He flips the turn signal. "You have an old Honda you're unable to part with?"

"Not a Honda, but I had an ancient Sundance I rode to the ground. Even when she died, I wouldn't let anyone get rid of her. I'm pretty sure Lily's long since been recycled at this point, and it's not the car ... *or*, not *all* the car. It's the nostalgia." And all that comes with it.

His eyes light up. "Yes! You get it."

Nick makes a turn down the street, and we head further into Sloane instead of toward Nashville.

"Where are we headed?" I stare out the window and wait for him to say he made a wrong turn, but he doesn't.

"This little tavern in town has rave reviews. I know you've mentioned how great the chicken is here, but I thought ..."

"Hot chicken," I say absentmindedly.

I tune out right after he agrees. "Oh yes, that's it!"

We pull into the parking lot at the Firefly Lounge, and my stomach churns. Is he still here? Will he see us? Will we blend in amongst the sea of Sloaners?

"Wow, I guess the food here *is* good." Nick cranes his neck to gauge the crowd waiting to get in. Some are smoking and talking, others are outside to be with their friends, cackling when a joke is thrown out there. "This is busier than I expected."

I hesitate to unbuckle my seat belt as he parks the car. "Sloane's a small town, and it's a Saturday night. There are limited options to eat here."

He pauses and puts his hand on the center console. "Would you rather get *out*-out for a night?" Ever the gentleman.

Yes, but I don't say it out loud. "Oh no, this is great. Their burgers are amazing." I paste a smile on my face and cross my fingers that Jase has already left for the night.

"Oh, perfect." Nick climbs out of the minivan and comes around to open the door on my side. Like I said, a gentleman.

I should warn him, but what do I say: hey, the minute we walk in there, there will be a thousand pictures of us? They'll be splattered all over our small-town gossip column tomorrow, along with pictures of me and my ex running a race together. You know the race, the one where I ran into your arms for no reason and asked you to kiss me? It might not have been the most genuine moment. Or, hey, my ex works here, and not any ex, but 'the one who got away' ex. Maybe not that, but I have to say something.

I step out of the van and take the hand he offers me. As we pace to the door, my thumb starts drawing circles on the back of his hand. "Hey, Nick."

"Yeah?" He bends his head down, and his ear is close to me.

At least he understands discretion.

"I haven't been back in Sloane in six years. There's a lot of drama getting dug up since I've been home. There will be a lot of ears tonight." *Tell him about Jase.* I open my mouth to continue talking but chicken out and pick at the skin under my nail instead.

Straightening, he winks and rubs my hand with his thumb. "Let's give 'em a show."

I want to agree with him and fight fire is with fire, but I can't be as free, or as me, as I want to be with Nick ... not with Jase so close.

Nick chuckles and smooths my hair behind my ear. "Hey, it's totally fine. You can lead, and I'll roll with it."

The moment feels too intimate, like it doesn't belong to him and me. Like he doesn't belong with me. Perhaps, more importantly, I don't belong with him, either. Brushing the intrusive thoughts aside, I reach out to open the door, but Nick beats me to it. He drops my hand and holds the door open for me. I smile, surprised by the gesture.

"Are you sure you're not Southern?"

His smile meets his eyes. "No, ma'am."

"You're right. If you were Southern, you would've had a great tip of the hat."

"Like this?" He gestures with a pretend hat on his head.

"Yep, like that."

A familiar voice bellows, "Two this evening?"

Peering up at Jase, his green eyes are darker than normal, his anger—no, *jealousy?*— apparent. Well, it serves him right.

"Yes, two please." I can't help being a little smug at his reaction.

"Booth or table?" Jase clicks his tongue while he checks out the seating chart.

"Do you have a preference?" My tone is sweet as sugar for my date, and by the twitch in Jase's eye, he notices.

"A booth would be great if you have it, man," he says to Jase.

"Coming right up, *man*," Jase replies, making fun of Nick. He picks up two menus and walks us to the corner booth I sat in when Jade and I stopped in a few days back.

We no sooner slide into the booth when Nick leans in. "Who's the friendly guy?"

I shake my head. Don't get me started. "You don't want to know."

"Ah, the ex." Nick makes an *okay* symbol with his fingers.

Jase comes back a few minutes later with a pad and pen in hand. "Welcome to Firefly Lounge. I'm Jase, and I'll be your server tonight. Can I start y'all off with something to drink?"

"I'll do a glass of Moscato." I keep my eyes glued to the menu. Two can play that game.

"Do you have a Lager on tap?" Nick strains to see the bar.

"We do, brewed right here," Jase answers.

"I'll do a pint of that, please." Nick opens his menu a bit more. "What's good here?"

Jase doesn't put his hand on his hip, but he's damn well close to it. "Everything."

"Ah." Nick sighs.

"I'll give y'all a minute." Jase backs away.

"So, how recent an ex is he?" Nick asks when Jase is out of earshot.

I pretend like I need to do math in the air. "Oh, about ... six years."

"Must have ended badly for him to still be like *that*."

I shrug. "The burgers are worth it, though."

Nick moves his attention to 'Burgers and 'Wiches' section.

THIS KIND OF LOVE

An old high school acquaintance, Molly, taps a microphone at the edge of the bar. She taps one more time, and the speakers screech. She winces and apologizes. "Sorry, y'all. Still getting' used to this new sound system. Trivia will be starting in about ten minutes. Grab your sheets now if you're playing."

"Trivia?" Nick moves his hand to his chin, considering.

I laugh. "Oh, Nick Scott, you have no idea what you're asking for?"

"Oh? It must be good if you're using my full name?"

"Kay's a mastermind," Jase announces. He nearly drops our drinks on the table.

"Oh, yeah, *Kay?*" Nick rubs his hand on mine.

I don't move. He's trying to antagonize Jase the same way Jase is trying to antagonize the two of us ... but Jase's nickname doesn't sound right on Nick's lips.

Jase gruffly interrupts my thoughts. "So, what'll it be?"

"Ladies first," Nick insists, scouring the menu.

"I'll have the—"

"Cowboy Burger?" Jase guesses for me.

"Yes." I look up at him for the first time since the host stand, and his eyes, while dark, look a little red around them. Has he been crying? I shake it off. Jason Cole has only cried twice in his entire life: first was his dad's funeral, and second ...

"I'll have the same." Nick brings me back to the present.

"Great, they'll be a few minutes," Jase barks. He pulls the slip off his notepad to hang it in the kitchen window.

"All right, all right." Molly beams from the bar. "Last call for trivia. We'll be getting started in a few minutes."

"You sure you're up for this?" I check with Nick, who is already halfway out of the booth.

"Oh yes, Dailey. I have to see if you're truly the Quizmaster you say you are."

I grin. "I am."

He chuckles. "All right, you hold the fort down, and I'll go get us a paper."

I can't help the comfort I feel when I'm talking to Nick. It's *easy* with him—fun, even. He almost makes me forget everything happening at work, home, and with Jase. Yet, when my gaze wanders, it's Jase's eyes that find mine from across the bar. He blinks them away, and the disappointment at the gesture slaps me in the face.

"Okay, we need a team name," Nick warns. He slides the pen and paper across the booth.

"How about: 'The Question Heirs?'" I beam.

Nick scratches his chin. "The Question Heirs," he echoes, emphasizing each word.

"What do you think?"

He ponders. "I think ... OH! The Question Heirs, like questionnaires?" A smirk tugs at his lips. "Guess you are pretty good at this. What's your secret?"

I shrug. "I watch a lot of TV."

"We'll see if it helps us this round. For all we know, it could be a legal round or dumb laws round; then, I'm our guy."

"Okay ... we're gonna get started," Molly calls. "Don't forget to put a team name at the top of your papers—the funnier, the better. First round: Sitcoms."

Nick snickers. "You had to know what she was going to say?"

I raise my hands in surrender. "Honest to God, I did not, but most trivia nights do have a TV round."

"I have got to get out more."

Molly clears her throat. "Question 1: In *Friends*, when Phoebe drags Monica out to Karaoke night, what song does Monica sing?"

I write down *Delta Dawn* without consulting Nick.

He peeks at the paper. "I don't even know what that song is."

"Shh," I whisper. "You can't say something like that here."

"At a bar?"

"No, this close to Music City," I reply, like it's obvious, which, to a Tennessean, it is.

Nick winks. "Got it."

I put my hand on his. "Quick learner, huh?"

Jase plops the burgers down on the table and walks away without a word. Could he be any more of an asshole? I'm lost in Jase-hate thoughts as Molly reads question two. "Which actress played former Senator Selina Meyer, who became the first female Vice President of the United States."

"It's Julia Louis-Dreyfus." I slide the paper and pen over to Nick. "Excuse me a minute; I have to head to the restroom."

"Sure. How's this?" He tips his fake hat.

"You nailed it." I chuckle.

Nick smiles, evidently proud of himself.

I step out of the booth, watching my step and for any busybodies. The bar seems focused on Molly and not me, and anyone not paying attention to Molly is glued to the hockey game on TV over the whiskey display.

I turn the corner, and Jase comes out of the kitchen, double revolving doors slamming behind him.

"You." Heat is coming out of my pores.

Jase crosses his arms. "Don't you have a date to get back to?"

"Yes, I do, and it seems like you're doing everything in your power to ruin it for me."

"Not *everything*." He sighs.

"Jase!" He's exhausting.

"Kay!" Jase calls back, eyes wide.

"Why are you doing this? We're not together. We haven't been together in a long time. I didn't mess it up; you did!"

He expands his arms out like an eagle. "Yeah, you're right. I did, but you don't know the full story. Every time I talk to you, you go between biting my head off and looking like you're going to kiss me."

Busted. "I am *not* going to kiss you," I all but shout.

Jase clicks his tongue on his cheek and inches closer. "So, why are you here, Kay? Of all the fancy places in Nash—why here? Why tonight, when I told you how busy we get after the race, when you knew I'd be here?"

I hang my head. "It wasn't my choice."

"Look at me, Kay."

I do and find Jase close enough I can smell his intoxicating cologne. I breathe it in deep. It's the same one he bought when he started playing football. He wore it at Homecoming and on the night we fell in love. He wore it the night we broke up ... and all of it is too much to take.

"This was a mistake, I'm sorry." I turn on my boot heels, but Jase reaches for my hand and spins me back around and into his arms.

His cool breath whispers in my ear. "What was a mistake?"

"This, all of it." I blink in rapid succession, trying to avoid everything that is Jase—his beautiful eyes inspecting me, strong arms holding me, nostalgic cologne clouding my judgment, heart full of ... *I don't know anymore.*

"Close your eyes," he orders.

"Jase," I beg.

"Kay," he echoes. "I've been waiting a really long time for this."

"For what?" I whisper.

"This." His lips close over me, reminding me of the incredible *need* I feel when I'm truly *kissed* by a man. I'm not talking a peck or soft kiss goodbye. I'm talking about holding on for dear life, feeling every heartbeat, palms getting sweaty and staying sweaty kind of kiss. I feel *it* and then some with Jase. Still. Even after all these years. The man has ruined me for all other men. *Damn it, Jase.*

There's a tap into a mic, and I hear Molly in the distance announce she's going to go through the answers to Round One.

Trivia.

Nick.

Fuckkkk.

I separate from his embrace as if a bucket of ice water was dumped on me.

"Wow." Jase breathes heavier than before.

I shake my head and get my wits about me. "Oh my God, what did we do?"

Jase wiggles his eyebrows. "Want to do it again?"

"No, I shouldn't have even done *that*. I'm on a date," I retreat. "I ... I have to go."

He calls after me, but he doesn't reach for me. If he would've, I'd have stayed.

"There you are!" Nick smiles as I approach the table. "So, great news, the answers you had were right, and I somehow got another couple right on my own. I think our team is in the middle of the pack right now." His voice drops when he notices my face flushed and hair a bit out of place. "Are you okay?"

I swallow and grab my purse to pull some cash out for the table. "Can we go?"

"Of course," he says. "Do you want a box for your burger?"

I shake my head. No. I don't need any reminders of tonight.

"Okay, let's go." Nick puts his hand on my lower back as we head out.

Everything in me tells me to keep walking, but I glance over my shoulder and find Jase watching me, *seeing me*.

I want to run to him, but I grit my teeth, betray my heart, and walk away.

Chapter 16
Then: Seven Years Ago

One step in front of the other, I take off into a slow sprint in the middle of the storm to get away from everything at home. I travel as far as my feet will take me: past Sloane High, through Rose's park, past the coffee shop, and all the way down Main Street. I run until my legs cramp.

I find myself in front of Jase's window. Picking up a small rock, I toss it up—horribly—and it hits the siding between Jase and Jack's rooms. I take another small pebble and try again, but this one hits the kitchen window. I duck behind the Magnolia tree.

Eric opens the kitchen door. "Come on in, Kate. The door's probably easier than the window with all this rain."

"Yes, sir." I shuffle over.

He takes one look at me soaking wet, and a smile forms on his face. "You look like you ran into the storm."

I don't deny it.

"Well, come on in." He calls Jase downstairs and tells him to bring a towel.

Jase appears, and everything else fades away. "Kay, is everything okay?"

I shake my head, and he comes over, wraps the towel around me, and pulls me in close.

"You're going to get wet," I tell him.

He pulls me impossibly tighter into his grasp. "I don't care."

I lose track of how long we stay like this, but it feels like forever. *I wish it was forever.*

A bolt of lightning flashes outside, and we jump apart.

Eric peaks out the kitchen window and winces. "It looks like it's getting bad out there. Why don't you kids go get warm?"

Jase puts his hand in mine and leads me to the sofa.

I shake my head. "I don't want to get the couch soaked."

Jase rolls his eyes. "My parents don't care."

Putting my hand on my hip, I tilt my drenched head toward my oblivious boyfriend.

"Kay, relax, we're not at your house. My mama would rather have you get the seat a little wet than have my football pads stink up the room. Trust me."

I close one eye. "Are you sure?"

"Yes!" He pulls me onto the sofa.

"Hey, Kate. Are you hungry?" Eric calls from the kitchen.

"No, thank you. Do you need anything? I can help with dinner."

He shakes his head from the kitchen. "Nah, this is my happy place. I've got it."

Jase puts his hand on my shoulder. "You don't have to be on edge, not here."

"I know." I brush my anxiety off a bit. "I can't help it."

He pulls me in to lean up against him. "What happened?"

I sniffle. "My dad found it."

THIS KIND OF LOVE

"Your notebook?"

"Mhm."

"The one with—"

I shiver. "He found all the poems and songs about his drinking and ... everything."

Jase rests his hand on mine. "What can I do?"

"Distract me, please."

Jase turns the remote on and flips through Netflix until he finds *Friends*, but I can't help glancing over my shoulder, half-expecting to see my dad behind me.

"It's okay." He pets my hair. "It's just us. You're safe."

I feel myself fading and give in to the deep pull of sleep in the place where I'm most comfortable in the world: Jase's arms.

He places a light kiss on the top of my head and lays down, continuing to hold me. "Goodnight, Kay."

"Goodnight, Jase," I mumble as I fade in and out of consciousness.

"I love you."

"Love you."

"Sweet dreams, angel."

His voice is the last thing I hear as I drift off to dreamland. I know he'll keep me safe in real life and in my dreams—which sometimes is the most dangerous place of all.

It's 4:02 p.m. when I clock out at Fran and Friends, toss my tips into the tiny pocket of my yoga pants, and throw my apron over my shoulder, "Bye, everyone. See y'all tomorrow."

Swinging open the creaky door to Jase's pickup truck he refuses to give a human name to, I hop into the passenger seat.

He leans in and gives me a kiss hello. "How was your shift?"

I collapse into the seat. "Exhausting. Breakfast was easy, but the church crowd was a lot today."

Jase grumbles. Just because Sundays are his day off doesn't mean he doesn't know how the diner can get when it gets hectic. "I'm glad I get to cook and not deal with actual people."

"You get to deal with me." I rest my head on my hand and blink.

"Aren't I lucky?" he jokes.

"Very." I tap his wrist.

He shifts the truck into gear. "You didn't text me when you got in last night. How were things at home? Did your dad calm down?"

I shudder. "No. I thought he would have fallen asleep early, but he stayed in the living room with all the lights off and scared the shit out of me when I walked inside. He tore all these pages out of the notebook, balled them up, and threw them at me one at a time until he ran out of ammo. And then, he picked up a bottle of whiskey. If Pop hadn't come down at that exact moment, I don't know what would have happened. Pop intervened so I could get upstairs—and then, out of nowhere, my dad was snoring."

Jase shifts his left hand on the wheel and places his other hand in mine. "How was this morning?"

I face his profile. "Like nothing ever happened."

He sighs. "I fucking hate that."

Smacking my lips, I focus on the clouds slowly shifting in the rearview. "It makes me feel like I imagined it, but I know I didn't. He just hates me so much."

"Kay..."

Wiping my eyes, I change the subject. "Anyway, I think we're doing well toward the New York fund." I dig into my work apron and grab a large wad of cash.

"Holy shit." His mouth falls open. "Maybe the church crowd is worth it."

"Yeah. A few more shifts like this, and we'll be able to rent a cardboard box in the city for a month or two."

"There's the positivity I love."

I lean back into the seat, slide my non-slip shoes off, and stick my feet on the dashboard. Jase rolls the windows down and turns the dial up as Taylor Swift comes on the radio with "Our Song."

I sing along with the radio while Jase pats the steering wheel in tune. When the song changes, he puts his right hand on the clutch and waves his fingers to me. Maybe I'm the lucky one.

"What's on your mind?" He turns the wheel.

"I'm grateful for you and excited to start our new life together. It's close."

"It is." He squeezes my hand.

Close, but it feels like forever when Dad's drinking seems to be getting worse, and he's picking fights with Mama more often than not.

Jase pulls into an abandoned lot and turns the car off.

I shift around, noticing the No Trespassing signs, but he waves them off and tells me not to worry. "What's the first thing you want to do when we get to New York?" He wiggles his eyebrows, trying to distract me from where he knows my thoughts are heading.

"I think get a big ol' slice of pizza."

"Like Joe's Pizza?"

"From what I've seen they're well done and cheesy enough it almost comes off in one bite."

"Like Joe's Pizza," he repeats and rubs his belly. "I could go for a slice of Joe's."

I laugh. "Later."

"Don't you think planning would be easier with some food?"

I roll my eyes. "Some of us ate lunch."

"Some of us waited for our sweet girlfriends. Maybe we could ..." his voice trails off, and he pulls me down in the seat with him, letting a cop car drive by, hopefully missing us.

"I thought you said this wasn't trespassing?" I shift up in the seat to cock my head toward the back window.

"It's not ... *exactly*."

I swerve toward him. "What do you mean not exactly?"

Jase shrugs. "Technically, we own the property; we just haven't done all the paperwork yet."

"Uh huh." I drum my fingers on the dash. "Who's *we?*"

He runs his fingers through his hair and looks out the window one more time before opening the driver's side door and stepping out.

"That's not an answer, Jason Cole."

Moving around the car, he opens the passenger side door for me. "It's my grandparents' property. It was willed to my parents—they haven't finished everything to make it *official*, but it's as good as done."

I take his outstretched hand and step out cautiously. "An abandoned lot?"

"Well, no," Jase answers. He moves to the cab of the truck, pulling out a backpack. "Come on."

"Jase, what if the cop comes back?" I keep my eye on the roadway.

"Let them. The house is in the Cole name."

"House?" I echo, walking after him.

"Should be right up here somewhere." He leads us past the lot into a wooded area and up a small rocky path.

"Somewhere? Haven't you been here before?" I glance up at him as he studies the sun compared to the trees ahead of us.

"Sure ... but not in fifteen years."

My hands fall to my sides. "You have no idea where we're going?"

"Oh hush, I have a plan. It's just not always as detailed as yours always are." Connecting his hand to his forehead, Jase squints up ahead. "Ah, there it is!"

I strain to see it, but all I can see is more woods.

Following Jase further up the trail, the house starts to come more into focus. For an abandoned building, it looks like it held up well enough from the outside anyway. It appears to be of gray stone, the colors tarnished to a dirty brown. The wooden porch has several holes from wear and tear and perhaps a woodland creature or two.

"I know it doesn't look like it, but this used to be something. From what my dad tells me, my granddad spent the better part of a year dressing this place up for my mom-mom to enjoy it. For her to have a beautiful place to relax, he put in this big wraparound porch with wood he chopped out back. If we go out back, there should be a decent view."

I put my hand in his, and he leads me around the house. Sure enough, the view's there. In between two Magnolias whose branches connect as if they are forming a big, wooden heart, I could see the Tennessee mountains and the most beautiful sunset. We get a lot of nice sunsets in Sloane, but the oranges and pinks hit differently up here—varying shades of sunshine and cotton candy, with a slight stripe of robin's egg blue cutting through the center. I would have missed the detail if we were at ground level.

"What do you think?"

"Wow." My breath catches. "This is ... I can see why your mom-mom liked it."

"Right? I know you want to move to New York, and if it's what you want, it's what we'll do ... but if it's peace, quiet, and security you're looking for, I can give you that here."

Here? He wants to stay in Sloane?

My heart drops, and I take a deep breath, swallowing the lump already forming in my throat. "I—Jase, I, uh, don't know what to say."

"You don't have to say anything. Sit here with me and take in this view, okay?"

I blink away a tear. It *is* beautiful, and he brought me here to show me a safe place where we could be together, but to stay here forever ...

I shake away the thought. Can't happen, won't happen. If I stay, I'll never be free ... but if I go, will I lose him forever? My lips quiver right as a small twinkle catches my eye. Between two tree, I see them and smile. "Hey, Jase, look!"

He turns his head from side to side but doesn't see anything. I put my hands on either side of his head and guide him in the right direction. "Right ... *there.*"

"Fireflies," he whispers.

"Tons of 'em. Catch and release?"

He takes off. "Race you!"

"They're so close it's not much of a race." I advance a few feet to join him.

We catch fireflies in our hands and set them free. We let our laughter fill the dusk until the sound of cicadas takes over. I'm so lost in the comforting sounds of our small town that I don't see Jase get up.

"Kay, come on, over here!"

Standing, I brush little pieces of grass off me and walk toward Jase's voice. "What's going on?" As I approach the porch, a broken window catches my gaze. "Oh no ... did you do that?"

He shakes his head and lifts a key between his thumb and pointer finger. "Nope, that's old. We're getting in the house the old-fashioned way."

I glance over my shoulder. "Are you sure we're allowed to be here?"

"Yes, I'm telling you, we own the house ... and I have a key." He swings the door open and tries flipping the switch, but the lights don't come on. "Guess we'll need to update a few things."

Leaves crunch behind me, and when I turn around, a flashlight meets my eyes.

I see a badge before I recognize what's happening.

"Evening, kids," the officer says. "You are trespassing on private property, and I'm going to have to escort you out."

I freeze in place and don't blink for some time while I think of what to say.

Jase holds up his hands, key well within view. "Hi, sir. I can understand how this looks, but this is my grandparents' property."

"This house has been abandoned for a long time," the officer replies.

I gulp.

The officer continues, "But the break in the window is new."

Panicking, I try to find the words, any words to explain we didn't break in, but all that comes out is, "I ... we didn't ..."

Jase kicks his heel but keeps his hands up and eyes glued on the officer's.

"Jase ... tell him."

He stays silent.

The deputy waves in backup from behind him. "Breaking and entering is a crime, kids. We're going to have to take you to the station."

Jase's eyes go wild at the other officers approaching him in the dark. Despite the fear on his face, his voice remains calm, steady. "This is my house."

The officer taps his foot. "I assume you have proper paperwork for that?"

Jase shakes his head.

The officer clicks his tongue. "Alrighty then, time to go."

I interrupt, "But..."

He twists, anger radiating off him, even in the dark. "Am I talking to you?"

"No, but ..."

"Kate ..." Jase warns.

"You're not letting him explain."

The officer gets right up in my face, close enough that I can smell the sweat pooling on his brow. Even after the sun went down, it's still a hot, August night. "That's enough, missy."

THIS KIND OF LOVE

I scoff, and a backup deputy yanks my arms behind my back as they shove me to the ground. I call out in pain as the cold metal cuffs are thrown on my wrists quicker than I know how to react. I scream again, but they push me back down into the grass.

"Let her go," Jase begs. "This was all me. Punish me. Let her go, please."

The lead officer puts his left hand on his hip, shining the flashlight brighter in Jase's face with his right. "Or *what?*"

"Nothing, I—it was all me."

"Let's go," the sergeant says and manhandles Jase in order to throw a pair of cuffs on him too.

"Wait, are you not going to let her go?" Jase cries.

"You *both* trespassed and broke the law."

They lead us down the path, out of the woods, and past Jase's car. Our Miranda rights are read on the way down, but I block out everything beyond you have the right to remain silent.

I squeeze my eyes shut. If I thought Dad was mad before, he's going to go off when he finds out about the arrest.

Jase lowers his voice, "I'm sorry, Kay." But it wasn't his mouth that got us into the back of a police car months before graduation.

"Me too," I mumble.

We ride to the station in silence. The trip feels endless, but still, not enough time to think about how I'm going to be able to hide this from Dad in a place like Sloane.

"I have a plan," Jase mutters. "Trust me."

An hour later, Eric and Pop show up to break us out of our holding cells. Disappointment is plastered on their grim, sunken faces, but here they are: the two most important men in our lives helping us out of our lowest low.

Pop clears his throat as we walk to his truck. "I won't tell your parents, but you're grounded. Indefinitely."

"Yes, sir." I hop into the truck and look back at Jase.

Eric isn't the yelling type, but he doesn't have to be to tell Jase what a mistake this afternoon was. He's getting a similar punishment: work, school, home, that's it. Home isn't my house—it's his. Jase's head is hung low, and he's apologizing profusely.

His sad eyes meet mine, and I feel my heart breaking, the weight of our mistake pulling us down.

I'm sorry doesn't feel good enough or strong enough, but I mouth it anyway.

He nods, and I know we'll get through this together—and—apart.

Chapter 17

Now

"**W**hat do you mean you *kissed* him?!" Amy all but shouts.

She's met with shushing and nasty glares.

"Sorry," she says to Meg, our yoga instructor, who's *way* too perky for seven o'clock on a Sunday morning. "What do you mean you kissed him?" Amy asks again, softer.

"I don't know." I follow the flow into triangle pose. "It just happened."

"How? Weren't you on a date with Nick? How'd you kiss Jase?"

I shrug.

Amy continues, "Also, how are you not in a complete knot like I am?"

"Ladies." Meg shuffles over to us. "Is there a problem over here?" Her hot pink spandex looks custom-made for her tan skin and bleached blonde hair. Meg's eyebrow is only slightly arched, but her voice is giving *pissed off*.

"No," we say in unison and exchange a look.

"You know what," Amy says, and warning bells go off in my head. "I can't quite get into triangle pose the way Kate can."

"Here, why don't you try this?" Meg calms once asked for help. She adjusts Amy's right arm. "Does that help?"

"Yes, thank you," Amy replies.

Meg walks away.

Amy mouths, "This is crap."

I shoot my best friend a pointed *you insisted on coming* look.

She throws back an *I wanted the tea* eyebrow.

"Then what happened?" Amy whispers.

"Nothing."

"What?" She speaks louder again, eliciting more looks from around the room.

"Nothing happened," I coo. "Trivia started back up, and I remembered I was on a freaking date ... with Nick."

"Yeah, but what if you needed to kiss Jase to get over him, and now you're over him and can focus on Nick?"

"Ladies." Meg circles back.

"We should probably go." I lean over to roll up my mat.

"I think that's best. You're always welcome to come back for another class, separately, if you'd like, or the club down the street offers Zumba—maybe it'll be a better fit." She shows us the door.

With one foot on the pavement, Amy shouts, "What a bitch!"

"Ame, shh, she can hear you."

"Good. She is a bitch. Who the hell does she think she is telling us to come back for separate classes or try Zumba?"

"I mean, we talked the entire class, and Yoga is about unplugging and breathing."

"Was I not breathing?" Amy's nose flares.

I cock my head. "You know what I mean."

"Anyway, you're over him now, right? You had all this tension built up for years and misremembered what it was like when you were a teenager?"

I shake my head. "I wish." We walk down Broad Street, away from the studio.

She sighs. "Damn. So, it was good?"

I sigh. "*So* good."

"Flannel Jim good?"

"Better than Flannel Jim."

She clicks her tongue. "Intrigued. Continue."

"So, Nick, perfect and well-meaning Nick, picked me up and took me to this 'little burger joint' he heard great things about online."

Amy gasps. "Oh no."

I nod. "Mhmm, and of course there's only one place actually *in* town and everyone and their mother was there after the run."

"Still?" She does the math in the air to figure out how long the crowd must have been hanging out at the bar.

"Yep. I'm sure you've noticed there isn't much to do around here …well, evidently, Saturday nights are trivia nights at Firefly as well."

She waits for me to keep going.

"So, we sat down, and Jase was our server, of course." I roll my eyes. "He was rude as hell to Nick."

"Um, yeah, you brought your new guy to your ex's work—not really a good move."

I point at her. "I agree, but it wasn't *my* move. I thought we were going to the city. Anyway, by the third plate slam, I got up to talk to Jase."

"And?"

"He kissed me instead."

"Oh. *Oh*," Amy adds, her eyes lighting up.

"Yeah." I bury my face in my hands. "I'm a terrible person."

Amy rests her hand on my arm. "You're not a terrible person ... you're confused."

I nod and run my hands through my hair, hoping it'll give me clarity on any of this, but my mind is a blank piece of paper, and the words aren't coming.

She nudges. "Let's try another angle. What does your gut say?"

"What does your gut say about what?" A familiar voice bellows behind us.

We turn around as Jase smiles coyly. This time, I do feel my cheeks burn.

His fingers brush mine. "I can only imagine that face means you were talking about me."

Outwardly, I glare at him, but inside, I'm mush.

"Oh, come on, Kay, I thought we were past all the glaring shit after last night."

"Jase," Amy barks.

Even as he says her name in return, his eyes never leave mine.

Amy takes a step back as her phone buzzes. "I should go."

"No," I beg, as Jase says, "Please."

"Actually, *we* were just leaving," I counter.

Jase's gaze intensifies. "Where are we going?"

"We ..." I gesture between him and I. "Are going nowhere. Amy and I, *we*, are on our way to get coffee."

"We are?" Amy checks.

I raise my right brow.

She slips her phone into her pocket and straightens. "I mean, we are."

"That's about as believable as a flying unicorn." He laughs.

Amy snorts, but not before a subtle snicker. Is he starting to win Amy over?

"Have fun, ladies." He waves his pointer finger at me, and I know I'll be thinking about this moment for the rest of the day.

I'm sipping my second cup of coffee of the day. This one is Mama's special blend with a touch of the French vanilla creamer she keeps in the fridge. I'm staring at an empty laptop screen, urging inspiration to strike, but nothing's happening. Nothing except memories of last night and running into Jase again this morning.

Hyla hops on my bed and paws at the blankets to get comfortable.

"What do you think, girl?"

Hyla sighs and rolls over for a belly rub.

"No? Ugh, I wish this coffee had an extra shot of ... something else." With this, a new blog idea comes to mind. I'm about halfway through when there's a knock on the door.

Amy pops her head in. "Hey, I wanted to see if you—oh God, it's a good thing I haven't seen you in the writing cave before."

I stop writing. "What do you mean?"

"Nothing. You look gorgeous right now."

"Thank you." I place my hands under my chin and bat my eyes at her, but when I glance at the mirror on my closet door, I inhale sharply.

"Told you."

My hair is in a messy bun at the top of my head with a pencil in it, my makeup has run quite a bit, and my oversized T-shirt is not in the least bit flattering. I look like a hot mess. "What's up, Ame?"

She takes a bag of Smartfood, a bottle of Moscato, and two glasses out from behind her back. "Any chance you want to watch *Penelope*, you know, for research to help me wrap up the cover feature?"

I stroke my chin, pretending to consider her offer. We both know it's an immediate yes. *Penelope* has been my "drop everything" movie since I was a little girl. It's the first movie Mama took me to see in theater. The day started and ended with Daddy being drunk out of his mind, but the middle was just the two of us: a haven with reclining seats, a big-screen TV, and enough buttered popcorn to make me forget the real world for an hour and forty minutes.

We peel back the covers, and both climb in, lining the pillows up straight. We lean back and sit facing the TV. Amy pours the wine while I turn on Netflix.

"How has everything gone with the article?"

Amy's face lights up. "You're going to love it. Reese is as amazing as you'd imagine—beautiful, sweet, funny. Interviewing her was like hanging out with an old friend."

I'm in awe. "We've been very lucky with cover models."

She hands me a glass, and we toast.

"I have to say..." She sips as I put my glass on the nightstand. "Sloane has surprised me."

"How so?" I meet Amy's eyes.

"Pleasantly surprised me," she amends. "It's got a lot of charm and good people."

"Gossips," I add.

"Hot men." She wiggles her eyebrows.

I click my tongue. "Ugh." I bring my hands up to cover my face. "What am I doing?"

"You're ... figuring it out."

I exhale. "No, I mean it, Ame; what am I doing? In Sloane? With my life? My family begged me to come down here and see my dad. I'm here, and I can't be within a hundred feet of him without having a panic attack. I finally find this perfect guy who gets me, and I've been sneaking around and kissing Jase. Honestly, what am I doing?"

She shifts to face me and puts her hands on my shoulders. "Kate, deep breath."

Inhale. Exhale.

"Better?"

I nod.

Amy holds up her pointer finger. "First of all, you are allowed to deal with your anxiety and trauma however you need to, and if that means waiting to see your dad, or not seeing your dad at all, I will support you. The big thing is being here with your family, and you are."

Inhale. Exhale.

"Second," she raises another finger. "Jase kissed you."

I lift my right hand. "I didn't stop him."

"Did you want to?" She quips.

I gulp.

She takes another sip of Moscato, then sets her glass down. "I didn't think so. Listen, is it ideal? No, but the fact of the matter is, we can't help who we're attracted to."

"It'd be a lot much easier if we could. Nick is a good guy. He doesn't deserve—whatever I'm doing, and Jase ..."

"Jase?"

I pull a pillow out from behind my back and bury my face in it. I mumble incoherently, and Amy peels the pillow away. "Um, repeat that?"

"It's complicated."

Her phone lights up with a text from Leo. She blushes and ignores it. "Is it, though? You've been in love with Jase your whole life, completely sabotaged relationships—"

"Hey!"

Amy raises her hand. "I'm not done. What happened back then sucked ... but that was *six years ago*, Kate. You've grown. He's grown. And despite spending half a decade apart, you're both still into each other. That doesn't just happen, you know?"

"I thought you were Team Nick?" I challenge.

She bumps my shoulder with her own. "I'm Team Kate, always. Nick's great, and from what I hear, Jase has made his fair share of mistakes, but he's also done a lot of things right, like loving you and protecting you. I'm here for whoever is going to make you happy."

"I'm not even here for Jase. I came to see my dad, and we all see how well that's working out."

"Again, you are allowed to deal with your anxiety and trauma however you need to. Or not. That's okay, too."

I squeeze her hand. "Thank you for coming down here. I didn't think I needed you here. I didn't think I needed anyone, but I was wrong. I've never needed anyone more. You're the best."

"I know," she agrees. "Ready?"

"Yes, ma'am." I press play and reach for the Smartfood, ready to have ourselves *a night*.

THIS KIND OF LOVE

A good night's sleep can do wonders. When I wake up, I have a sense of clarity and purpose I haven't had in a long while. Maybe it was Amy giving me permission to feel however I need to that made me realize I need to start taking control of my life—mistakes and all. Time to start ripping off band-aids.

I dial Nick's number and pace in my room, waiting for him to answer. He picks up on the second ring. "Hey, beautiful."

"Hey," I answer. There's a big lump already forming in my throat. I can't do this on the phone. He deserves better.

He laughs nervously. "Uh oh, I don't think I like the sound of your voice dropping."

Me either. I dig my free hand into my hair. "What are you up to?"

"Not much. What's up?"

"There's a park in the center of town, across from the high school. Want to meet there in an hour?"

"Sure. I'll see you soon."

Fifty-five minutes later, I'm sitting on a bench in the middle of Rose's Park, which is lit up with twinkling lights, even in the morning. Birds are bathing in a mini fountain nearby, chirping and dancing.

It's nearly empty for eight o'clock, and I'm thankful for the lack of eyes on me. Nick's footsteps echo as he transitions from the concrete of the sidewalk to the marble path. I hold my hand up to wave, and his wide grin reaches his blue eyes. His long, black overcoat reaches his knees, blue jeans and sneakers sticking out.

"Jeans? I didn't think you owned anything but suits," I joke.

"Oh, I don't. I borrowed these from my neighbor at the hotel."

"Ha." I smirk but look away. "Listen, Nick ..."

He sits next to me on the plastic bench and puts his hands on mine. "It's okay. You don't have to do this ... I get it. It's not me, it's him."

I gape at him. "What? How'd you—"

He shakes his head and says, "Sometimes a guy knows these things."

"Oh."

"... and I saw the paper this morning." He hands it to me.

The paper's folded over to page 4—*Matilda's Column*. On the top of the page is a big, half-page, semi-grainy photo of Jase and me running straight ahead but looking at each other. A look that could look like love but certainly looks like we've got *history*. History based on secrets and lies but history, nonetheless.

"Nick, it's not—he's my ex."

He cuts me off. "It's okay, Kate. You guys have a past. I get it. If it were just a past, I would wait it out until you're ready, but it's not finished."

"I'm so, so sorry. This whole thing wasn't fair to you?" I put my head in my hands. "Gosh, why couldn't it have been you?"

Nick laughs and plants a sweet kiss on the top of my head. "Hey, really, it's okay. It's not the right time, and I'm not the right guy."

Sniffling, I look up. "You're a good guy, Nick Scott."

He cocks his head. "Not what the ladies in my basement would say."

Our laughter fills the air and lingers long after he leaves with a tip of his invisible hat.

Some time passes before I stand. I intend to walk home, but my legs have a different idea and, instead, I pace to Jase's door. The front porch light is on, almost as if he's waiting for me or for someone else. I knock twice before I chicken out and trip on the front steps.

The front door opens, and Jase calls after me. "Wait."

I stop in my tracks and turn around to see Jase pulling at the screen door. He stands on the porch in a pair of ripped jeans and quarters drinking T-shirt, muscles peeking out from his sleeves. He looks impossibly hotter than yesterday.

"Been thinking about the kiss, huh?" He runs his hand through his buzzed hair, and it takes everything in me not to jump him.

I don't back away, either. I stand there on his porch and stare into his perfect eyes. "This was a mistake. I'm sorry. I should go."

His arm reaches out. "Kay."

I look up at his pleading eyes with my confused ones.

"Do you want to come inside?" He holds the door open.

"I, uh ..." I bite my lip.

"Kay?"

I swallow. "Okay."

"Okay," he repeats.

I don't know what I'm expecting, but I'm hit with a strong sense of nostalgia. The first floor is wide and open-concept, with big windows around the side and beautiful hardwood floors stretching through the living room and giving way to the tile in the kitchen, separated by an island. The kitchen cabinets are light grey above the marble countertops and a side-by-side fridge.

I turn to face Jase. "Wow. You made it happen."

He sticks his hands in his jean pockets, and heat rises to his cheeks. "Yeah."

"It looks good."

"Want a tour?" Jase extends his hand, and without thinking, I take it.

Lightning runs right through me like it always does when I'm with him. My phone vibrates in my pocket. "One sec," I say to Jase, and answer, "Hey, Mama."

Her tone is flat. "Som ... something ha ... happened."

"I'll be right there." I hang up and rush out the door.

He chases after me. "Kay!"

"I've gotta go. I think something happened with my dad." Tears fall from my eyes.

Jase grabs his jacket from behind the couch and pulls his keys off the hook. "Let's go."

"You don't have to come with me."

He shakes his head, keys in his mouth, while he pulls the door shut but doesn't lock it. "Don't be ridiculous, of course, I'm coming with you."

I climb into the passenger seat of his old pickup truck. "Guess this is an upgrade from the Sundance." I inhale the faint new car smell from the air freshener hanging off his rearview.

"Her name's Missy." He mumbles under his breath and puts Missy into drive, heading into the unknown. Together.

Chapter 18
Then: Six Years Ago

"Oh, Fucking Christ." I wince in pain.

"It wouldn't hurt as much if you held still." Jase uses both hands to push me back down into the chair.

The tattoo artist assures me he's almost done.

Almost done is *not* done, and I close my eyes to fight the pain, suppressing another screech as Greg turns the machine off.

"There we go. Sorry if it was too much. Typically, the shading hurts less than the outline." Greg scratches his chin.

"Evidently, not for me." I yank my arm back and instinctively massage my wrist.

Greg and Jase both stop me.

"Oh no, you don't," Jase says. "It needs to be wrapped first."

I frown. "How come you didn't scream?"

"I have a much higher pain tolerance than you do. Obviously."

I grit my teeth.

"Y'all want a picture?" Greg pulls out his phone.

Jase wraps his arm around my shoulders and pulls me into him. "We sure do. Come on, Kay, be a good sport and stick your wrist out."

No.

"Kay," he begs. "For me, *pleeease.*" He draws out the word and bats his eyelashes at me, and I sigh.

"Fine."

Jase puts his wrist next to mine under a desk lamp on the empty tattoo station one over.

"Perfect." Greg takes one shot and crops the picture to get it right. "Want me to send it after we get these all wrapped up?"

"That'd be great," Jase says. "I can settle the bill whenever."

As he follows Greg to the cash register at the front of the shop, I drop my gaze to my left wrist. I blink to adjust to the new art on my arm under the plastic wrap and exhale. It's cute. I can't believe I let him talk me into this.

"Ready to go?" Jase holds up his right arm with his new mason jar and firefly. As matching tattoos go, they're not bad, but it might as well be two names in a heart—my mama will have a heart attack all the same.

"My parents are going to kill me." I bury my head in my hands as I come back to reality and feel the gravity of this decision in a whole different way.

"Oh relax, this is better than getting arrested ... again." He holds the door open for me.

I whack him in the gut as I pass him. "It's not funny. I was grounded for *months.*" Glancing down at the small insect on my wrist, I mumble, "This will probably be about as long."

"Puh-lease. For one, you're eighteen, an adult in the eyes of the law ... and court system."

I give him a warning look. Still not funny.

He smirks. "Two: we're moving to New York in a few months anyway, if your parents would rather spend time angry at you, I don't get it, but they're gonna do what they're gonna do, which leads me to three: you can't control their reaction."

I squint. "I'm not sure they're going to agree with your logic. It's not that they're going to yell at me for making a decision that impacts my body. It's about having respect for my parents while I'm in their house. It's a courtesy. I should have asked or told them."

"I'll never understand this immense guilt you carry around, but man, is that shit deep."

I shrug. I want to fight him, but he has a point. The guilt of disappointing them is *strong*.

Jase takes his jacket off and wraps it around me as we walk home. "Here." He adjusts the sleeves down past my wrist. "This should help."

"Until dinner when Mama asks why I'm wearing a jacket at the table."

He sighs. "Work with me here, Kay."

"I'm just saying."

Pop's pulling into the driveway as we walk up. He steps out of his pickup truck and tips his hat in our direction. "Katie girl, Jase."

"Hey, Pop!" I rush over to give him a wide hug while being careful not to directly rest my left wrist on his back.

He sniffs the air twice and says, "Hmm, smells like a couple of new tattoos."

They have a smell?

"Yes, sir. Mine." Jase covers.

"Uh huh, and the bandage on my granddaughter's wrist is ... for fun?"

I cringe and let go of Pop, looking down at my shoes.

"You know I was born a day, but it wasn't yesterday." His knowing eyes stare at me.

"Yes, sir," we reply in unison.

Eric comes out of Jase's house with a long apron on, a half-filled-out crossword puzzle in one hand, and a spatula in the other. "Oh good, you're home. We're having breakfast for dinner. How many pancakes ..." He sniffs the air. "Does it smell like a couple of tattoos to you?" he asks Pop.

"Yes, sir," Jase says.

"Ah." One word. One syllable. No true *reaction*, and certainly not a bad one.

"Hey, Eric, you have some extra pancake batter tonight?"

His friend smiles knowingly. "Sure do. Come on in and wash up, kids."

"But ..."

Pop holds his hands out to me. "I've got this. You go." He's covering for me. *Again.*

"Thank you." I hug him again.

"Hey." Pop shrugs. "At least y'all didn't get arrested again."

"Told you." Jase grabs my hand and pulls me into his warm, welcoming home for dinner and understanding.

Breakfast for dinner is one of Jase's favorite meals, but I've never been a fan of eggs, so I'm grateful Eric has *options*. I skip the scrambled eggs and instead opt for an extra serving of French toast casserole and a pancake.

I take my seat between Jase and Jack at the table, and Jase pours himself a glass of orange juice.

He leans over and points to the casserole. "You know that has eggs in it, right?"

"I'm sure, but they're not staring at me, so..."

He rolls his eyes and picks up a big bite of potatoes on his fork. "You're weird."

I bump my shoulder into his. "But I'm your weird."

"Yeah, you are." Jase bumps back.

Jack pretends to gag. "You're both weird and gross."

"Leave 'em be, Jack." His mama scolds him and sets a glass of wine on the table, smiling over the glass at me. "Nice of you to join us tonight, Kate."

She's always been sweet as pie. I smile back. "Thanks for making room for me."

"You know there's always room for you. Go ahead and eat up."

Dinner at the Coles is normal. Everyone takes turns talking about their day. Funny stories are shared because they're welcomed. Laughter echoes through the room like it belongs—and it does. It always has.

After dinner, Jase's mama does the dishes, and his dad dries them. The Coles excuse Jase and me to rest our tattoos, and Jack heads upstairs to 'work a paper.' Though we all know by 'work a paper,' he means texting Lindsay Harris.

Carrie turns the sink off after she passes the last dish to Eric, but instead of drying it, he places the still-wet plate on the counter and pulls his wife in close. He spins her around the kitchen like they're on a dance floor at a Firehouse. There's no music playing, but they don't need it. They're humming along to the same tune and gazing at each other with love as sweet as a sugar high, even after they've been married for twenty-five years.

"I want that," I say to Jase, staring at his parents move in sync. "I want that kind of love."

He places a kiss on my hand and squeezes. "I want *this* kind of love."

His smile lights up the room, and I lean into him. "You have this kind of love."

Jase pulls me in tighter, and I listen to his heartbeat in sync with my own as I drift off to sleep. This kind of love. Our kind of love. Forever.

The next morning, I wake up in my own bed, wondering if the matching tattoos were a dream, but when there's a *clink* at the window, I look down at my wrist still wrapped and know how real it is.

I unlatch the window. "Yes? May I help you?"

"My fair maiden." He bows. "Wondering if you'll come down from your high tower to get coffee with me?"

"Coffee, you say?" I place my hand on my chin.

"Oh yeah, turns out I didn't get a lot of sleep last night."

"We weren't even out late." My messy ponytail flips from one side to the other animatedly.

"I was worried about you and what would happen if your parents found out about …" He wiggles his brows. "You know."

"Shhh!"

"Your mama and dad already left for work." He shrugs.

I check the time. "Shit, it's later than I thought."

"Where do we stand on the coffee?" Jase wiggles his brows.

"Meet you down there." I grab my wallet and keys and run out of my bedroom door and down the stairs.

THIS KIND OF LOVE

The silence is unsettling, but I owe Pop a big thank you for covering for me and the reprieve it's brought.

Java House is hectic for a weekday afternoon, but Jase sashays up to the counter like he owns the place, ordering a vanilla latte for me and a cappuccino instead of his normal black coffee.

We take our drinks to go, and he mentions a pitstop on the way home. Instead of making the right turn to go home, we move left toward the high school and walk down the field full of dandelions.

Jase leans down and picks a handful to give me. "My lady." He bows again.

"Not that I don't appreciate it, but where did this Shakespearean thing come from?" I wave my hand over him.

"Blame the exhaustion." He stretches and lays down on the grass.

I plop down next to him and point out dinosaur and dog shapes in the clouds.

He traces them in the grass, and we laugh about peak fatigue until he gets serious and asks how my tattoo's feeling.

My eyes shift to my wrist. "Okay ... if I don't touch it. How's yours?"

"Feels okay, too. I'm glad we got them."

I smile, admiring the detail in Jase's design. "Kind of ties us together, doesn't it?"

"In the best way. So ... I was thinking."

This gets my attention, and I turn toward him. "Oh?"

He pulls out a folded-up piece of paper from the pocket of his basketball shorts.

"Uh oh." I rest my head in my hand, elbow on the grass. "Should I be worried when *you* start pulling out lists?"

Jase answers without hesitating. "Yes."

"What do we have here?"

Jase folds the paper closer to him and mumbles about patience. "We've been talking about life after Sloane, about going to college, finding new jobs, and living in New York ..."

"Mhmm?" My stomach starts to turn.

"I've been writing down the ideas we've had and crunching numbers, and I have a plan."

"Oh?" I sit up.

Jase winces preemptively. "I'm not the planner, so you've got to tell me if you hate it."

"Jase, are you kidding? I'm sure I'm not going to hate it." I hold back the tears. He came up with a plan for us.

I lied. I hate it.

Well, I don't hate the plan. I hate that it means we'd barely see each other because we have nowhere near what we need to be able to afford a tiny studio apartment on the outskirts of New York City while going to community college part-time and working full-time.

"How is it *that* expensive?" I grab the paper with his carefully outlined facts and figures.

He shrugs. "I've run the numbers multiple times. You're still waiting to hear from Ithaca, right? They have a good writing program; maybe scholarship money could come in ... maybe we get something a little further out of the city to get started, and maybe we bring up Lily—she's better on gas than my truck."

Maybe. Pulling out my cell phone, I look up the distance between Ithaca College and NYC and cringe. "It's more than a little out of the city ..."

"Maybe more affordable?" Jase offers.

I shrug. *Maybe.* Living in upstate New York isn't the same as living in New York City.

Jase puts his hands on mine. "Hey, what's the most important thing in all of this?"

"That we're together and we're safe."

"Yes. We will be, Kay. No matter where you want to go, I'll go with you. Taking this detour could be better in the long run. It could open doors we can't imagine now."

I process what he's saying. Going to a great school with a great writing program could be better than hoping and praying writing on my own will take off without any formal training or connections. He has a point.

"You're right." I sigh. "Ithaca's not New York City, but it's not Sloane, either. If it means we can afford to put food on the table, then it's all worth it."

"There you go." Jase pulls me in. "Though, I didn't say anything about being able to afford food ... we'll have to re-crunch the numbers when your acceptance letter comes in."

"*If,*" I correct.

"*When,*" he affirms.

Jase has always had my back. He's always believed in me, even in the ways I don't ... especially in the ways I don't. He's never doubted, never wavered. Not like I have.

"Here." Jase tears the stem off a dandelion and wraps it around my ring finger, tying it carefully. "Until I can get you a real one, let this serve as our promise ring. *When* you get into Ithaca, we'll move to New York and start our life together."

It's a stem from a weed he picked in a field full of weeds, but this moment warms my heart more than a real ring could. Dandelion or not, he made a promise, and Jase has always kept his promises from the very first day we met. So, when he holds his pinkie out to me, I loop mine in his, believing every word.

Jase's phone rings, and he mouths: *Sorry.* He picks up. "Hey, Mama, I'm out with Kay." His tone changes, and he says he'll be right there.

Panic sets in, and the world spins. Endless possibilities circle my mind.

He hangs up and helps me stand up. "Come on, we have to go."

I run close behind and lose my dandelion ring in the process. "What's going on?" I ask, breathing heavier than a runner should.

"There's been an accident." He doesn't slow down to wait for me.

He jogs straight home, and I follow, ditching what's left of my coffee in a trash can by the park when we pass. My skin grows clammy, and my heartbeat thrashes in my ears.

The closer we get, the faster he goes until he stops in the driveway staring at his house. *It's going to be okay. It's going to be okay. Please be okay.*

The door is gaping open. His mama's wailing can be heard from the street. Police cars line the driveway with their lights flashing, the officers split between the front lawn and inside.

My mama and dad come outside right as Nana and Pop pull up. They rush to Jase, who's frozen in place.

"Jase, go see your mama," my parents say in unison.

"I'll go with you." Pop puts his hand around Jase's shoulders and walks him inside.

"What's going on?" I ask Mama as Jase and Pop step inside.

"There's been a terrible accident, sweetie. His dad ..." She doesn't finish her sentence, and she doesn't need to.

THIS KIND OF LOVE

From the corner of my eye, I see Jase collapse on the ground, screaming. Jack pulls him in for a hug on the floor, holding him to help with a pain I can't understand.

His dad—his hero—is gone.

In that moment, part of Jase is, too.

Chapter 19

Now

The PA system at Sloane Memorial jolts me out of a rocky sleep. I shift my head from side to side, but trying to stretch out the strain of sleeping in an uncomfortable waiting room chair with my head pushed against the wall is impossible. I wince, adjusting to the harsh lights. There's consistent beeping in the background and an angry tone that draws me fully awake.

"What's going on?" My voice is groggy.

Amy looks up from the book she's reading in the chair across the aisle and half smiles at me. "Oh good, you're awake. Will you please help them settle this debate so we can move on?"

"There is no way he's the baby daddy." Jase's gaze doesn't lift from the old episode of *Maury* that's airing.

"Yes, he is!" Nana shouts. "The baby looks like Ryan."

"Ryan's the baby daddy," Amy adds.

"*Suspected* baby daddy," Jase amends.

"How long was I asleep?" The clock on the wall reads nine a.m. ... three hours of sleep after being up all night in the emergency room awaiting some sort of news. "What'd I miss?"

Amy shakes her head. "Just whatever this is about." She gestures between Jase and Nana, both heated in the father or not debate.

"Whatever what's about?" Mama asks as she enters the waiting room. A weary Pop shuffles in by her side.

We all stand, palms sweaty, facing Mama, anxious for an update.

Nana steps forward and places her hand on Mama's shoulder. "How's Andy doing?"

Mama wobbles backwards, then recovers. She runs her hand through her long, dark hair and sighs. For the first time, I notice the gray strands shining under the fluorescent lights. There are dark circles under her eyes, and her frame droops deeper than yesterday.

"He's..." Mama swallows, and I can hear the gulp. "Not doing well. He's going to have to stay in the ICU for at least a few days while they run some tests and continue to monitor him."

"What happened, Mama?"

Jase moves to help Mama sit down on the nearest chair and holds her hand.

She sniffles. "They said he was having a fine day. He had a slice of pizza and a cup of pudding for lunch, and a short while later, his eyes rolled to the back of his head, and he started seizing."

I lean forward. "What could have caused it?"

"The doctors said it's a side effect of one of the meds he's on, and they've put him on something else, but he's not out of the woods yet."

"Sure, but what needs to happen for them to say he's going to be okay?"

Mama rocks her head from side to side. "I don't know. They asked us to step out for a few minutes."

"I'm sorry, Mama."

She waves me over and pats the seat on the other side of her.

I sit beside Mama and lean back. "You know, these seats aren't exactly comfortable, but if you want to try and nap on my shoulder, I'm sure Jase could find a blanket for you."

He stands. "Yes, I'll be right back."

"Oh no, it's okay," she rebuts.

Jase is already gone, and Mama's almost asleep on my shoulder, anyway.

Nana stands as Pop grabs her hand to help her up. "Maybe they'll let me see Andy when they're done pricking him. Want me to stick him once for you, Katie girl?"

I smirk and mouth, *No, thank you.*

Nana's way through a depressing time is to crack a joke. She's already told me she'd prefer her funeral to be a standup show than a cry fest.

Amy nods as Nan and Pop head toward Dad's room. "Here for you," she mouths.

Jase turns the corner back into the waiting area.

Amy pretends to read, but I see her eye glancing over the pages to watch him cover Mama in a blanket, tucking her in as best as he can in a hospital guest chair.

"Thank you."

The blanket has *Sloane High School* imprinted on it, and I question him with my eyes.

"I keep a blanket in my car for emergencies."

"I don't think my mama would want to be covered in a blanket you've rolled around on with unknown company."

Jase has the decency to step back, his expression hurt. "I think you've confused me with my brother."

"Jack's gotten his act together, I hear." I'm aware my voice is a little too loud, but as Mama snores, I relax a bit, knowing I didn't wake her with my outburst.

Jase snorts. "Is *that* what he was telling you at the Pumpkin Festival?"

I adjust, trying not to disturb Mama. "Who told you we were talking at the Pumpkin Festival?"

Amy sets her book face down in her lap, eyebrows up, fully invested in *this* story.

Jase shrugs. "Oh, you know, no one and everyone."

"You better shut your mouth, Jason Cole. This is how things without merit make their way through the town."

He laughs. "Oh, I know full well how it turns out. There's no truth to it?" His voice is a little light, almost hopeful, and I'm not sure what to make of it.

I pretend to gag. "Ew, he's like a brother to me."

Jase shutters. "He *is* a brother to me, so, good."

Our gazes lock. It's like a moment years ago when the only thing that mattered was him and me. His green eyes shine into mine, and I can't remember anything but how much I love him. *Loved him*—past tense, back then, before I grasped how much a broken heart aches.

Amy clears her throat.

I blink and turn away from Jase.

Nana strolls into the room in a huff. They wouldn't let her see Dad because his health is too fragile to allow for visitors right now. When they allow people back in, it'll be one at a time.

Pop shrugs and takes a seat.

I stand, put my hands on my lower back, and stretch. "I'm going to grab some coffee from the cafeteria. Anyone want anything?" Several arms raise. "All right, a round of coffee coming on up."

"I'll go with you." Jase stands.

Amy beats him to it and points to the chair he vacated. "Read the room, lover boy."

Wordlessly, he sits back down.

Amy tips her ball cap toward him and follows me into the hall.

My best friend waits for the elevator doors to close before turning her attention to me. "Where were you yesterday that Jase gave you a ride to the hospital?"

Pushing the button for the lobby, I sigh. "I needed to see him. I ... can't explain it."

"I can."

"Care to share?"

The elevator doors open, and we ride to the cafeteria.

"I've seen the way you look at him, and I haven't seen you look at anybody like that the entire time I've known you."

I glance at my watch. "It's because I hate him, and the list of people I hate is very small. In fact, both people on it are in this hospital. There's something for you."

"I don't believe that." She reaches for the coffee carafe. "I don't think you ever hated Jase, or your dad, for that matter. I think you hate what they did to you, and I think you hate how you reacted, but I don't think you truly hate them."

I blink away. It doesn't matter. The two men I cared about most in the world broke my heart. I'm not dumb enough to let them do it again ... am I?

THIS KIND OF LOVE

Amy pours another cup of coffee and waves her hands in front of my face. "How much cream for Nana?" Her foot tap and eye twitch tell me it's not the first time she's asked.

"Grab a few. She can put them in upstairs."

She stirs hazelnut creamer in her own coffee and places it in a carrier while I toss her analysis over and over again in my mind. You know, even I'm ashamed to admit Jase is chinking my best friend armor. Blame the way he looks at you and the far-out gaze you get on your face every time his name comes up."

I pick up the coffee carrier and walk to the elevator while Amy grabs the last coffee and follows me. "Are we done here?"

"Okay, okay. Let me ask one more thing," she begs.

I relent. "Fine."

Amy holds up her pinkie. "You have to promise me you'll make me your maid of honor when you get married."

"Ame."

"I know, I know, you 'don't love him.' Except you totally do, and he loves you, too, or he wouldn't have driven you here, much less sat in the waiting room all night."

Maybe. I intertwine my pinky with hers.

The elevator dings, and the doors open wide to a sleepy Jase, standing there, jacket on, looking ready to leave. He slips his phone into the front pocket of his blue jeans and shifts his expression to us. "Oh man, a pinkie promise? I interrupted something serious."

Amy and I unwind our pinkies and shift our free hands back down.

"Coffee?" Amy hands Jase his cup.

"Sure. Thank you." He accepts the cup for what it is: part caffeine, part peace offering.

Amy pulls the holder from my hands. "I'll be taking those." She walks back to the waiting room, leaving me alone with Jase by the elevators.

"I, uh, don't think the door can close with how you're standing, so ..." His voice drops, and I jump forward.

"Are you leaving?" *Please don't.* I try steadying my voice, but I can't hide the note of disappointment.

He digs his hands into his front pockets and squints his right eye closed. "I didn't realize how late it was. I have to go open the bar, but I can come back tonight if you want?"

I kick an invisible rock on the floor. "No, it's okay. Thank you for bringing me and staying through the night."

"Of course." He steps closer and pushes the down button to call the elevator. It opens, and Jase moves inside. "Hey, Kay?"

"Yeah?"

"I'm here if you need to talk about ... you know, all of this."

I smile. "Thank you."

He tips his hat, and as the door closes, I let my mind wander—to all the could have, should have, would have beens. To the where would-our-life-be nows—if he hadn't broken my heart and if I hadn't left.

Chapter 20
Then: Six Years Ago

The collective stench of white lilies and chrysanthemums is paralyzing. The nave is lined with well-wishers and sympathy baskets, trying to bring peace to a family who can never be whole again. It's heartbreaking and harrowing, and through it all, the Coles stand there, united, full of pain and full of grace.

The service is long and agonizing. The pews are overflowing with guests dressed in black, paying their respects. The preacher asks everyone to hold their condolences until the end—*the family needs some time*, he says. But when the service concludes, I'm not sure they've had enough time to come to terms with what's happening. If anything, it's made it worse. Carrie's sniffling turns to wailing. She's grieving the love of her life. How can anyone say anything to ease her suffering?

Nana and Pop greet Jade first, and she reaches out to pull them into a tight hug. She wasn't here when it happened, and she blames herself. It's not her fault. It's no one's fault. These things just happen sometimes. The Coles are like family to me, sometimes more than my own family, but being here today feels like I'm at a stranger's funeral.

Jase and I have barely spoken since the night it happened. My mama baked lasagna for the family, and I brought it over with her, but Jase wasn't home. I've tapped on his window every night since, but he hasn't answered. I've called, but it's only gone to voicemail. He hasn't been at school or driven past the house. Not that I can blame him. I don't know what he's going through or how deep the pain he's feeling runs, but I know he *is* hurting, and I want to be here for him like he's always been here for me. He hasn't missed anything in my life over the last thirteen years, even when I haven't called ... especially when I haven't called.

But he won't let me in now, and it's breaking me that I can't hold him and let him know he's not alone.

"I'm sorry, Jade." I sniffle.

She wraps her arms around me and pulls me into her like she does with the rest of my family. Unlike the rest of my family, she doesn't let go. She clings to me like a T-shirt after a summer storm. Jack taps her on the shoulder and gives her a signal to pull back. When she does, there's a mix of confusion, anger, sadness, love, and immense grief in her hazel eyes. She shakes her head. "How'd this happen, Kate? I can't believe he's gone. My dad. Gone just like that." She snaps her fingers, and its echo ricochets like the first pop of a firework.

I squeeze her hands. "I don't know, babe. I'm sorry. What can I do?"

She frowns.

It's clear what she really wants to ask: bring him back, and what I want to say: I would do anything to make it happen if I could.

Giving her hands a final pat, I shift to Jack as the man behind me hurriedly shakes Jade's hand and tries to move past me in line. His point is clear—if I'm not going to get in and get out, I should step aside.

"What an asshole," Jack mumbles.

"Jack..." I warn.

He shrugs. "What? My dad *died*, and he's acting like it's another stop on his to-do list. We don't need people here who don't give a fuck."

He has a point. It's a funeral, not a matinee.

"I'm sorry, Jacky."

He pulls me in for a hug. "Thank you."

Jase stands between his older brother and his mama, pulling her to his side. She's a wreck. Her husband of twenty-five years is gone in a senseless accident. There's no one to blame. There's nothing to reconcile. His heart gave out in the car, and he lost control. He wasn't driving drunk or erratically. He wasn't a bad person, and he didn't believe in violence. He was a family man through and through—always wanting to spend his free time dancing with his wife and playing various sports with his kids. He ate right, was in shape, and ran for fun. There was no history of heart disease in his family. There were no signs.

It doesn't matter. Jase's mama knows it deep down, but she's looking for them, anyway.

Carrie's face is red, blotchy, and bloated. She hasn't stopped crying, slept a wink, or stood up on her own in five days. She's grieving her soulmate while my dad, the abusive town drunk, is alive and well and sitting in the fourth pew. Life's not fair.

"I'm sorry, Carrie." I wish there were something better to say, but there's not. We all know it's bullshit.

She sniffles but doesn't say anything.

Jase doesn't take his eyes off his mama.

I pat her hands with my own and take a seat in the pew next to my mama. "I wish I could take their pain away," I mumble.

"We all do," she replies.

When the line wraps up, Pop stands to meet Jase, Jack, and the other pallbearers up at the front of the Church. Nana tries to pull Pop back, but he insists on going. Eric was like a son to him, perhaps more than my dad, who's constantly pushing him away. Nothing will keep him from honoring his memory. She nods at this and lets him go with a warning to *be careful*. My eyebrows furrow at the exchange. What's there to be careful of?

As the cantor sings Leonard Cohen's "Hallelujah," the pallbearers move the coffin slowly down the nave. Grief glues the rest of us in our pews, and echoes of cries remind us that life is never as long as we'd like.

Mama and Nana rush to ensure each of the buffet burners is on. Mama insisted on organizing the luncheon, and Carrie agreed—grateful it was something she didn't have to think about. Nana stirs the meatballs in the oversized crockpot and pours in jars of homemade red sauce. Mama puts Dad to work cutting the rolls as she takes a baked ziti out of the oven and replaces the tin above a burner she's deemed ready. Pop and I greet people as they come in either house and direct them to the buffet or bathroom.

"Well, I can't say the occasion doesn't leave something to be desired, but you're at least good company." Pop tilts his hat my way.

I smile. "Right back at 'cha." I scan the room for Jase.

"Maybe he needs some time on his own," Pop offers.

I offer a prayer card to the next family in line.

THIS KIND OF LOVE

The distinctive creak of the kitchen door fills the room, and familiar footsteps enter. There's chatter and mindless condolences and 'what can we do for you's.' *They're back.*

Pop stretches his hand out for my pile of prayer cards. "Go," he whispers.

I hurry down the hallway, past the living room, and into the kitchen. Jase's face is drained of color, and his eyes look lost. His gaze meets mine, but not fully. He doesn't acknowledge I'm here, just that I'm another person in an already packed kitchen.

Nana sashays a tray of cookies from a guest to the dining room table, where desserts will be served. I dodge out of her way but keep my attention on Jase. He doesn't seem to see me, though. He doesn't see anyone, really. I close the distance between us and reach for his hands, but he recoils as if I burned him. "Jase." I blink back the tears welling in my eyes. Let me help. Don't shut me out.

"Kay, I can't do this," he announces.

"What can I do to help? Do you need water? Ziti? Pineapple Upside Down Cake?" *His favorite.*

"No. I can't do *this*." He motions his hands between him and me. "Us. I can't do us."

"What? Do you want to lie down? Take a nap?"

"No." His voice is strong, firm. "I need to be alone."

"Okay." I back away. "I'll call you later."

"Kay ... I don't need to be alone for now. I need to be alone, period. I can't be in a relationship or move to New York with you. I need to be here ... with my family."

What? My voice cracks. "Can we ... can we talk about this later?"

"No, Kay. No, we can't." Over the hum of people talking, over the low sympathy songs on Spotify in the background, his voice is loud and clear. *He's* loud and clear—he's done with me. Done with us. Forever.

I hold it together until I stumble out of his house, into mine, up the stairs, and into my bedroom. Only then, when I'm truly alone, do I let myself cry. I let myself fall apart.

He's grieving. He's been holding himself, his mama, his siblings, and his house together by a thread. I know he's said things he doesn't mean ... but he doesn't call. He doesn't toss a pebble at my window. He doesn't smile when he sees me in town, answer my texts, or acknowledge I exist. For three months.

Hearing he got accepted to Sloane Community College makes it clear his plans are here—and mine aren't.

How can he not miss me? He told me I was everything to him. And now ...

If I could stop the dreams and the plans.

If I could stop the hoping, pining, and loving ... stop my heart from aching.

If I could, I'd stop every bit of it.

But I can't.

Moping around in my room every night for months has only made my stomach turn and my eyes dry out—it's hardly been the summer I imagined having.

THIS KIND OF LOVE

Screw this. I'm moving to New York. I'm going to live the life we, no, *I* dreamed about. Deep breath. One thing at a time.

-Pack for Ithaca
-Register for elective classes
-Research a safe running path on campus
-Schedule interviews for waitressing jobs
-Imagine who I'll be a year from now

I'll be better *then*. My pointer and middle finger absentmindedly touch my wrist. Maybe.

"Fuck him." I turn my playlist on and turn the volume *up*. Taylor Swift's "All Too Well" is exactly the energy I need to start moving on.

Clink.

Oh really? Was the music loud enough to finally make him come over? How very much like a rom-com.

Clink.

I talk before I open my window. "Okay, we can talk—Jack? What are you doing?"

Jack's halfway up the tree already. "You didn't answer your phone."

I pick up my cell. "'Hey' is the big message you had to climb my tree for?"

"Yeah." He climbs in the window. "You haven't really been around. I've been worried about you."

I scoff. "Yeah, well, when your brother broke up with me at your dad's funeral, in front of half the town, and stopped returning my texts, I kind of got the message." Eventhough it took me weeks to do so.

Jack puts his hands in his pocket, nervously looking around my room.

"What's going on?" I gripe.

"I wanted you to hear it from me. Well, I wanted you to hear it from Jase, but it doesn't seem like *that's* going to happen. I guess I'd rather you hear it from me than ..."

"Jack, spit it out." I throw my hands on my hips, waiting for this big announcement.

"Jase has a girlfriend." His words are quick, but it doesn't stop the air from whooshing out of my body.

"He what?" I'm unable to take back the vitriol in my tone. My eyebrows are glued to the top of my forehead, and my blood pressure has spiked to a level it refuses to come down from.

Jack hangs his head. "I'm sorry, Kate ... I walked in on them, and I, uh, didn't know."

My muscles go slack. "What do you mean you walked in on them?"

Jack scratches his ear but doesn't answer the question.

My chest starts to ache, and my thoughts spiral out of control. Were they having sex? Does she know about the spot on his neck? The spot that's mine. Did she like his tattoo? Does she think it's cute? The tattoo was his idea—the one that matches mine. Does she know? Does she care? *I can't breathe. I can't breathe.*

Jack's eyebrows draw together, and he reaches for my hands. "Kate, breathe."

I shake my head. I can't.

"Yes, you can. Take a deep breath in and out." His gaze peers into mine. "In and out."

I focus on the kindness in his eyes, the bridge on his nose, the line on his forehead—little details to keep me from falling deeper into panic.

THIS KIND OF LOVE

When the oxygen pulses back through my veins, I realize there's no point in being upset. Jase said he was done with me, with us. His life is his to spend with whoever he wants. It doesn't matter what I say, how I feel—nothing is going to change it. It doesn't matter if it was him throwing pebbles; I am going to New York, anyway.

"Ugh," I groan. If only it were as simple as to choose not to care. Maybe one day it will be.

Jack sits next to me and puts his hand on my knee. "I'm sorry. I didn't want to be the one to tell you." He pauses and removes his hand to take a crumpled-up flyer out of his jeans pocket. "I wanted you to know what you could be walking into here."

He hands me the flyer, and I open it up and roll my eyes. "Sayonara Seniors Night?"

"What?" He looks over at the flyer then turns it over. "No, on the back."

"You're having a party ... Oh." Air catches in my throat when realization dawns on me. Jack is already in college. *He's* not having an end-of-high-school party. *His brother is.*

"Yeah, *oh*," he agrees. "I'm sure my mama would agree this isn't the way to go about anything, but she's out of town this weekend, and even if she wasn't ... she's been letting Jase get away with pretty much anything since ...."

I fold the flyer and put it on my nightstand.

Jack continues, "You're more than welcome to come."

I don't mean to, but I flinch.

He winces. "I didn't mean anything by it. You know you're more than Jase's ex—you're my friend, too. I don't know about you, but I could use a friend these days."

Hearing his words feels like a punch to the gut—both *Jase's ex* and that Jack could use a friend. "I'm sorry," I mutter. "I guess I assumed when Jase was done with me, you guys would be, too."

Jack smiles. "Oh no, you can't get rid of us that easily. You're still an honorary Cole—and if you ever want to be an actual Cole ... there's more than one option."

"Jack!" I shout and cut my hand right to his gut when he winks at me.

He doubles over but laughs. "What? It was funny." When he stands, he smooths out his jeans. "So, you'll come to the party ... for me?"

My eyebrow arch. "Still laying it on a little thick there, *bro*."

Jack raises his hands. "Come as a friend?"

"I'll think about it." I escort him to the window.

"You know, I've always wondered why you and Jase used the tree and window when the door is easier."

"Get it now?"

He shakes his head. "Nah. It's hard to fit your body through a window."

"Bye, Jack." I help him out and close the window, but when he looks back and waves, I don't feel the longing I felt for the other boy next door.

The other Cole.

The one who got away.

No one's home when I head downstairs. I leave a note on the kitchen counter, letting them know I'm next door and I'll be home before curfew. The entire house has been more on edge over the last few months, partially due to the reminder that life is precious and not guaranteed and partially due to college being a few weeks away. Mama has been extra emotional because she's *losing her baby*. Me. A note's the least I can do to try and prevent a meltdown.

Breathe in, breathe out.

Okay.

Oh-kay.

Standing on the front porch, I take several deep breaths. Then, I take a few more. I step aside as recent grads walk in the house with a case of beer in hand.

"Kate?"

My brain's still a little hazy when I look up to see Jack standing in front of me in a pair of jeans and a pullover sweater. "Do you want to come inside?"

Hesitantly, I look over his shoulder and see people filling every square inch of the house. The line up the stairs of girls in short skirts waiting for the bathroom gets longer by the second. The red solo cups thrown throughout the living room make me shudder. There are couples making out in the hallway, but I'm sure there are even more in the bedrooms and bathrooms. I back away. "I'm sorry, Jack. Thanks for inviting me, but this was a mistake. I'm gonna go home."

Jack reaches out to stop me. "Hey, I know this is a lot, but please, please don't go."

I close my eyes. He asked me to come—for him—because he could use a friend, and honestly, couldn't we both?

"Okay."

As soon as we step inside, Jase comes out of the kitchen and turns the corner to the hallway. His solo cup is halfway to his lips when he sees me, too. The entire world freezes as we stare at one another. He blinks and looks away first, and my eyes burn.

"Go talk to him." Jack pushes me toward Jase, but in the time it takes me to consider his suggestion, the world unfreezes, and Jase disappears into the crowd.

I shake my head. "I guess he didn't want to talk to me."

"Come on." Jack rolls his eyes. He grabs my hand and leads me around the corner behind the stairs to Jade's room.

He knocks three times softly, and sure enough, his brother answers, "Yeah?"

"Go on." Jack encourages me, and I enter the room.

"Hey ..." I shift my feet nervously in the doorway.

Jase looks up, blinking in surprise. "Kay?"

"Surprised I found you?"

"What?" His eyebrows crease. "No, I thought you were here with Jack."

I look back and extend my hand toward the door. "I'm not here *with* Jack."

"Oh." He sighs in relief.

"Jack invited me to come as a friend."

"Ah, 'as a friend.'"

"Ugh!" I scream, throwing both arms in the air. "What the hell is the matter with you? First off, I would never—he's like a brother to me—but second, even if it changed and I was 'here with Jack,' it's my damn business since you broke up with me, need I remind you."

Jase hangs his head. "I know."

"You know? That's it?"

Jase stands, heat radiating off him in waves. "What do you mean, that's it? My dad died, Kay. I needed time to heal—alone."

"Oh, okay, and now you're done healing alone, you can heal with another girl like our relationship means nothing to you?"

"My dad died without warning, and you want to move to New York. I can't leave my family behind, and you won't stay. It's kind of the end of the road for us, don't you think?"

"*Why would I think that?* I think you're judging me without talking to me. I would never force you to go to New York, especially after what happened, but it doesn't mean I want to lose you, either. I want to talk to you and be here for you. Let me be here for you."

He scoffs. "Oh, you'll be here for me for what—the next two weeks? Aren't you leaving for Ithaca? Why even wait?"

The tears fall, ignoring the commands I'm giving them to go the hell away or to at least pause until I'm out of this damn house. The house that used to give me love and safety now only brings pain.

The door creaks, and in walks the cheerleading captain with bleached-blonde hair, a perfect smile, and long, tan legs.

"Hey, babe." Lindsay greets Jase but pauses when she sees me. "Oh, hi, Kate. Sorry, I didn't mean to interrupt anything ..." She doesn't make any attempt at walking away. Instead, she plants her feet further into the ground as if she's grown roots. Her hair always looks blown out and perfect, and I hate to admit it, but she looks even more perfect *with him.*

I thought I couldn't breathe before, but nothing has felt like the punch to the gut like this moment is with Jase and Lindsay and seeing our entire relationship blow away like smoke.

The world spins around me. I falter before I can steady my stance and get out of the house and into my own. Seconds after I step foot in my room, a dark shadow looms large in the doorway. Dad's feet are planted firmly into the carpet and his arms are pushing against the frame, knuckles white from the pressure he's applying. His eyes are bloodshot, his face is beet red, and he's foaming at the mouth.

The hair on both arms stand. "Dad?"

"You stupid bitch!"

"*What?*" I blink three times in quick succession.

"You fucking whore! Who do you think you are?"

"Dad, what?" I object.

He screams and trips into the room, catching his fall on my dresser, which he then deliberately flips over onto the floor. The loud thud shakes the house, and Pop barrels up the stairs.

"*Andy!* What are you doing?"

Dad doesn't listen. He slams the door behind him and flips the lock. "You're a liar. I didn't raise you to be a liar and a whore and a runner. You're gonna hide in New York instead of dealing with your problems. Who are you?"

I flinch every time he lunges toward me in his drunken stupor.

"No wonder he ended things with you. No one loves a whore." His glassy gaze stares into mine, but it doesn't connect with his eyes. Almost like he's looking through me, but it doesn't make the words sting less.

I'm vaguely aware of Pop trying to break down the door, but I can't turn my attention there. I just can't. I close my eyes and ask Dad the question I've been wanting to ask him for some time. The question I'm scared to death to know the answer to. "Do you, Dad? Do *you* love me?"

"No." He sneers, and spit falls to the ground by my feet. "I only love your mother."

There are inaudible shouts and cries, but I can't hear anything over the sound of my heart breaking in two. I only know I'm breathing because I can feel each gasp for air pointedly. *Take a deep breath. Keep breathing.*

Even though I asked the question. Even though, deep down, I knew the answer. Feeling it and hearing it are two different things. A child should never have to hear their parent say they don't love them.

One more bang and Pop's in the door, calming Dad down to get him to leave.

Before I can think better of it, I grab a duffle bag, throw random items from my closet and dresser into it, and zip it, while Pop moves Dad to my parents' room. I scurry out of the house, turn Lily's ignition, and back out of the driveway, leaving Sloane and the broken pieces of who I used to be in my rearview mirror.

Chapter 21

Now

It's mid-afternoon by the time I peel my eyes open in my childhood bedroom. I'm holding Hyla, who has forgiven me for leaving her in a stranger's company for the night once I climbed into bed and offered her little spoon. She is not a big cuddler, save for when she can find a warm, sunny spot she can bathe in.

"Hey, baby girl, do you want belly rubs?"

Hyla rolls over onto her back as if she's doing me a favor. Maybe she is.

I glance at my phone. No missed calls. I fire off a quick text to Mama, asking if there's any update on Dad and when visitors will be allowed. I don't know if I can face him, but if something happens and I don't …

I used to think I'd feel relieved with him gone because he couldn't hurt anyone anymore. But now? Now that I know he's been sober and turned his life around? On the other hand, in his grand quest for turning over a new leaf, I haven't been a part of it … he hasn't called. He hasn't asked to speak to me when Mama's reached out. He hasn't hitched a ride with Nana and Pop on their visits up north. My lungs constrict, and I gasp for air, trying to steady myself.

MAMA: "Sounds like it's still gonna be a while."

I exhale. I don't have to figure out a plan right now.

"Hey, Hy?"

Hyla snuggles further in bed.

I pull back the covers and see her looking at me from the corner of her eye, but she doesn't get up until after I've changed into fresh clothes and grabbed my running shoes.

"What do you think, girl?"

From the incessant jumping and tail wagging, I know she's on board. I grab my earbuds right as the doorbell rings. "Hold that thought." I bolt down the stairs and swing open the front door.

Carrie is standing on the porch in a long, black maxi dress, hair pulled up into a messy bun, and arms full of grocery bags.

I step aside to let her in, and she puts the paper bags down to pull me into a tight hug.

I cling to her. "Oh, I've missed you."

"You've been gone far too long."

When she pulls back, I gesture to the bags. "What is all this?"

"Oh, you know, a little something and nothing at the same time."

We head to the kitchen, and she unloads meals into our freezer while I put a large bouquet of lilies in water. I inhale the soft, sweet aroma. "This is so sweet of you, Carrie."

"Oh, this is nothing. Your family was there for me endlessly when I lost Eric."

I avert my gaze.

She points at me. "Including you."

"I don't know how much I was there then ... I stayed away from it all and then left town."

Carrie clicks her tongue. "Oh, sweetie, I know my son pushed you away. Stupid boy."

I glance at the firefly on my wrist: a token of the promise we both made—and broke. "It wasn't *all* him."

She pats my hand. "He's grown up a bit. Listen, all of this to say: life is short. Appreciate the time you have with who you have. They won't be there forever."

"I love you."

"Love you more. Alright, well, I should get going. Tell your mama I'll call her later to check in, okay?"

I nod and walk her to the door, considering her message: *Appreciate the time you have with who you have. They won't be there forever.*

Putting in my earbuds, Hyla and I head out for our run. Hyla's leading the way on what's become our traditional path, making the couple of turns we need to get to Main Street. We take a pit stop past the high school to pick up a few dandelions before continuing.

It's barely three o'clock, and the bar is packed. Jase seems to have made a name for himself, which can be hard to do in a town like Sloane. I'm sure Lindsay was there every step of the way. The jealous pangs are as fresh and strong as they were the day I found out they were a couple.

Hyla and I turn around back and run down the alley right as the bar's back door swings open. Jase hurls a bag of trash into the dumpster and catches us as he turns to the side. His head tilt is cuter than I'd like it to be. He crosses his arms and lets me start.

"Hi." I'm a little breathless. Good start.

"Hi," he echoes.

We stand there, staring at each other, waiting for the other to say something more. Taylor's singing in my ear about forgetting Calvin

Harris existed, and while I can normally relate, standing in front of my ex, I'm having thoughts that are anything but hate or indifference. After six years, I haven't been able to forget about him ... or how important he once was to me. Last night made that abundantly clear.

Hyla barks once and pulls me toward Jase.

Well, this is new.

"Hi to you, too." Jase bends down to pet Hyla.

"Seems like you made quite an impression on my dog," I remark.

Jase smiles from ear to ear and scratches my pup's butt.

"Careful, keep treating her like that and she'll get dog hair all over your black uniform and not think twice about it."

"Oh, that's okay, right girl?" he asks Hyla as she rolls over for belly rubs. Jase complies. "I doubt you came here for me to give all my attention to your dog," he adds hopefully.

Hyla looks at me with puppy dog eyes while getting the belly rubs of her life. Can we keep him?

I shake my head. "We were out for a run."

"Uh huh, and you always run past the front of the bar ... and behind it?"

"Oh, I, uh ..."

"Kay."

I shift my feet, take the buds out of my ears, and pull a bundle of dandelions from my pocket. "I wanted to thank you for taking me to the hospital last night and staying. I know you could have been home with your family instead."

His eyebrows scrunch together in a look I don't recognize.

I hand the flowers to Jase, and the second his hand touches mine, it sends a shock right through me.

He shuts his eyes and inhales. He felt it too. For all that I don't know about him now, I still *know* him. He knows me, too. He understands me in ways no one else does or could.

"Come inside with me?"

Hyla stands, ready to follow him.

I need a minute and move side to side to think.

"Don't overthink it." Jase grins at me. "Come on, I want to show you something." He takes my hand and leads me through the doorway.

My other hand is holding Hyla's leash. "Where are we going?"

"You'll see." His eyes shine.

Hyla's tail wags.

The butterflies in my stomach overpower my logical brain. I follow Jase, and my heart beats quicker in my chest. I shouldn't get attached. It'll only lead to getting hurt again, but I can't help it: I love Jason Cole—*loved. Loved Jason Cole.*

"Hey, Jimmy," he says.

"Boss." Jimmy nods as Jase walks us behind the bar to a latch in the floor.

"Jade's Jimmy?" I eye him a little closer. He's tall, built, and has a buzz cut and caring eyes. *He's cute.*

Jimmy grunts and Jase keeps moving.

On the wall right by the bar is a picture I haven't seen in years—one of us as kids, catching fireflies. "Jase." I point at it in awe.

It clicks: the picture, the name: Firefly Lounge, him always being here, Jimmy calling him 'Boss'—Jase doesn't just work here.

"Jase, is this your bar?" I think back to the first time I stopped in here with Amy. There were signs, and I missed them.

"Yes." He looks back at me.

"No, no, no, let me rephrase. Is this *your* bar?"

"Yes." He points to the liquor license above the photo of us. *Jason Cole.* He swallows. "Although technically, it's *our* bar."

Dazed, I turn to him. "What?"

"Come on." He opens the hatch to reveal a set of steps leading to a wine cellar.

"Oh, I don't think Hyla can go down there …"

Hyla flies down the old wooden steps like she's done it her whole life.

"What were you saying about Hyla?" Jase smirks.

I purse my lips and follow him down. I'm met with an immediate chill from a drop in temperature, but it's not unwelcome. The mostly gray space has a large wine block in a third of the room, with a variety of vintages lined floor to ceiling. The rest is almost apartment-like, with a small couch pulled out into a bed, a desk by a tiny basement window with ample light sneaking in, and a kitchen bar with a humming mini fridge.

"This is not what I expected down here."

Hyla sniffs around, and Jase finds her a bowl for water.

"What did you expect?"

"A bunch of cobwebs, honestly." I laugh. "It's … nice."

"Thank you." He places the flowers on the desk as he walks by. He folds the couch bed back in. "I thought you'd like it."

I sit next to him on the couch. "Ooh, this is even comfy for a throwaway couch."

"Why do you think it's a throwaway couch?"

"It's in a wine cellar … oh my God, do you live here? I'm so sorry."

Jase shakes his head. "You've been to my house."

I narrow my eyes, "Not an answer."

"I don't live here, but sometimes I do stay the night if it gets too late." He pauses. "I'm not with Lindsay, Kay." His voice is a little higher than normal, and his jaw clenches. What isn't he telling me?

"Oh?"

"Oh," he repeats plainly. "In fact, I haven't been with Lindsay in six years ... and not even then, if I'm being honest."

I feel the heat rising to my cheeks. I want to ask him why and what happened, but I'm scared to know the truth.

Jase blinks at me but doesn't say anything.

"What?"

"You don't know?" He studies my face. "You don't know." His voice turns serious.

"Know what?" I raise my eyebrows and cross my arms to fight the sudden chill. Must be from the cellar. The chill sends shivers down my spine. Not the chill in Jase's voice, not that, never that. "You and Lindsay were ..." I can't say it.

He steps closer and stares intently at me, not breaking eye contact. His voice cracks. "When my dad passed, I fell into a deep depression. Lindsay asked me out, and I said yes, because I thought she could distract me from ... everything."

I blink away.

He continues, "We went out a few times, but it didn't mean anything."

I shake my head in disbelief.

"Everyone, including Lindsay, knew I was wrapped up in you. Jack invited you to the party thinking if I saw you, I'd come to my senses. He was partially right. When you left, I ended it, but it was already too late."

Standing, I pace back and forth, trying to process what he's telling me. I run my fingers through my hair. "You let me believe you moved on like that." I snap my fingers together. "Like we meant nothing to each other."

Shoving his hands in his pockets, he sighs. "I was angry and scared. I lost my dad, and you were moving to New York. It doesn't excuse anything, but I was a stupid kid. I was lost and didn't know what to do." Jase's eyes plead with me to believe him.

I try swallowing the lump in my throat. I try to get the night, the whole conversation with Jase and my dad's insults out of my head, but I can't. They're right there, taking up space. *I only love your mother.*

Jase shoves his hands in his pockets and bows his head. "Listen, Kay. I was young and dumb back then, but I've grown up since then. I bought a bar." He gestures around him.

I follow his gaze, taking it in. "You bought a bar. You're practically an adult," I joke.

He snickers. "Well, yes, but I meant I bought a bar to get my life on track. It also reminded me of you. The wine cellar is what sold me on it—it's a safe place to think, write, and be."

"To write?" Why would he get the space to write? Oh, my God. He got it *for me* to write, in a safe place, in Sloane. Jase is several feet away from me, but piecing together his admission hits me like a punch to the gut. "You bought this bar for me?" I blink back the tears starting to form behind my eyes.

"I mean, it's not New York or anything, but yes, I bought it after your dad stopped drinking. I figured he wouldn't want to come in here and see me, and I was hoping he wouldn't want to see me enough to actually stay sober." His voice breaks.

He bought this bar to try and keep my dad sober and keep me safe from his abuse. Of all the beautiful things he's done for me, this is ... this is beyond comprehension. I can't calm my beating heart ... nor do I want to.

I rush to close the gap between us and hop up into his arms, wrapping my legs around his waist. He holds onto me. I'm not thinking about what to say or do next, and he knows it.

"Kay?"

I tie my hands around the back of his neck. "Shut up and kiss me, already."

"Yes, ma'am." He wiggles his eyebrows and closes his lips over mine.

In that moment, every wall I've carefully constructed over the last six years crashes down like they're hit by a tidal wave. All that matters right now is him and me. Us. We'll deal with the rest of it later.

Chapter 22

Now

Clink. Pulling back the covers, I hop out of bed and open the window. Jase is at the base of the Magnolia tree in black joggers and a baseball tee, red roses in tow.

"Hi." He finger waves.

My palms get sweaty. "Hey there."

"Want to join me for a run?"

The wind blows a gentle breeze, and I take in the sweetness of his cologne. "I'd love to. I'll meet you downstairs."

I take the steps two at a time, feeling like a kid heading to a carnival. Opening the front screen, I smile at the boy next door, all grown up.

He bites his lip. "I wasn't sure how you feel about roses, but it's time I up my flower game."

I inhale deeply, getting a whiff of fresh baby's breath in each nostril. "Well, I'm partial to dandelions, but these are beautiful. Thank you. I'll put them in some water."

Hyla runs down the stairs, nearly running him over.

"Hey, girl. I've missed you, too. Is anyone else home?"

"Just us. Amy has one more interview, and everyone else is at the hospital."

"How's he doing? Any word?"

We step into the kitchen, and I shake my head. "Not really. They're capping visitors to limit stress."

"How ironic; they want to limit stress for a man whose excessive drinking and behavior has stressed everyone around him for years."

"Right?" A smile spreads across my face. He gets it. He's *always* gotten it. Jase puts Hyla's leash on, does all of one jumping jack, and shouts, "Race ya!" as he starts running.

"You don't believe in stretching?!" I yell.

"Never did. The best stretch is the run itself." He runs backward and faces me.

"I'm pretty sure that's the exact opposite of what any doctor would say."

"Good thing I'm not a doctor." He's halfway down the street.

I do a few quick stretches, then take off after him and pass him.

"Oh, it's gonna be like that then? It's the perfect fall day. I thought we could go for a nice jog, keeping pace." Jase calls after me.

"Oh no, this is a full-on sprint now. We'll see how well a 'no stretching policy' does for you when you get a Charley horse."

"Come on, that's kind of mean," Jase replies.

I throw my hands up in the air. "You're the one who wanted to run."

"Yeah, because I thought it would be fun. You know, now that I think about it, there are other fun things we could have done ..." His suggestive tone trails off when I look at him, but his gaze studies mine, looking for an opening.

I cross my arms.

"I'm kidding. We're taking this slow." He adjusts his hold on Hyla's leash as we move further down Main Street.

THIS KIND OF LOVE

"Yes. Taking it slow." I shift my gaze down briefly. "I've been thinking ..."

"Oh no," he jokes.

"I owe you an apology."

His eyebrow arches.

"I was a total asshole to you."

"What?"

"You know ... then. For six years, I've held onto things being your fault because it's easier than admitting the truth." I stand still. "I'm as much at fault for everything that went down. I pushed you and ran away. Instead of being here for you, giving you space, and trying to make it work, I doubted you. I left when you needed me."

He paces over to me. "I don't blame you for wanting to leave an abusive situation."

When I avoid his gaze, he places his fingers under my chin and lifts it. We look into each other's eyes.

"I don't blame you. You needed to go, and I needed to stay. It never changed my feelings for you, not ever."

"It's just ... knowing now what I wish I knew then ..."

"Kay, everyone makes mistakes. The only one judging us for them is Hyla."

I look down, and sure enough, there's Hyla, head tilted, waiting for us to get a move on. I roll my eyes and then see something shift across the street in front of the high school. It's almost stuck. "Wait, what is that?"

Jase cocks his head. "I don't know, a cat?"

"It doesn't look like a cat. Come on." We head over closer, but when I realize what it is, Hyla and I pull off to the side of the road.

"Where are you going?"

I point. "It's a turtle."

"Okay ..."

"Can you go help it get across the road?"

He glances from me to the turtle and back again. "Seriously?"

"What?"

"Well, if it's a snapping turtle, it could hurt me." This normally confident and suave man almost sounds ... scared? Of a turtle.

"Jase, it could be run over. Can you please help it?"

"Why can't you help it?" he counters.

Yep, he's scared of the turtle.

I look down at Hyla, who is blissfully unaware of the animal hanging out in the street. "Because I'm trying not to let a certain pup know there's a little creature for her to scare the life out of. "

"Kay Dailey, you have got to stop getting me in hairy situations."

"You'd be our hero. Forever and ever for saving the poor little turtle. Besides, you've gotten me into plenty of trouble yourself."

He sighs. "You better make this worth my while."

"Oh yes, when we get where we're going, I'll make sure you're compensated." I wink, and he puts his hand on his chest.

Hyla seems to have caught on, and she starts to whine. "Oh, sweetie, he'll be right back. He's off to be our hero and save a poor little turtle."

"I'll be back, Hys!" Jase shouts from across the street. "I have to help an animal, even though it could take my arm off."

Hyla wags her tail, acknowledging Jase, and sits with a huge grin on her face.

The turtle whips his head back, and Jase jumps a foot off the ground.

I roll my eyes. "Alright, fine. I'll get it. You stay here with the pup."

He pounces at the chance to take the leash. "Your turn, Dr. Doolittle."

THIS KIND OF LOVE

Picking up a large stick, I tiptoe toward the turtle as he snaps his head again.

"Not as easy as you thought, huh?" Jase scoffs.

I inch the stick closer, and it grabs on. I dash across the street, place the stick and turtle in the field, and back away. "Easy peasy, and we're back on track." I dart down the road.

"Hey!" Jase calls after me. "Play fair."

I laugh and pick up the speed. "Come on, slowpoke."

"Slowpoke?" Jase points his finger to his chest. "Really? Oh, Dailey, you are in for it."

As Jase chases after me, Hyla by his side, I feel the butterflies I caught all those years ago anytime I was anywhere near Jase. My heart is the fullest it's been in years.

We jog for miles through town a couple of times, then a few laps on the field at the high school, spending hours together. It's like I've finally come home.

The clouds cover up the sun, and Jase grabs my hand.

"Where are we going?"

Jase plugs his nose and pokes my shoulder. "I don't know if you've smelled us lately, but I, for one, could use a shower."

I bring my shirt up to my nose and sniff. Jerking away from my tee, I gulp. "You're right. Where is this shower you speak of?"

"I, uh, was thinking my place?" He shoves his hands into his short pockets.

I blink seductively. "Your place, you say? I thought you'd never ask." I pretend to faint, but Jase doesn't look amused.

He picks up Hyla's leash from the grass where we let it fall. She stands at attention, ready to follow her new best friend anywhere. "What do you say, girl? Will you go back to my place without mocking me?"

Hyla wags her tail. *Oh, yes.*

Jase gives me a knowing look.

I start walking off the field. "It's not you, I'll have you know. She's embarrassingly easy to please. I've seen her try to run across traffic for peanut butter ..."

"Tell yourself whatever you need to, Kay." He pauses long enough to scratch behind my girl's ears. "But lucky for Hyla, my peanut butter is always well-stocked."

We're at Jase's house before I know it, and sure enough, his peanut butter options are plentiful—both Skippy and Jif, with crunchy and smooth of each. Jase is scooping a spoonful of Skippy's smooth into a recycled takeout food container, and Hyla's tail is going crazy. She's practically drooling. Get it together, girl. It's just peanut butter.

"Why do you have all this peanut butter?" I take in his kitchen with a marble breakfast bar and countertops, stainless steel stove and fridge, new tile backsplash to match the tile floors, recessed lighting, and floor-to-ceiling windows on the wall leading out to the wrap-around deck which would overlook the sunset.

"You never know who's going to come by," he answers whimsically, like having four different choices of peanut butter is normal in any pantry.

"What do you use it for?" I counter, not letting it go.

He blushes. "I'm trying to make a peanut butter milk stout."

My eyes light up.

"Unfortunately, I can't quite nail the recipe."

"Well, if you ever need a taste tester ..."

Jase chuckles. "Duly noted. Alright, upstairs. Shower's straight ahead. Take any towel out of the closet and use whatever soaps and shampoos you find up there." He places a hand on each of my shoulders and turns me toward the steps.

I linger on the stairs, thinking about what the last few years must have been like for him, here, without me, but when Hyla barks and sells out my location, I bolt up the soft, carpeted stairs, two at a time.

"Find everything okay?" Jase shouts up.

I jump. *Not yet.* "Yup!" I call back and find my way to a hall closet outside the bathroom. I wince and open the door. "Ah, towels." I pull one up to my nose. It smells ever so faintly like flowers and Jase. I hold it close for a minute and hang it over the door since there isn't a towel rack in the bathroom. I step in, turn the tap on, and let the scorching hot water pour down my head, through my hair, onto my shoulders, and continue down my bare back.

It's cleansing—letting the water run its way down. For a few short minutes, I don't have to worry about what's happening at the hospital or what's happening with Jase. I don't have to think about New York or what I'm missing at work. I don't have to know what life will look like when this is all over. I don't have to make decisions that will impact the rest of my life, not right now, anyway. All I have to do is massage shampoo through my hair and rinse it back out. Then, I'll worry about the conditioner and body wash, but one step at a time. I breathe in and out while shampooing, taking note of my breath, and feeling my shoulders relax. I've got this.

Ten minutes later, I step out of the shower to dry off and realize I don't have anything clean to wear. After a few minutes of snooping, I discover an old long-sleeve flannel shirt in Jase's closet, the same one I thought was fun to try on a time or two before he got new clothes and before I outgrew the idea of wearing his shirt with nothing underneath it. I would think better of it now, but all I have are my sweaty running clothes.

I slip his flannel over my head and let my shoulder-length wet hair dry as-is. Tiptoeing down the stairs, dirty clothes in hand, I hear Jase singing along to a song his Echo is playing. He stirs the pot on the stove.

"Wow, something smells good." I step foot onto the tile floor. I peek in the oven to see what he's cooking, and my eyes light up. "Are you making mac and cheese?"

Jase keeps jamming along, then tosses the noodles into the pot when it boils.

"With spirals? But I thought shells were 'the best.'"

"They are!" Jase glances over his shoulder. "... but it's your favorite meal. I might as well make it how you like it."

"It never mattered before." I cross my arms under my chest.

Jase stirs the mac. "Back then, I was a stupid teenage boy who didn't realize I should bend a little to get what I want."

"What is it you want?" I let my voice drop on the last word, huskier than I've let it be in some time.

His head tilts subtly enough that I can tell it got him. Turning slowly, he starts to speak, but when he sees me standing in the middle of the kitchen with his shirt hitting mid-thigh, his mouth drops.

"What were you saying?"

Jase's eyes scan me slowly. "I ... uh ..."

I walk past him to the stove and flip the burner off. "You were about to tell me why you were making spirals."

THIS KIND OF LOVE

I expect him to stall or string words together or *something*, but what I don't expect is his direct, sultry response. "You. I want you, Kay."

The way he draws out my name with his accent, full of want, makes me bolder than I've been in years, the kind of bold I only am when I'm around him. "So, what are you waiting for?"

He's in my arms, and I'm in his, and in the kitchen I've always dreamed we'd dance in one day, he shows me what I've been missing all these years.

It's better than I remember. *He's* better than I remember. My heart beats as the last piece of the wall around it disappears.

"You're a menace." Jase surveys the half-boiled noodles. "I can't *believe* you let perfectly good spirals go to waste."

I pull my shirt back over my head. "Oh, yeah, all me."

"You're the one who turned the stove off." He gestures to the pot.

"Well, yeah, because I didn't want it to over-boil on us."

He drains the noodles into a colander and rinses out the pan. "Guess shells will have to do, then."

I give him a pointed look, and he replies with an oh shucks gesture. "Oh!" I say, pieces all coming together. "You did this on purpose, so we would end up with shells but you're not the bad guy."

"I don't know what you're talking about." Jase turns his attention back to the pot.

"Uh huh. Here I am thinking you've changed, and here you are being the same person you've always been." I'm joking, but when he turns, there's hurt all over his face.

His voice drops. "I would hope I've learned a few things since you left ..."

I wiggle my eyebrows. "I did see firsthand some things you've learned."

He doesn't laugh. He looks at me, blinking, expressionless.

"Jase ..." I step closer. "I didn't mean anything by it. I was joking."

"I know." He bows his head. "I ... I really am sorry for everything that went down between us. I was hurting, but I've spent all this time wishing I hadn't pushed you away."

I purse my lips. "I know." Sighing, I clap my hands together. "I regret leaving."

He smirks. "Quite the pair, aren't we? So, now what?" He holds his breath, waiting for me to say something.

I shake my head. "I don't know."

He offers me an out. "Mac and cheese?"

"Mac and cheese," I reply, taking it.

"Well ..." He approaches the stove again to take in the boiling and pour shells right in. "Brace yourself, Dailey, my Mac and cheese game has improved."

"It couldn't possibly; you're using the same noodles."

"Oh, I know I've always been a big shell guy. It's never gonna change, let's be real, but my cheese game has improved."

"Oh?" I'm intrigued.

"Wait and see."

I laugh and let him have this point. As we sit down to dinner, I admit it is pretty good. We're mid-conversation about each of our days, about a funny story about a customer at the Firefly, and our old days working at the diner together. It's all *easy*. It's easy to talk to him, laugh with him, forget the last six years that happened without him, and imagine what our life could be like right here, with dinners together and Hyla lounging in the living room.

And when we clean up the dishes and kitchen, it's easy to imagine how normal our life could be, just us. When we go lay on the hammock on the wraparound deck and watch the sunset, it's easy to imagine growing old together, and when we fade off to sleep, I can hear Jase say my name and kiss my forehead. I can hear him say goodnight and sweet dreams. I can feel his heartbeat against mine. In the last moments before I fade off to dreamland, I can't help but imagine how this could be forever, if it weren't for my traitorous heart warning me about a life in New York City calling my name.

Chapter 23

Now

"You're hogging the blanket." Jase pulls it back to his side of the sofa.

"Am not." I pull it back, right as he lets go, and the full blue throw ends up in my left hand. "Okay, *now*, I might be hogging the blanket."

He smirks and gives me a kiss. "It's okay. As much as I would love to watch another episode, I really should get to work. My mama's coming in to finalize the menu for a fundraiser she's hosting."

I fold my legs under my butt. "Oh, nice. What's it for?"

Hyla struts over, and Jase leans down to scratch her ears. "She's been trying to find ways to honor my dad since he passed, and she recently found out October is Sudden Cardiac Arrest Awareness month, so we're doing something at the bar to raise money for impacted families."

My mouth parts. "Jase, that's ... so lovely."

He nods. "Yeah, I'm proud of her for channeling her grief into something that'll help other people. We all are."

"I'd love to help with whatever she needs."

"I'll let her know. I'm sure she'd love that. Hear anything from your mama?"

THIS KIND OF LOVE

I flip over my phone from where it's resting on the arm of the sofa and tap it twice. "Nothing."

"You're welcome to stay here and binge *Friends* as long as you'd like, or ... you could come to the bar with me and keep me company?"

"As nice as it sounds." I give him a slow, sweet kiss. "I should get back. Thank you for today."

"Thank *you*. I've missed this. Us."

I smile. "Me too."

When Hyla and I head back to my mama's house, I redirect my thoughts from thinking of this as the new-normal and Sloane as home. My apartment, job, life ... everything is back in New York. My stomach turns. Why does moving back to New York sound less appealing than it did a few weeks ago? When I came down here, it was always for the purpose of a visit, to help Mama through Dad's health crisis, then go back home ... but lately, New York feels further away and less like home.

I no sooner reach my room and settle in to work on a *Case of the Mondays* when the call comes. I answer immediately. "Hey, Mama."

Pop's deep voice on the other end of the phone sends a jolt right through me. "Katie girl. Your dad's asking for you."

He meets my silence with his own, letting me process everything.

I close my eyes. "I'm on my way."

When I get to the hospital, Mama pulls me into a warm embrace. She doesn't say anything. She doesn't have to. It opens the floodgates, anyway.

"Oh, Mama. I hate this. I hate that he did this." I don't disguise the anger in my voice.

She closes her eyes, but to her credit, she doesn't leave.

"I hate that he told everyone who would listen he was a family man my entire childhood, but he missed every school play, track and field event, and family dinner because he couldn't stay awake to hear how my day was. I hate that he's guilted good people into caring about him when he doesn't care back. I hate how he treated you, how he thought you were his, regardless of the shit he put you through. I hate that he pushed me away. I hate that I left. I missed out on time with everyone I love because I let the bully win."

I sniffle and fall forward, head in my hands, resting on my lap. I hate him, but I hate myself more for letting him win and change the course of my life.

While I'm wallowing in self-pity, I hear two sets of feet approach: Nana and Pop.

Nana places a kiss on my forehead. "You may have been louder than you meant to be, Katie girl."

I hang my head further. Oh God.

Nana continues, "But for what it's worth, I think he needed to hear it. I also think you need to tell him directly."

I look up at Nana, completely drained. "I don't think I can. I don't think I can see him."

Mama pats my back and places a strand of my hair behind my ear. "You are a strong, independent woman, Kate Elizabeth, and you can do this. If you don't want to talk to him, that's okay, too. You don't have to do anything you aren't comfortable doing. It doesn't make you any less strong to walk away or head back to New York. Do you hear me?"

"Yes, ma'am." I stand.

"Do you want me to come with you?" Mama asks.

I shake my head. Even though on my walk to Dad's room, the only thought going through my mind is how I'd rather be doing anything else, anywhere else, than this, here. The closer I get, the louder the monitors beep, and while I'm vaguely aware of them, I'm more conscious of my sweaty palms and my stomach flipping over in dread.

A bubbly nurse comes out of Dad's room with a laptop. She pulls the courtesy curtain closed and smiles when she spots me. "Hello there. Can I help you find the right room?"

"I'm—um—looking for Andy Dailey," I whisper.

"Oh yes, you're in the right place. You must be Kate?" she guesses, dimples on display.

I swallow.

"Your dad's been asking for you. He'll be happy you've made it."

The nurse disappears down the hallway and leaves me standing outside of Dad's room under a wave of emotions. *He's been asking for you.* Why, so he could tell me what a failure and disappointment I am? Been there, done that. What a pathetic piece of—I pull back the curtain and gulp.

"Kate?" Dad puts the pudding cup and spoon in his hands down on the tray table next to the bed. "Is it really you?" His voice cracks. He coughs, and it's like he's hacking up a lung. His whole, frail body moves with it. He must have lost fifty pounds or more since I last saw him. His hair went from salt and pepper to all salt, and it's receding. If I passed him today, out on the streets, walking around, living life, I wouldn't recognize him. The man in the hospital bed in front of me, hooked up to three different monitors, is my father—and I wouldn't even know it if the chart didn't say it was him.

The thought hits me like a ton of bricks, and the tears come crashing down. I've spent six years thinking about this moment. Would it happen? Would I ever see him again? What would happen if I did? While most of the scenarios I've played out in my head involve me *never* seeing this man ever again ... some part of me, deep down, let myself think about it. *The* scenario always ended up the same way: me yelling and screaming at him, strong enough to give him a piece of my mind. I would leave because it was my choice. I would tell him off, and I would go back to living my quiet, peaceful life. I didn't consider a situation where it wouldn't be true. I never thought it would be possible to see my dad again, after all this time, after all the pain he caused, and *not* let him have it, but here we are. Tears. Actual waterworks. While my brain says to stop, shut them off, be stronger than that ... I can't.

I take a seat, but the sobs don't stop. Jase swore he would protect me, and he didn't, and it *stung*, but it didn't hurt as bad as hearing "I don't love you" come from the one man who always should have. My heart is breaking all over again as I replay the scene and his words over and over again in my heart. *You fucking whore. You're a liar. I only love your mama.*

"I know you hate me." Dad finally breaks his silence.

I sniffle through the aches. "Yes."

"I hate me, too," he admits, tears free-falling onto his hospital gown.

Chapter 24
Then: Five Years Ago

I'm putting away groceries when my phone vibrates on the counter. Shuffling the chicken to my right hand, I shift my phone to my left ear and push play. "Hey, Nana."

"Morning, Katie girl," she says. I can tell she's on speaker.

"I was just about to call you. What time are y'all getting here?" I put the chicken in the fridge and grab the strawberries.

"Slight change of plans." Nana's voice drops.

I let go of the strawberries. "Is everything okay?"

"Well ..."

Pop interrupts. "It's fine, sweetie, all good. We need to postpone a bit, is all."

A loudspeaker echoes in the background, the words indistinct. Nana whispers she'll call me back.

Despite the rushed tone and the change of plans, the thing I get held up on is Pop saying it's fine. If it *was* fine, he would've said everything's 'miserable as usual' in his normal cheerful way ...

A nagging feeling lingers through the night, especially when Nana doesn't call back, my gut pushing me to uncover what's going on. Where are they? What's happening? Why is there a loudspeaker?

I try calling Mama to see if she'll tell me anything but it goes straight to voicemail.

Something's *off*.

I want to be there with them, but I can't. I can't risk seeing my dad and having him yell, scream, and carry on.

I can't see Jase and Lindsay. It'd be too much. I still think about him. Them. What their life must be like. Is it everything they've always wanted? Does he ever think about me? Or were we always destined to be a thousand miles apart?

By three a.m., I can't take it anymore. I start Lily's engine, but I can't put her into drive. What would I even do in Sloane? Would I head right to Sloane Memorial and wander through prison-like walls with grimy lights until I find a hospital bed with Pop's name on it? What if I see Dad or Jase instead? Would it be worth the drive, worth the heartache?

I *can't*.

I dial Nana, and she picks up instantly. "Katie girl!" she feigns excitement, but it's there, the speaker in the background, again.

"Hey, Nan. Wanted to check in."

"Oh, we're good, sweetie. Nothing to worry about. Can I give you a call back, though?"

"Sure." There *is* something to worry about. I can feel it in my bones. She doesn't want to tell me.

I try Mama again. This time, she picks up.

"Hey, Kate, I can't really talk right now. Can I call you back?"

"Mama...what's going on with Pop? I know something's wrong."

She sighs. "Hold on." A loud door closes on the other end of the phone. There are footsteps before she says, "Okay. Please don't worry. It'll all be fine. Your granddaddy was diagnosed with liver cancer. He's been going to treatments, and everything's been looking good. He fell walking around Walmart yesterday. He's with a doctor to make sure he's okay."

I barely hear what she says after *cancer*. Pop, who's always been larger than life, who's been here for every birthday, Christmas, and moved in to help wrangle Dad. Who's here to help him?

"Kate?" Mama asks, but I hang up.

The lump in my throat hardens, but I don't let the tears fall, go back inside, or answer when Mama or Nana try to reach me. Answering would make it real, and it can't be real. It can't be. He's the strongest person I know, the only man remaining in my life.

The one who stayed.

This was all a dream. It didn't happen. I didn't go. I didn't hear. He's fine.

When Nana and Pop come visit a few weeks later, I keep up the charade until I can convince myself it was never real at all.

Chapter 25

Now

Four knuckles rap against the door. "Hey girlfriend, you ready for dinner?"

I don't answer.

Amy knocks again. "Kate?"

I want to reply, but a mix of tears and snot erupt from my face, and I reach for a tissue.

She opens the door and rushes over to me. "Hey ... what happened?"

I grab another tissue and sob.

Amy kneels beside my bed and grabs my hands. "Did Jase do something?"

I shake my head. "N ... no."

"Is it your dad?" She rubs comforting circles on the back of my hand.

I close my eyes.

"Okay, I'm coming in. Scoot over."

I wiggle my legs and butt a few inches to the right, and Amy climbs in next to me. "Want to talk about it?"

"He's awake."

"Did you see him?"

"Mhmm."

She purses her lips. "Did you say anything?"

I move my head from side to side.

"Did you want to?"

"Yes ... and no. I don't know."

Amy wraps her right arm around me. "Have I ever told you my mom left my dad for my brother's best friend?"

"What?" My mouth drops open as I stare at my best friend.

She winces. "Oh yeah. They hooked up at my brother's wedding ... talk about awkward. All that to say, I get how complicated family can be."

I squeeze her hand.

"And, with the help of some good old-fashioned therapy, your girl made it through."

"I'm glad you did." I pause. "Think you could recommend someone?"

Amy bumps my shoulder. "Of course. Everyone could use a Martha."

"Everyone could use an Amy, too."

I yawn, and Amy moves the covers back to step out of bed. "Love you, girlfriend. Try and get some rest."

She's barely out the door before my cried-out frame falls into an empty, dreamless sleep.

After a few days of steady recovery, the hospital schedules Dad's discharge to a home healthcare program. While I can't predict the weather, I would've bet anything there would be thunder and lightning the second he steps foot in the house. Some things you feel deep in your gut. The sky lets loose as soon as the front door swings open.

"Kate! Amy! Can you give me a hand?" Mama calls up the stairs.

"I can help, Liz." Nana rushes in front of us to run down the staircase.

Mama and Pop struggle to get Dad in the house with his wheelchair. Our little deck and awning do little to shield the rain once it pelts sideways.

I freeze in place. For a few weeks, it felt less like hell and more like Mama's. Now that he's back ...

Amy and Nana lift the chair, and Mama helps Dad get comfortable. "How's that feel?"

"Oh, you know, miserable as usual," he quips.

I snap, "Don't."

"Kate," my mother chides.

"I'm sorry, Mama. I just ... need some time." I backpedal up the stairs as memories creep into my brain like Halloween nightmares: Dad whacking a glass out of my hand to have it shatter on the cold, hard ground; my jaw stiffening in defiance as he slams the front door time and time again; his Cheshire cat smile haunting my nights; his sneer; how he said only loves my mama.

My whole life, he's been an emotionally abusive alcoholic. It doesn't change overnight. No matter how many people he's fooled into believing him, he hasn't fooled me.

There's a light tap on my door, and I say, "Go away," expecting it to be Mama or Amy.

To my surprise, I hear a whispered, "Katie girl, it's me." I suck in my breath. I've never been able to say no to Nana, which is how Amy and I ended up in Sloane in the first place.

THIS KIND OF LOVE

She knocks again, then sticks her head in. "Can I come in?"

"Sure."

Nana smiles and sits on the floor, patting the carpet next to her. "You want to talk about it?"

I shake my head. *No.*

"Okay. Mind listening to me then?"

I lean my head against her shoulder. "How are you doing with all of this, Nana?"

"If I say I'm 'miserable as usual,' would you smack me, too?"

"I didn't smack him," I argue.

"I know, sweet girl, but I wouldn't blame you if you did ..." Point made, she's mad, too. "You know, I didn't think I was going to survive when I went through this with your pop."

I scrunch my eyebrows together and pull my head off her shoulder. "Dad's drinking?"

Her voice droops. "Your grandfather's."

"Pop doesn't have a drinking problem," I object.

"Not now, but he did for quite a while," Nana says. "It nearly broke me. It did break your father."

"What?" I try reconciling what she's saying with the calm, gentile man I know. The man who has been here for every event in my life, big and small. The man who has held me, lied for me, protected me ... loved me. The man who has been every bit the father my dad refused to be.

"Katie girl, your pop wasn't always the person he is now. For a long time, he had an extensive problem. He refused rehab, therapy, and me. He saw whiskey as a solution, not a problem."

"Oh, Nan. I'm sorry." I put my hands on hers, and she squeezes mine.

"I know, baby. I know. He eventually got help, but it took him getting arrested on your dad's birthday for him to realize he even had a problem."

"Pop got arrested?" *How many secrets does this family have?*

She nods. "He got a DUI, and he swore that was it, the end of it. It was, but the damage was already done, physically, mentally, and emotionally. It took me a lot of years to forgive him. I don't think your dad ever did." She sniffles and uses her sleeve to dry the falling tears.

I study Nana's face. "How could you ... forgive him, I mean?"

She blinks through the tears. "Because I loved him—still do, you know, and the things he said and did were the disease. It took a long time. Len spent a lot of time in rehab before he transitioned to AA. Hell, he's still in AA. I drive by sometimes to make sure."

"But what—why didn't you tell me? How come everyone in this family has kept secrets from me? Did you think I couldn't handle it ... any of it?"

Nana brings her knees up and rests her head against them in a posture I've done a thousand times before when I don't feel safe or when I feel like the world around me is crashing down. "That's not it. You needed to leave, Kate. You needed to get away from your daddy like you need air to breathe. Nothing was going to stop you, and we sure as hell weren't going to try and guilt you into staying."

I look down, ashamed of how selfish I've been. I didn't know Pop was a recovering alcoholic. How could my family think I wouldn't put my interests aside to be here for them through it all.

"I'm sorry, Nana."

"Sweetie, listen. We were living on autopilot for way too long. You leaving was the swift kick in the butt we all needed to get our shit in gear, so don't you ever be sorry. You hear me?"

I nod.

We stay in this moment for a while before I whisper something I swore to myself I would never admit to anyone. "I almost came back ... when he got sick."

"I know." She smiles knowingly.

"How, Nana?"

She pats my knee, stands, and moves toward the door. "Oh, sweetie, Lily's old engine damn near knocked through the phone."

She knew, and she didn't call me on it.

"Hey Nan ... I love you."

"I love you, sweet girl." She pauses. "You should tell him. Anger and resentment is a burden you shouldn't have to carry after all these years. Let it out. Lighten the load."

With Nana's encouragement and Mama's pleading, I find myself at St. John's church four towns over with Dad, impatiently waiting for an AA meeting to start. When the leader welcomes the group, I bolt, flinging open pearly white doors in my wake.

"Kate! Wait, please." The last part comes out as a desperate plea. I can't stop. It's like my feet are programmed to walk right to the car. I don't know what I was expecting, but it sure as hell wasn't him at the front of the parishioner room out of his wheelchair, standing with a wooden cane, running the meeting like he has his shit together. Like he isn't trying to fool his family with his 'recovery.' Whipping around, I let the rain hit my face in all its fury. Drops quickly fall to the ground and ricochet back up.

"Kate," Dad says again.

I can't tell if it's tears or a side effect of the downpour we are stuck in.

"What?" I'm exasperated.

"I thought you'd be proud of me." His voice wobbles as he speaks, but all it does is harden my glare.

Spitting, I reply, "You thought I'd be *proud* of you? I'm happy you think you've gotten your life together. If you're not fooling anyone, and you've really overcome your addiction, then I'm happy for you."

He nods as I unload a lifetime of baggage.

"But I don't forgive you. The things you said and the damage you caused are reprehensible."

"Kate—" he pleads.

I put my hand up. "Don't."

I drop into the driver's seat and slam my steering wheel three times in a row. When I pause, he's still there, studying me through the windshield, eyes guarded, almost like he's seeing me for the first time.

I hesitate, then unlock and push open the passenger side door.

Dad slides in wordlessly, the rain sticking his clothes to his frail frame. It takes all his body weight to get the door to shut. He closes his eyes and sniffles. "Kate, I fucked up." He inhales, and his whole chest moves with his breath. "I fucked up everything for a long time for everyone I love, and I'm sorry. You deserve better. Your mama deserves better. Your nana and pop deserve better. Hell, *I* deserve better than that version of me."

I don't say anything, just listen and process.

"I was angry at my pop forever. I didn't understand how he could let alcohol come before our family. I didn't understand until I did it, too …

but at the time, I didn't think I had a problem. I need you to understand that. I blacked out a lot—I don't think I can remember a full day of your entire childhood, only pieces here and there." He cries and brings his hand to his eyes. "I honestly thought we had a good life until it hit me one day, and I stopped. Your mama, bless her heart, helped me get help, and I—" Another sniffle. "I'm ashamed."

I close my eyes and exhale. "You ... called me a whore. You kicked ... me out of the house. You told me ... you told me you didn't love me."

Dad weeps. "I don't remember that. Oh my God, I'm so sorry. It isn't true."

I sit in silence.

"Kate, please tell me you don't believe any of it. I never, *ever*, would have said it sober. It's not true."

He puts his hand on mine, and I flinch and look away.

"Oh, I feel like a monster."

"You are," I reply coldly.

He runs his hands through his hair. "No. I'm not that person anymore."

"I wish I could believe that." I wipe away the tears as they fall.

"Let me prove it to you. It's not going to happen overnight, but please let me try. What do you say?"

I gulp. "I don't know."

"Okay." He pats my hand before opening the door. "'I don't know' isn't no. I'll take it and prove it to you."

As he heads back into his meeting, I can't control the cackle from escaping.

Turning back around, Dad asks cautiously, "What's ... what's funny?"

I run my hands through my hair. "It's not funny, but it's ... you know, this is probably the only time we've had a sober conversation."

His face falls. "I hope it's not the last."

He turns around and waves, and I pull out. While there's a long way to go, and I sure as hell don't forgive him or forget what he said or did my whole life, '*I don't know' isn't no.*

Though, it isn't yes, either.

Chapter 26

Now

"What did he say?" Jase spins a small rock in his hand.

I toss my pebble into the lake, watching it skip five times before it disappears. I click my tongue. "He said he feels like a monster, and he doesn't remember any of it."

"Do you believe him?" Jase flicks his wrist, letting the rock go wild. Seven skips.

"Nice." I admire the ripples his pebble causes in the water. "I don't know. Kind of. It was weird seeing him sober. When my mama said he hadn't been drinking, it was kind of like sure, he's in the hospital, but seeing him leading a meeting ..."

Jase gives me space to process my thoughts.

"It was weird. It made me angry. I don't know. He never cared to get sober for me or Mama. Your dad passed, and Pop thought it would be a wake-up call about how precious life can be. Instead, he spiraled. I left, and he never called. I've spent all these years feeling unworthy of love. I've been angry. *Hurt*."

"Kay." Jase steps forward. He takes my hand and lifts my chin with his other hand. "Listen to me. You are worthy of love. You are worthy, and you are loved. Okay?"

I lower my head.

"Your dad was drunk the entire time you lived at home. It's going to take some time to adjust. It's okay to doubt him and distrust him. It doesn't happen overnight."

"I don't forgive him," I mumble.

"You don't have to." He takes off his jacket, wraps it around my shoulders, and we sit on the cold ground, Jase's jacket and arms around me.

As we sit together in our spot, I'm reminded of how *nice* it is to be here with him. When I'm going through it, and when I'm not.

I can't give up what I've built in New York. I've worked too hard to build my life, my career, and he can't come with me. He built his life here, and even though this moment isn't enough, it needs to be. I squeeze him tighter, and when he puts his head on mine, I know he knows.

Clink.

Hyla stretches, then sits with her tail wagging, waiting for Jase to pop in.

He doesn't disappoint. As soon as I open the window, he hands me a coffee carrier with two cups and a dog bone secured, before tossing his legs in.

Straightening, he leans in for a quick kiss before bending to greet Hyla. "Good morning, baby dog."

In a short time, Hyla has gotten used to a certain kind of life—a spoiled one.

"How's my girl?" Jase smiles up at me, hands still scratching behind Hy's ears.

I take a long sip of my vanilla latte. "Mmm, much better now. How'd you even climb up here with a coffee carrier?"

"Branches are my friends." His attention shifts to my bed, bag wide open, clothes thrown about. "What's going on?"

I smile. "Oh, you know, packing."

"So soon?" Jase tries to mask his disappointment by drinking some of his coffee.

I'd bet money it's black. I avert his gaze and answer casually. "Kind of one too many Daileys in this house now."

"You could stay with me," Jase blurts out. He blinks like the offer even surprised him.

"Very sweet offer, but I need to head back home."

"New York isn't home, Kay, and you know it. It doesn't make you feel like Sloane does. I know it. I can feel it." He puts his coffee down on my desk and steps closer.

I take a slight step backward. "Jase."

"Kay, please stay."

"I can't. You know I can't. My whole life is in New York." I turn away, but he takes hold of my hand.

"But I'm here." The crack in his voice almost breaks me.

"Jase, I ..."

The knock on the door jolts me out of this moment. "Kate, we should hit the road so—Oh, hey, Jase."

"Ame, can you give us a few minutes?"

"Yes, of course. I'll meet you downstairs." She steps out.

I turn around, but he's already gone, and it's like a dumbbell set was placed on my chest. "Bye, Jase," I whisper into the silence and blink the tears away.

Hyla's tail falls.

Me too, girl. Me too.

As Amy and I pack up the car a few minutes later, Mama preps sandwiches for the road.

Nana and Pop hug us goodbye, and Dad waves by the door, letting me tell him what I'm ready for.

I wave back and hug Mama.

"Ooh, I love you, sweetie," Mama coos in my ear.

"I love you, too, Mama." I squeeze, and she does too.

"Don't let it be six years before you come back, okay?"

"Okay."

"Drive safely," she calls.

We hop in the car, and this time, when we pull out of the driveway, a gray, cloudy smoke clears from my lungs, and the thought of coming back doesn't feel as strange ... leaving does. My heart starts to crack the further we get out of Sloane, and by the time we get back to New York, I'm left with pieces. I miss him. I miss them.

But this is my life. This is the life I've chosen for myself. I love my life.

I loved my life.

Then.

THIS KIND OF LOVE

Before I went down there and messed with everything I'd built over the last six years.

The first week back is a blur of Starbucks lines and meetings, catching up and making small talk, avoiding Lucy, watching Amy and Leo flirt shamelessly and get awfully close to becoming *something*, just like Nick and Barista Betty at what's now *their* Starbucks. It's like the days pass around me, and I'm *stuck*.

I think about him ... and them. I want to reach out, but I know it'll make the transition back to my real life harder. Instead, I put on stockings (update: they're still evil) and heels, and I paste a smile on my face in every approval meeting. I review Amy's Reese cover story and sigh at how perfect it is because, of course, she absolutely killed it. I volunteer for more articles than normal for the February issue. Throwing myself into my work got me through the pain the first time; I can do it again.

Twisting my key in my apartment door, Hyla's collar jingles as she rushes to greet me. I give her pets and know she will help me through this. Hyla and therapy. I open my laptop and log into Zoom, ready for my first session with Gina, who comes highly recommended by Amy's therapist. As we talk, I find myself nodding along and adding in small pleasantries but not sharing a single thought deeper than I would share with strangers on my blog.

By the time the session is over, Hyla's retreated to the bedroom, ready for *Friends* re-runs and a treat as I dig into *another* pint of Half-Baked. Two pints haven't helped, but I have a good feeling about the third one.

My phone buzzes right as I put on "The One with Unagi," and my heart skips a beat as I check hopefully. It's not him. It's never him.

"Ugh." I flip back the covers and bring the pint back to the freezer, dropping the spoon in the sink. Sighing, I steady myself on the counters and take a few deep breaths. Catching a glimpse of the cabinets out of the corner of my eye takes me back to my dream cabinets, in my dream kitchen, of my dream house, with my dream guy.

It brings me to my knees.

He's not here. He hasn't called. I let him walk away. I ran back to New York without him. I let him go *again*, and he left *again*. The tears come before I can stop them. They flood my face until I fall asleep on the kitchen floor for the second time in a month. This time, the exhaustion holds me through until the harsh morning light.

My phone vibrates on the tile floor. "Hey, Ame."

"Hey. I'm gonna be there in a sec. Can you buzz me in?"

I sigh, staring down at the ice cream stain on the front of the work shirt I wore yesterday that I never changed out of. "Where's your key?"

"Buried. Be there in five."

Wetting the bottom of my shirt, I try dabbing and rubbing the stain out, but it doesn't look like it's going anywhere. Giving up, I push the button to let Amy in.

The knock on my door makes me jump. She hasn't knocked in ... ever. "It's open!"

She knocks again. *What the hell?*

I open the door as I say, "What's gotten into—oh. Hi."

"Hi," Jase says breathlessly. He's standing there in front of me, eyes wilder than I've ever seen them.

"What are you doing here?" I check behind him for Amy.

"She's not coming, Kay."

"What?"

"Amy called for me."

Hyla rushes to him, her tail wagging more than it has since we left Sloane.

I blink furiously, willing the sleepiness out of my eyes. "What're you doing here?"

"I lost you once. I'm not going to do it again."

I shake my head, trying to wake up if this really is a dream. I can't keep torturing myself with thoughts of Jase in New York.

Jase steps forward into the apartment. It feels a lot smaller with his big frame standing inside. He sets a corsage down on my counter.

"What are you doing?"

"I'm here to bring you home."

"Jase—"

He holds his hand up to stop me. "If you don't want to move back full time, I get it, and I won't push you, but then I'm either moving here or we're doing long distance. I can't do life without you. I refuse."

I put my hands on my hips. "You refuse? What if I say no?"

He swallows. "Then will you at least be my date to the SCAA fundraiser this weekend?"

I gesture to the corsage. "I'll do anything for nice flowers."

"I should've brought more with me."

I roll my eyes.

He puts his hands on either side of my face. "If your life is here, I'll come here."

Placing my hands over his hands, I squeeze.

"I love you, Kay. I've always loved you. Even after six years, it didn't go away. It just grew stronger."

"Yes." I interrupt.

"Yes, what?" He leans closer to me.

"Yes, I'll at least go to the SCAA fundraiser with you."

He barely lets me get the words out before he leans his head down. "And then?"

"And then, we'll see." As his lips close over mine, I know this is exactly where I'm supposed to be: safe and with Jase.

Chapter 27

Now

The fundraiser begins right at sundown with a slideshow video from the American Heart Association sharing the importance of knowing what sudden cardiac arrest can look like, helpful resources, and how to get CPR certified.

For a town as chaotic as Sloane, it can be hard to capture adequate attention to command a room, but Carrie does it with ease. When she walks to the microphone, a hush falls on the room. "Hello. Thank you all for joining us this evening. My name is Carrie Cole, and I lost my husband, Eric, six years ago after he suffered a cardiac arrest while driving. One day, he was healthy—young, active, no history of heart disease, and then the next, he wasn't here anymore." She sniffles.

Jade nods to encourage her mama to keep going.

"It's taken me a long time to grieve his passing—I don't know that I'll ever be done grieving if I'm being honest. We were together for twenty-five years. Twenty-five years, can you believe it? We had three beautiful children together. When he passed, I was lost. We all were in different ways. Grief isn't linear. It isn't logical. And it certainly isn't the same for everyone. It took me a while to realize that each of our reactions was normal and that we each needed different things, even if we didn't get it at the time."

I didn't get it then, either, but I do now. Jade tried to find what her parents had with the wrong partner, Jack ran to the military, and Jase pushed me away—they did all of this because it was safer than getting hurt again. It's always safer to run than risk getting hurt again.

Jase reaches for my hand and brings it to his lips. *We're not running again.*

Carrie continues, "We were so focused on what we *lost* that it took us a long time to realize Eric was still with us in different ways. He's in every recipe I make ... I mean, honestly, he is. He wrote notes on each recipe in our cookbook, so I can't screw anything up."

This elicits some chuckles.

"He gave Jade the courage to stand up for herself and what she deserves."

Jade smiles at Jimmy. He winks back.

"He gave Jack his love of the Peace Corps, and he taught Jase to catch fireflies, which he still does from time to time. He's all around us, and if he had one thing to say, it'd be that life is too short. Say what you need to say, don't hold anything in or back, tell your loved ones what they mean to you with your whole being, take care of yourself, and take care of each other, even when it's not easy. Especially, when it's not easy. Thank you."

The room erupts in applause. There isn't a dry eye in the house when Carrie steps away from the podium.

Dad wheels over to me. "Hey, Kate, can I talk to you for a few minutes?"

Jase eyes me. "You okay?"

I nod. I'll be fine. "Sure. Let's go sit down."

THIS KIND OF LOVE

He parks at a nearby table. "I'm glad you're here. It's great to see you."

"A few months ago, I couldn't imagine us having this conversation, or any conversation, to be honest."

He lowers his head. "Me either."

"I've been thinking a lot about the last few times I've seen you, actually, and Carrie's right about one thing: life is way too short. If lightning came down and struck us tomorrow, I wouldn't want our relationship to end like that."

"Me either," he cries. "I love you, Kate."

I nod but don't say anything back.

He continues, "You and your mama are everything to me. I'm sorry for all the years I didn't say it ... or said the opposite. I'd love the chance to prove how much you mean to me now."

I gulp. "I'm not sure I can forgive you or trust you to be honest., If I said otherwise, it'd be a lie. Maybe one day that will change."

His shoulders sag.

"In the meantime, I'm choosing to let go of the anger and resentment. I've held onto them for a long time, and it's been eating me inside. I can't do that anymore. I need to be at peace with knowing we'll never get back the time we lost, and you'll never be who I needed you to be growing up—but I hope, in the future, you will be."

He places his hand on mine, and I let him.

Jase strolls over and tilts his head. "Everything okay?"

A heavy weight dissipates from my chest, and I sigh. "Surprisingly, yes. Letting go of what I can't control and working on what I can."

He places a gentle kiss on my forehead and sits down next to me. "I'm proud of you."

I lean into him and focus on the steady beat of his heart. I could get used to this.

Before we leave Sloane, Jase nudges my shoulder. "Hey, Kay, I have something for you."

I shift my gaze up to his eyes. "What's that?"

Standing, he wiggles his hips, like he would do as a teasing teen. "You'll see." Ushering me outside, Jase hands me a jar. "Come on."

I smile and follow him into the woods, right to our spot. It's just as beautiful as it's always been, with its calm water, deep dark sky above with a flash every so often from the fireflies that surround us.

I catch one in my jar, and when I turn around to show Jase, he's on one knee with a diamond ring.

My eyes fill.

"Kate Elizabeth Dailey, I've loved you since I was six years old, and I promise I'll love you every day from now until forever. Will you marry me?"

A lightning bug lands on the ring. A sign if I've ever seen one.

"Jason Everett Cole, my mama's known you were trouble since we were six years old."

He smiles. "Is that a yes?"

"It's a yes."

I guess you can still meet the guy next door, fall in love, and live happily ever after, after all.

Epilogue
One Year Later

"Okay," Jase huffs. "I think this is it." He places the last of the moving boxes on the laminate floor.

"It's a good thing we got a bigger place," I tease, eyeing up the mounds of overflowing boxes.

Jase raises his hands. "Hey, don't look at me. Hyla's stuff takes up the entire kitchen."

Hyla smiles as if pleased with herself.

I shrug. "Well, to her credit, New York real estate is a hot commodity, so she might as well claim her spot."

"You're not kidding," Jase replies.

I shuffle toward him. "Do you ever miss it?"

He arches a brow. "Sloane?"

"Mhm."

"What's to miss? I still co-own the bar and get to do the art, branding, and fun stuff from the comfort of my home with a killer view, I might add, while my best friend does a hell of a job managing the day-to-day on-site. I couldn't have made a better decision for Firefly than having Jimmy as my business partner."

"And he's an even better life partner for Jade," I chime in. "I ... uh, just want to make sure you're happy here, that's all."

He lifts my chin and places a soft kiss on my lips. "Kay, I'm *only* happy where you are. New York, Sloane, anywhere in between—none of it matters without you."

"Promise?" I lift my pinkie.

He intertwines his pinkie with mine. "Always."

"Speaking of happy." Jase smirks as he pulls our first newspaper out of the back pocket of his jeans, unfolded to Engagement Announcements. "You'll never guess what I saw."

I reach for it and smile when Nick and Barista Betty are pictured front and center. She's in a knee-length white sundress, and he's in a suit. They're wrapped in each other's arms and grinning in a way you only do when you've found *The One*. "Well, would you look at that. Love is in the air."

"Knock, knock, the unpacking committee is here," Amy announces as she enters our new apartment, pizza in hand. Her boyfriend, Leo, is right on her heels. "Oh gosh, what did we walk in on?" Amy attempts to shield her eyes with pizza.

I let go of Jase. "Nothing, Ame. Just making sure my husband still loves me after a year in New York."

Amy all but drops the pizza on the counter. "He better. You're a catch."

Jase chuckles. "Trust me, I'm never letting Kay go again."

"Good. Hey, Leo, do you still have their housewarming present?"

Leo pulls a wine bag out from behind his back. "I do."

I raise my brow and accept the gift. Pulling a bottle out of the bag, I gasp. "Oh my God."

"What?" Jase peers over my shoulder. "Oh, you guys, it's perfect."

Amy blushes. "We had the label custom-made."

I can't stop staring at the intricately designed label with a wedding picture of Jase and me in our gown and tux chasing fireflies down at our spot in Sloane. In a picturesque font, it reads:

Kay-Scato: For nights you never want to end.

I hug the bottle to my chest. "I'm going to save this forever."

"Well," Leo says. "Then, it's a good thing we brought more."

Amy steps into the hallway and sashays back with three more bottles and a corkscrew.

"You two are ridiculous," I quip.

"But you love us. Now, which box has glassware?"

Jase escorts Amy to the kitchen as there's a thunderous thump in the hallway.

What the hell?

Voices of varying volumes leak in through the gap in the door.

I tiptoe to the peephole to check out what's going on. "What the—"

Nana, Pop, Jade, and Jimmy arguing in the hallway was *not* on my bingo card.

When I open the door, they hush and throw their arms around me, so I'm enveloped by a large group hug.

"What are you guys doing here?"

"Well," Jade steps out of the embrace. "We couldn't get in our normal summer trip since y'all were too busy packing and Amy was focusing on that promotion she just got ..."

"Hey!" Amy shouts from the kitchen.

"Sooo, we thought, why not surprise you with a few extra hands to unpack and set up your new home."

My heart swells as I look at them. They came all this way for me. For *us*.

"Besides," Nana interrupts my thoughts. "I've got an itch to beat everyone's asses in a game of Rummy."

I laugh and move out of the doorway. One by one, they pour into the living room and exchange hugs and hellos with Amy, Leo, and Jase. When things settle down, Hyla makes her petition to be Queen of the house by moving person to person to ensure she's well-pet.

It turns out, unpacking goes a lot quicker when you have a dozen extra hands to help and everyone has a common goal of pizza and game night.

We're setting up the table for Rummy when I catch Jase staring at me. "What?"

He wraps his arms around my waist and pulls me toward the big bay window.

"I think they're ready to play soon."

"Oh, we have plenty of time. Let's enjoy this moment, just the two of us." He points to the sun setting in the distance: varying shades of sunshine and cotton candy, with a slight stripe of robin's egg blue cutting through the center.

I glance up at my husband and see my face reflected in his beautiful, stormy eyes; I can't help but smile. "I can't believe we're all together—it's so different from the last time I moved."

He nods. "Better?"

I tear up. "Indescribably. When I left Sloane all those years ago, I never would have imagined we'd find our way back to each other."

Jase tucks my hair behind my ear. "I never stopped imagining it."

"Hey Kate, Small Town Boy, y'all ready or what?" Ame calls.

He tilts his head at me and mouths: "Small Town Boy?"

THIS KIND OF LOVE

"Inside joke. Come on, let's go let Nan kick our butts."

"Yes, ma'am," he replies, tipping an invisible hat and leading me to our seats.

Nana shuffles with a gleam in her eye. "Already, ladies and gents, this here is what we call Rummy night...."

We play for hours, laughing until we cry, soaking in every minute of it, and all the while, I'm just as grateful for the loved ones who came to help—as I am for my parents staying in Sloane.

A year into therapy, and I'm starting to be strong enough to set and share my boundaries with them. The biggest: to respect my new safe space here in New York with Jase. I still talk to Mama regularly, keep her up to date on my blog, and send *plenty* of Hyla content, of course, but I only talk to and about my dad when I feel strong enough to do so.

I respect Mama, Nana, and Pop for keeping their relationship with my dad and supporting him through his disease and recovery—and they respect me for letting go of the resentment but protecting my peace. Nothing will ever erase the pain of the past, but I'm moving forward, day by day, with the person who understands and loves me more than anyone else in the world and my *our* soul dog—and there's nothing better than that.

Acknowledgements

It takes a village y'all, and I wouldn't be anywhere without mine.

First, A MILLION THANK YOUS to my dream team at Rising Action Publishing.

To Alex, who saw my vision for TKOL and trusted me to see it through. To Tina and Hailey for showing me how to clean up the messy bits in the best way. Y'all get me. You do. You've made this book 800x better—and the journey's been everything and then some. I'm a genuine fan of every single title the team puts out and I'm still pinching myself that I get to be part of this #pubfam.

To Rising Action and Simon & Schuster, thank you for distributing this book in multiple formats worldwide, so we can get it into readers' hands. I'm forever grateful.

To Lauren, my absolute favorite author, mentor, and friend ... I'm so, so thankful you answered an email all those years ago and have kept answering since. Thank you for taking the time to read and blurb for me. Everyone, go buy LL's entire backlist, seriously. It's chef's kiss.

My behind-the-scenes gems: Lucy, who absolutely slayed this cover—I can't thank you enough. To Maegen and Dolan for taking the time to make me the prettiest GIF. It's perfect, and so are you two! To Katie and Kathleen, thank you for your editing and insight. To Cathie and Eric, thank you for offering a safe space in the writing community. Thank you to my incredible Betas: Sonia, Kaitlyn, and Linton. Your invaluable insight molded TKOL into what it is today.

To Don, thank you for being my biggest supporter, taking me on writing retreats (with nom nom pizza and wine), and being the better half of my favorite love story. You're everything to me.

To my fur babies, angel Hyla, Rose, and Ellie—snuggling and loving you is my favorite part of the day, every day.

To my mom, my first and forever best friend. I'm lucky to have you. You're a superhero. Thank you for your endless sacrifices, love, and believing I can do anything I set my mind to.

To Markie, thank you for spending your *entire* childhood listening to me sing off key and repeatedly read the same chapters out loud until I got them right. Your support is unmatched.

To the beautiful family Don's brought into my life. From day one, they've been mine and I've been theirs: Donna, Paul, Annie, Jamie, Neil, Pike, Warner, Pete, and Copper. I love you. Thank you for your love and encouragement.

Early readers flagged Amy for being "too good a friend." Who could be as selfless, kind, and wonderful in real life? *Enter The Great Gatsby Cheers GIF.* I'm lucky to have a whole crew that inspired Amy through a million little moments like:

- Sonia encouraging me move in with her (for basically nothing), being my Kelly Clarkson karaoke bestie, and always being a listening ear, hug, or giving the tough love I need.

- Bancroft driving me to college for *months* while I learned to drive stick, being the Wednesday night bartender to my Trivia host, and my brother from another mother.

- Gabe, who can always use a hug from Aunt Ah—and then tries to steal my dessert.

- Zollo walking me home from Friendly's in a snowstorm, wonderful nights at the diner, drinking coffee, playing cards, and bonding over our love for Don. #NoSecretAlliances

- Kitara showing up every single time I have a mental breakdown, always being up for a coffee date and book recommendation for #BookClub, and my soul sister.

- Johnny Rockets secretly installing an inflatable dinosaur in our front yard, scouting out Christmas Day Eagles tickets, and being up for any adventure.

- Harry and Kaitlyn for being the most thoughtful, fabulous double date partners, delicious cooks, and conversationalists.

- Jessica planning AC/OC beach trips, Konstantine BFFAEAE singalongs with Z and Don, and always being up for a Disney marathon.

- Lauren going viral for #Joots. She's an #Influencer, pizza party queen, and exactly who I want to be when I grow up.

- Will and Taj for Disney singalongs, walks on the beach, mental health check ins, and hosting a podcast the world desperately needs. #WorldsJustSpinning

- Monica for always having my back and never thinking I'm crazy, even when I am a little crazy. Like bringing the wrong shoes to Disney and breaking them on the first day. #ToTargetWeGo.

Thank you for keeping every bartender love note. You're my sister from another mister, and I love you so.

- Tara for forever being one of my best ladies who sees through B.S., can quote any scene from any episode of *Friends* or *The Office*, and matches my palette. We were destined to find each other. Seeing you become a mama has made my heart swell.

- Alisa, Dan, McKenna, Jax, Paisley, Renley, and Tango, for being kind enough to buy a house we love, so we can see it all the time like Halloween movies and firepits, brisketathons, and birthday celebrations. We love y'all to pieces.

- Julia, who has been a constant source of love and light. She's the first person standing and cheering, the best at keeping secrets and giving advice, and my absolute rock in a world that's anything but steady. The family tree says cousins, but my heart says sisters.

- Kathleen, who has seen me through my highest highs and lowest lows, is my words of wisdom, my shoulder to cry on, and my forever coffee date. Best. Friends. Forever.

- Erin for being the first person I told about my childhood, and the person who didn't judge but held me stronger and better than I ever could myself.

- To my Apple Crew: It's once in a lifetime that someone can find a beautiful band of girlfriends like you. The show up any day, any time, for anything kind of people.

- To my work team of dreams: It's rare to find people who completely share your brain—but somehow, we do.

- To my Swiftie and #TrueCrime sisters, Mel and Riley, who never think a conspiracy is too farfetched to consider. Y'all are real ones, that's for sure.

Thank you to all of them for showing up. And even though a few (*cough DG fam) are mad Alex and I vetoed a shirtless man on the cover, I hope they'll forgive me ... eventually.

All of this to say—there will always be more Amys than aIMees. Hell, thank them, too.

Most importantly, thanks to YOU for reading. This wouldn't be possible without you.

About the Author

Ashley Detweiler is an American author who writes contemporary romance. She believes in happily ever after (blame her husband), the power of coffee (blame her Poppop), and is fundamentally a dessert person (thank her mom). Ashley lives outside of Philadelphia with her (summer after) high school sweetheart, two furbabies, and as many books as she can fit in the house. *This Kind of Love* is her first novel.

Looking for more Romance? Check out Rising Action's other love stories on the next page!

And don't forget to follow us on our socials for cover reveals, giveaways, and announcements:
X: @RAPubCollective
Instagram: @risingactionpublishingco
TikTok: @risingactionpublishingco
Website: http://www.risingactionpublishingco.com

Mira lost the Oscar for best screenplay. Again. She could deal with it, except she lost to Preston Green. Again.

Overworked by her self-imposed expectations, Mira has to refocus her writing. She also needs to take a damn break, but time off has to be forced upon her. Luckily, an opportunity to get away and pull herself together comes along with the added bonus of getting time with a director she would kill to work with. A film shoot in the south of France is exactly the combination of rest and work that she can go for. Unfortunately, it's Preston's film.

Weeks of picturesque movie magic with her nemesis make it hard to remember her past heartbreak and his annoying way of always being out of her reach.

A steamy rivals to lovers romance exploding with banter, Take 2 will have you reaching for the popcorn and smiling straight through to the credits.

Angie Johnson wants nothing more than to keep her parents' struggling Idaho farm running, maintain her career as a NICU nurse, and find a man to marry before her father passes away from cancer. Unfortunately, even if she had time to meet someone, the online dating world is full of dead ends. That is, until she meets Daniel Smoot, a man ready to settle down on her timeline. Unfortunately, in order to reel him in, Angie may have told him a little white lie: that she, who is afraid of heights, is very into extreme sports.

Remington James the Third has his own set of problems, and finding a woman is not one. He's in town to convince Angie's parents to sell their land to his family's development company. In order to get on their good side, he takes a job at the farm and volunteers to help Angie snag Smoot by training her in extreme sports and the intricate art of seduction. What he doesn't plan on is falling for the woman whose life he's been ordered to uproot.

A wholesome romance about choosing love over your bank account, Extreme Romancing in Idaho will steal your heart.